Hallmark
PUBLISHING

# The Game Changer

## A Parkwood Mystery
## from Hallmark Publishing

# JENNIFER BROWN

The Game Changer
Copyright @ 2019 Jennifer Brown

Print ISBN 978-1-947892-41-5
eBook ISBN 978-1-947892-72-9

www.hallmarkpublishing.com

# TABLE OF CONTENTS

# CHAPTER 1

M ARY JEAN, MY EDITOR AT the *Parkwood Chronicle Weekly*, sat over my three-paragraph article with a red pen and made maddeningly slow circles and comments. A million of them.

"You've repeated the word giblets quite a few times here," she said, not looking up.

Mary Jean—or *Mary Mean* as I'd heard a couple of the middle school carriers call her behind her back—used this method of editing for every piece submitted to the *Chronicle Weekly*. Print it out, deliver it to her desk, and then sit there while she pored over it with one of the thousands of red pens that rolled around in her desk drawer.

*Mary Mean* was a misnomer. Mary Jean was perfectly nice, with kind eyes behind her cheater glasses, of which she had an entire drawer full, just below her drawer full of red pens. But Mary Jean was old school. The whole *Parkwood Chronicle Weekly* was old school. My life was old school.

At least that was how it felt compared to the life I'd left behind when I moved here a year ago.

But the life I'd left behind included getting phased out of being the youngest lead reporter on the homicide beat—a job I was good at, I might point out—at a certain very high-profile Chicago newspaper. And then getting phased out of a three-year relationship with a very high-profile newspaper cartoonist named Trace, who'd completely broken my heart when he refused to follow my career to Missouri. And then, most heartbreakingly, getting phased out of a friendship with the best and sweetest bulldog ever—my little Tink— because he belonged to Trace, too. So, yes, the life I left behind was much more modern and cosmopolitan than my life in Parkwood, but it was also a life that had been phased into nonexistence.

However, if I'd ever used the word *giblets* in a story at my old paper, it would have been something along the lines of, *The body was discovered buried in the bottom of a stand-alone freezer in the suspect's basement, frozen among packaged ground beef and chicken giblets. Forensics examiner Lucy Fang and her team are working to decipher the significance...* Not, *Giblets are the secret to the chewy bits, and chewy bits are the secret to happy potatoes.*

Mary Jean made a circle and flicked her eyes up at me. Seeing that I was watching her, she half-turned the page toward me. "See. Right here." She tapped the circle she'd just made and read aloud, "'I really like Esther's new giblets,' said customer Roy Bunson. Most residents agree— when Esther put giblets in her gravy, she took dinner, and possibly giblets, to a whole new level.'" She glanced at me again. "Do you hear it? Do you hear how that many giblets in such short space may sound a little...off?"

I winced. "Yes, ma'am."

She returned to the paper. "You've got to read things back to yourself." She tapped her ear with her finger, the point of her red pen dotting her temple. "That's what I'm here for. To teach you how to listen to your words before you release them into the world. You're your first and most important editor."

It wasn't that I was so in love with giblets. And it wasn't that I didn't know how to self-edit. It was that giblets were just as good for bulking up an article as they were for bulking up gravy, and every *giblet* got me one word closer to my word count goal—a goal I struggled to hit with every story I wrote.

I was bored. It had taken me a year to admit it to myself, but there it was. Giblets this, sale on soccer cleats that. Sale ads. Obituary after depressing obituary. I missed reporting on the homicides that led to obituaries.

When I'd chosen the job in Parkwood, I was freaked out and fraught. I could have held out for a bigger paper, a bigger town. But at the time, no other offers were coming in—I was too young, too inexperienced, too overpaid, and the industry was too saturated and shrinking too rapidly. I was far from the only out-of-work reporter in the world, and I had student loans to think of. And then when it became obvious that my boyfriend Trace wasn't willing to relocate to be with me, I was desperate to get out of Chicago altogether to mend my broken heart. Parkwood had extended an offer and a charming, sleepy community filled with trees and historic homes and smiling strangers seemed like the best place to catch my breath, lick my wounds, regain my pride and get over Trace. If I could accomplish that, I could try again. Except, I hadn't yet tried again. And I hadn't yet gotten over Trace.

Don't get me wrong—Parkwood, Missouri, population 4,944, was an adorable little town. One supermarket, one high school, one bowling alley, three gas stations, a bank, more chain pizza joints than you could shake a ball of mozzarella at, and not a single designer shoe store to be found.

No daily rush hour traffic jams. No pollution. Lots of little kids playing on really green lawns. Your mail carrier, produce clerk, and librarian actually knew your name. And the dogs here looked really happy all the time—if you didn't think it was possible for a dog to smile, just take a look at a Parkwood dog on a walk and you would change your mind. Parkwood was small and sleepy, but it was also really nice. The kind of place you see in allergy medicine commercials. Until I moved here, I didn't think this type of town really existed.

Mary Jean mercifully finished destroying the article and slid it across the desk, then removed her cheaters and set them on her disaster area of a desk and attempted a smile. "Don't look so glum. It's just a rewrite. Didn't they ever make you do a rewrite at that Chicago paper of yours?"

"Of course they did." *I just wasn't writing about giblet gravy in the first place.*

"It's still missing something, though." She picked up her glasses—a different pair this time, that seemed to appear out of nowhere—and lightly chewed the plastic earpiece before pointing at me with them. "Did she give you the recipe?"

I shook my head. "I tried."

Mary Jean's eyes narrowed. "That Esther Igo can be stubborn as the day is long. She knows the town is itching for it. She's toying with us. And you pressed her?"

I nodded. "She wouldn't budge." Although, to be fair, I hadn't pressed all that hard. I liked Esther, and if she wanted to keep her recipe to herself, I didn't see what the harm was. "But, I mean, why would she reveal it? It's her new prized recipe. People are lining up for it. If everyone can just make it themselves, won't they stop going to the Hibiscus?"

Mary Jean gave me a curious look and then laughed.

"First of all, if someone around here gives you their prized recipe, you can guarantee it's missing an ingredient or two. Or maybe has an extra one added. Or a measurement that's just a little off. That way yours comes out okay, but not quite as good as theirs. They look generous, but they're still the better cook."

"That's devious," I said.

"That's tradition," she corrected. "Secondly, nobody would stop going to the Hibiscus for any reason. People have been going there since Parkwood was a stop on a dirt trail and the Hibiscus was a table in Esther's great-great-grandmother's kitchen. That is also tradition. People want the recipe to the new giblet gravy. That doesn't mean they want to make it."

"But wh—" I started, but then thought better of it. The answer was likely to be *tradition*.

"Go read that through," Mary Jean said, pointing at the article. "Pay close attention to the giblets. And then, I need you to go back to the Hibiscus and get that recipe. Offer her something in return." She gathered up what seemed like the most random and unchecked assortment of papers and whisked away from her desk.

I followed, clutching the article in one hand. "Offer her something? What do I have to offer Esther Igo?"

"A deal," she said over her shoulder. "Offer her a deal. Tell her she can read the article and make whatever changes she likes before it goes to press."

I gasped and nearly fainted. I could feel the cosmic force of all of my University of Chicago Journalism School professors and all of their professors and the professors before them gasping and nearly fainting with me. "Let her see—I can't do that. That's…unethical. It's censorship. It's partiality. It's—"

"It's not a big deal and we do it all the time." She slapped the random papers on our part-time receptionist's desk. "Joyce, I need you to file these," she said.

Joyce set down her sticky bun in slow motion, licked

two fingers clean, pulled out an earbud in even slower motion, swiveled in so-slow-she-was-almost-backward-in-time motion, and said, "Huh?"

"File these, please," Mary Jean repeated. She turned to me and put a motherly hand on my shoulder. I must have looked as much in the throes of journalistic panic as I felt. Plus, sometimes I was pretty sure Mary Jean saw herself as a surrogate mother, since mine was so many miles away. She was always trying to feed me, make me wear a jacket, tell me I looked like I needed sleep—it was as if she had a direct line to my mom. "We've been making that deal since this paper opened. We aren't reporting cutting edge exposés here, Hollis. We're running a small-town paper. It's for the people, and they have expectations. Whether or not we have a job on Monday morning depends on whether or not our customers keep reading. And they'll keep reading if they can get their eyes on that recipe."

Joyce was slowly picking through the random papers. She'd gotten a manicure over the weekend—extra long, extra pointy, and extra shiny. It looked nice, but also cumbersome. "Where exactly am I filing these? I think this is your dry cleaning receipt, Mary Jean."

Mary Jean ignored her and headed back toward her own desk. "You should hurry over to the Hibiscus so you can get back before the parade clogs up the square. Eat something while you're there. You look hungry."

"I do?" I looked down at myself. How exactly did I look hungry?

"Afterward, go on over and cover the parade, then take the rest of the day to rest up for the game tonight. You'll be covering that, too."

Oh. Right. The game. The high school homecoming football game. The biggest event in town. Everyone would be there.

And I would be there, too. Not to cover the game itself. That honor would go to long-time reporter Ernie Holden, who would sleep through one hundred percent of the game, but would still somehow instinctively know what had happened when he woke up, like he had been telepathically tuned in. Or like he had been using the same article for thirty-five years and just changing the names. Which was much more likely, especially since that article used the phrase *Can you dig it?* and referred to the quarterback as *One cool cat.*

No, I would be at the homecoming football game to cover a much more riveting story: the new hot dog roller. That's right, ladies and gents, no more pulling wilted dogs out of murky boiling water. Thanks to the tireless fundraising efforts of the Glove and Handbag Club, Chapter #1696, Parkwood was catching up with the rest of the world and heating up their game-time protein on rollers. Bleacher snacks were about to reach a whole new level.

And I, with just over $60,000 left in student loan bills, was going to crack that case wide open. *Eat your heart out, Trace.*

I took my article back to my desk and sank into my chair.

Lucky me.

# CHAPTER 2

TRAFFIC ACCIDENTS WERE A SOCIAL event in Parkwood, and when they happened, they caused a huge
headache. The entire town simply had to get a gander at the
accident, no matter how small, so they could relay the story
that evening over dinner.

And when it came to fender benders with Wickham
Birkland—or anything with Wickham Birkland, from
trampled azaleas to missing mail—there was no such thing
as small.

Wickham was Parkwood's most notorious bad mood
waiting to happen. He skulked around town with a scowl
and a list of grievances as long as his uncut hair (unsurpris-
ingly, his list of grievances began with his ex-barber), and
when you were the new kid in town, one of the first things
you learned was that you should try your level best to never,
ever cross his path in any sort of way, but especially not in
any sort of bad way. And that was exactly what had happened to the poor soul who had the misfortune of running
through the stop sign at the intersection of Oak and Tutor,
just two blocks north of the Hibiscus.

There was a lineup of lookie-loos four blocks long. Betty
Ramp—I knew her from a story I'd penned about the new
First Methodist Sunday bulletin format (they were shaking

things up with Cambria font!)—was toting lawn chairs and a pitcher of lemonade up the sidewalk for the older folks who'd abandoned their cars for a better show. Betty Ramp was thoughtful that way.

An unlucky police officer was having a heck of a time trying to direct traffic. I'd never seen him before. He must have been new to Parkwood, likely filling the opening left by Officer Jamie Martin, who'd retired and moved to the coast just a few weeks earlier. This new officer was closer to my age, and was tall, dark-haired, and had a muscular build that didn't look half bad—okay, actually looked really good—in a uniform.

Nobody was paying him the slightest bit of attention. By the time I drove up to the stop sign, he'd given up on hand signals, as several cars had simply taken up residence right smack in the middle of the intersection, their owners sitting on someone's open tailgate sharing a bag of cookies. He pleaded me with his eyes to just move on. They were nice eyes, I couldn't help noticing.

Like a good reporter, I quickly surveyed the accident, even though I knew the *Parkwood Chronicle Weekly* would never report on such things. *People don't want to read about accidents, Hollis*, I could hear Mary Jean saying. *They want to read good news. New babies and award-winning cakes and spelling bees.*

"Just as long as they're not spelling g-i-b-l-e-t-s," I whispered to myself as I tried to assess the situation.

A man had popped into the front of Wickham Birkland's Mercedes, knocking a big hole into the grill and shattering the headlight. My windows were rolled up, so I couldn't hear what Wickham was saying, but from the looks of things, he was either throwing an utter fit or dancing the Y-M-C-A. Or maybe practicing to be head cheerleader for tonight's homecoming game. I tried entertaining myself by making up the cheers and seeing how they aligned with Wickham's furious body language. "Hey-hi-ho-hoo! We're the team that's gonna beat you!" I giggled. "It works! Jump to the left! Jump to the right! Raise your fists up high and—" A knock on my window startled a squeak out of me. The officer was right on the other side of the glass. His nametag read HOPKINS.

Sheepishly, I pushed the button to roll down the window. Now that I could hear, I could definitely tell that Wickham Birkland wasn't cheering. In fact, the police chief had arrived and was now standing between him and the other guy, and probably for good reason. Wickham was looking a little more than unhinged.

"You think you could keep traffic moving, ma'am?" the officer asked in a very official voice. It was a smooth, baritone voice—I couldn't help noticing that, too.

"Sorry," I said. "I was just cheering…um…" I squirmed. "Sure, I'll move. But… Can I ask you a question first?"

"I'm directing traffic, ma'am." We both looked at where traffic should have been, but obviously wasn't, moving. He sighed, closed his eyes briefly, refocused on me. "What's your question?"

"Do you have any thoughts about Esther Igo's new giblet gravy, by chance?"

The Hibiscus Café—a local institution and hub of activity at any time of day in Parkwood—was abnormally quiet. Everyone was still at Oak and Tutor, watching Wickham Birkland dance circles of anger around the man who'd crashed into his Mercedes.

The scent of gravy and butter rolled out as soon as I pulled open the door and my mouth immediately began watering. Esther's gravy may not have been something I got excited to report on, but I have to admit there really was something special about the new recipe. Even I wouldn't have minded getting my hands on it, and I lived on a diet of microwavable macaroni and cheese for one.

"Well, Hollis Bisbee! You're back again! Welcome, welcome!" Esther, in many ways the matriarch of Parkwood, was a fluffy woman in every possible sense. Her graying hair was a fluffy cloud of curls, her fluffy-ruffled apron concealed a fluffy figure, and even her words were fluffy. When you walked into the Hibiscus, the fluffiness enveloped you and you felt like you were…home. Not just any home—your childhood home.

My childhood home in Chicago was filled with my mom and her twin sister, Ruta. Mom and Aunt Ruta were one and the same and neither were fluffy in any sense, nor could either make gravy—or much more than toast—to save their lives. But they were tough and scrappy and never let me get away with feeling sorry for myself over anything. They were all *pick yourself up by your bootstraps* and *rub dirt on it* and *there are no white knights or horses here, sister, so don't bother with that damsel in distress bit.* I'd repeated that last one to myself a thousand times while adjusting to Parkwood.

Boy, did I miss those women. I made a mental note to give them a call later.

"Yep, I'm back," I said, making my way to the counter while flashing what I liked to think of as my reporter smile—all teeth, confidence, and sincere, trust-me eyes. The smile I used to have to rely on to get an experienced police officer to give up the goods on an investigation I was now using to get a chef to give up the goods on a recipe. "I just can't get enough of that gravy, Esther."

"Oh, you're too kind. Did you know I had to whip up an extra batch this afternoon? Yesterday, I ran clean out before the dinner hour even got here." She leaned in and whispered. "I'm telling you, it's the giblets that have people begging for more."

I slid onto a stool at the counter and Esther immediately poured me an iced tea. "I heard old Wickham's giving somebody the business out on Tutor," she said.

I took a sip of the tea. It was so sweet, it made my uvula recoil. Esther served two flavors of iced tea—sweet and syrup-sweet—and I was still trying to get used to it. "I got caught up in it. Looked like he was fit to be tied."

She clucked her tongue. "That Wickham's been looking for trouble since the day he was born, and one of these days, he's going to actually find it. You mark my words about that. You having the turkey sandwich again, honey?"

My stomach growled. Turned out Mary Jean was right— I was hungry. "Sounds great. Has he never been in real trouble before?" With Wickham's temperament, I found this hard to believe.

Esther scribbled something illegible on a pad of paper, ripped it off, and pressed it through a window. A meaty hand pawed through and grabbed it. I'd never seen the chef attached to that hand. I'd often wondered who it might belong to, until my neighbor Daisy told me it was good that I didn't know; some mysteries were best left unsolved.

"Small-time trouble, sure," she said. "But his daddy got himself in real hot water once. Caught some teenagers throwing rocks at a dog. Well, Jeffrey Birkland loved animals and didn't take to that very kindly. Beat the living tar right out of those teenagers. All three of them, single-handedly. Put 'em in the hospital. Two of 'em were never the same again. He showed no remorse. He went to prison, spouting 'eye for an eye' the whole way there. Most people think that's why Wickham is the way he is—learned it from his daddy. Maybe they're right. I'm no brain shrinker, so I couldn't tell you. Personally, I suspect anger is just in the Birkland blood."

I thought about how red Wickham's face was as he shouted and waved around the front of his car in that intersection. If it was possible for anger to run in blood, Birkland blood seemed as likely to hold it as any.

"'Hup!'" a deep voice called from the window where Esther had passed the order earlier, and a plate appeared. Esther hurried to grab it.

"Voilà!" she said, setting it in front of me while refilling my tea with the other hand. "Open-face turkey sandwich, extra gravy for my extra special guest this afternoon."

I took a deep breath, inhaling the intoxicating scent, then picked up my fork. "Speaking of the gravy," I said, digging in. "Mmm...you really outdid yourself."

"You like it?" Esther's whole face lit up when she smiled, and in that smile it was easy to see why everyone wanted to be at the Hibiscus, even if they had the same dishes in their recipe boxes at home.

"I love it." I swallowed. "And speaking of—"

The door opened, and a child's shriek interrupted me, followed by sheer, utter chaos. My next-door neighbor and best friend, Daisy Mueller, and her entourage of children, were making the entrance they made everywhere they went.

"Willow! I swear, if you don't stop doing that, I will take you home and let the dog babysit you, and I mean it this time. Brant, do not walk on the booth tables. I said get off of there! And where did your shoes go? Lucas, what on earth are you doing? Come help me with your sister! Where is Jake? Jake? Jake! Darn it, Jake, did you put muffin up your nose again? How many ER doctors have to tell you that could go to your brain? You ever see someone with Blueberry Brain? It is ugly, son. Really ugly. Just—here, blow it out. Brant! Get down from there! Hey, Esther, sorry to be late. These guys got into some chocolate and have been a sugar and caffeine tornado ripping right through my house all morning."

To me, Daisy's house seemed to be a tornado all the time. Then again, I was childless, so what did I know about kids and caffeine?

She handed Esther a basket of Mueller Muffins—her fledgling baked goods side business. So far, Esther was her only client, but she was a good client. Daisy's muffins fairly flew off the shelves at the Hibiscus.

"Oh, hey, Hollis. I didn't know you'd be here this morning." She blew her bangs out of her eyes and checked her phone. "Good grief, I guess I meant to say this afternoon," she corrected.

I wiped gravy off of my bottom lip with a napkin. "I was just trying to get a little extra for the story," I said.

"Extra?" Esther, said curiously. "What kind of extra?"

There was another child-shriek, followed by a crash, followed by raucous laughter. Daisy looked up at the ceiling, counted to five, then said, "That's it! I'm calling the dog now. He owes me one anyway." Judging by the way the kids all giggled and cheered, my guess was they didn't find her threat to be as menacing as she'd meant it to be, if for no other reason than they didn't own a dog. Daisy rushed off to find the source of the ruckus.

I took another bite of turkey. The diner door opened, and another customer walked in. A few seconds later, it opened again and two more entered. The wreck had apparently cleared. Soon, the Hibiscus would be hopping and my chances of getting Esther's undivided attention would be severely diminished. I couldn't decide if that was a good thing or a bad thing. My eyeballs were already floating on a sea of sweet tea.

"What kind of extra?" Esther repeated, refilling my glass, even though I'd only taken a tiny sip.

I swallowed. "Well. Okay. You know."

She raised her eyebrows. "I do?"

I nudged her. "Yeah, I think you do." This was so uncomfortable.

She scratched her head contemplatively. "I don't think I do."

"Mary Jean wants the recipe."

She set down the tea pitcher and crossed her arms. "Oh, she does? Well, I don't give out my prized recipes. She should know that by now."

"She thought..."

Her eyebrows—fluffy as they were—went up so high they were concealed behind her fluffy bangs. "She thought...?"

I took a breath to steel myself. "She thought you might be interested in a trade."

She uncrossed her arms and put one hand on her hip. "What sort of trade are we talking about?"

I took a gulp of tea this time. Then another. Then pointedly looked at the pitcher, hoping another refill would stall me from having to say the words aloud. She didn't budge. That Esther could drive a hard bargain when she wanted to. "You're sure you won't just give it out? For the good of the people?"

"Exactly what kind of trade is Mary Jean looking to make?"

She was channeling my grandmother—God rest her stern soul—and instantly, I felt like I was ten again. My throat didn't want to let the words out. To make this bargain would betray my oaths as a journalist. Not that I took actual oaths, of course. But I thought them. And I stood by them.

"You can look over the article and make any changes you want before it goes to press," I mumbled.

She brightened. "Is that so?"

"Yes, ma'am. If you want. But you don't have to make changes," I added. "If you have strong beliefs in the first amendment, for example."

"Oh, honey," she said soothingly. "Are you worried that my writing will outshine yours? That's so sweet." She laid a hand on my arm and squeezed. "You shouldn't concern yourself with that. I'm sure your article is just fine and I'll make very few changes. Did you mention my giblets at all?"

I caught Daisy just as she was strapping Willow into her car seat. Two of the boys were climbing around the minivan like moles.

"Boys!" she was yelling wearily. "You need to get back in those seats. If I get pulled over, I'll tell on you both. Do you want me to tell on you?"

I snorted. "You're threatening to tattle on your kids to the police?"

"It's all I've got left," she said. "They've been running me ragged all morning. My threats are getting weaker as the minutes pass. You get your story?"

"More like she got hers," I said. "But, yes. She's going to

give up the recipe, and all I have to do is add a whole lot of glowy language about the Hibiscus."

She snapped Willow's seatbelt and slid the minivan door closed, silencing the babble inside. She leaned against the door.

Daisy was thirty-one and adorable—small and mighty, with blond hair cut short and choppy, which I once accused of being stylish but she claimed was accidentally so, because she'd had to keep getting up to pull Brant away from the litter box while her at-home stylist worked on it, and also more than once had to cut out a piece of gum that nobody would admit to having lost there. Eventually, she decided it was just *a look* and she would go with it.

Daisy was a great—if not exhausted—mom, but also a whiz in the kitchen, especially with baked goods. She could take flour, sugar, and whatever she had in the back of the pantry and turn them into something you'd be proud to take to the company picnic. She seriously had no idea how impressive her baking skill was. She thought it was "just a thing," and refused to admit that it was "just a thing" that she did better than anyone I'd ever known. Including Esther.

Daisy was also outspoken, incredibly intelligent, completely sleep-deprived, was the only person I'd ever seen look good in overalls, which she wore all the time. Also, she was the most intuitive person I'd ever met. She could tell you where her kids were at all times, just based on the sounds she wasn't hearing.

Mom and Aunt Ruta tried to convince me that was just mother's intuition and everyone had it. I didn't have the heart to remind them about the time they left me at a gas station in the middle of Nebraska on our road trip to Yellowstone when I was seven. There were some conversations you just didn't want to open up again with Aunt Ruta.

Daisy closed one eye against the sun. "You do know Esther's going to leave like four ingredients out of that recipe, right?"

"That is so devious," I said.

She shrugged. "It's tradition."

"All I know is Mary Jean said get a recipe and I'm getting a recipe. Story ready to go to print. What I'm more interested in talking to you about is murder."

"This again?" She glanced through the van window, pounded on it with the flat of her hand, and pointed threateningly at a kid I couldn't see.

"Yes, this again. You know you're interested. You said you were interested. You've said it multiple times. I've even got a name for it. *Knock 'em Dead.* What do you think? The *Knock 'em Dead* podcast."

"I think you've got a fixation," she said, starting toward the driver's side door.

"And so do you." And that was the truth. Daisy always initially acted horrified when I brought up true crime, but within minutes she was spouting off facts and opinions and hypotheses right along with me. We'd spent many a summer evening sitting in her backyard, our feet in a plastic baby swimming pool, talking serial killers and suspicious widows long into the night.

It only made sense that we could put our deep-seated and somewhat mortifying love of true murder mysteries, books about serial killers, and missing person podcasts to good use. An idea began to simmer. And then bubble. And then boil. And then overflow.

Just about every evening ended with the same words:

*We should do this professionally. We should make a show. A podcast!*

But in the morning, when the enchantment of mystery wore off, we were both hit with reality: I had a job at the newspaper and she was trying to get a small baking business off the ground. Who had time for podcasts?

But as every day—and every gravy story—rolled by, I was starting to be willing to make the time.

Daisy raked a hand through her hair. "I enjoy small talk," she said.

"Mm-hmm, and you especially love small talk about big crimes," I said. "Come on, Daisy. I'll buy the equipment. I've got the name. You know you like the name—I could see it in your eyes. I've researched it and planned it out. We choose a theme, and do four or five episodes on that theme, then we move on to a new theme. So not just one murder per episode, but lots of them. I've already got our first theme. I'm ready to go."

She had a hand on the door handle. I could see her thinking. She opened the door a crack and yelled inside. "I saw that, Jake! Cut it out or you'll answer to your father, I swear it!" She slammed it shut again. "I don't know. I've got a lot going on, with the kids, Mike's new freelance job at home, the muffin business...And, besides, I'm just some random woman who bakes things. You're the expert reporter. I'll sound stupid."

I gasped and swatted at her arm lightly. "Don't say mean things about my best friend. You will not sound stupid. C'mon, I miss exciting stories," I said. "Tonight, Mary Jean's got me working on a story about hot dogs. *Hot dogs*, Daisy. My career plan was not to write stories about hot dogs. Unless those hot dogs were a murder weapon or used to rob a bank or—"

"How could someone rob a bank with a hot dog?"

This. This was exactly how our bests conversations started. I felt a jolt of excited energy. If I could ride this wave, the *Knock 'Em Dead* podcast was as good as made.

I put my hand in my pocket and stuck my finger out like it was a gun and pointed it at her. "I've got a gun."

"No, you don't. You have a Ballpark Frank. I can smell it. It needs mustard."

"Well, I mean, a frozen hot dog could be a weapon. And it wouldn't smell."

She thought it over. "Not really. A whole pack, maybe. But I just don't see myself being too intimidated by a thawing hot dog. How much could that hurt? Ouch, you gave me a small bruise."

"You're missing the point. Actually, no, you're not. These are the kinds of things we would talk about on *Knock 'em Dead*. It would be great. People would love us. I can't do this forever." I whipped out the notebook that I always carried in my bag and waved it at the Hibiscus. It flopped open to reveal Esther's recipe. "Not if this is all I get to do. I've got to have an outlet. And you can't do that forever without some sort of time out." I pointed at the van window, which currently had a kid's face smushed against it, nostrils flared. "You'll go insane."

"Oh, honey, I'm already there. Firmly and utterly."

I stuck out my bottom lip. "Please? Just give it a try?"

"Can I use it to promote Mueller's Muffins?"

"Of course! Promote away!"

She sighed. "Okay. Why not?"

I jumped and squealed, then wrapped her in a quick hug. "You won't regret this. We're going to have so much fun. *Knock 'em Dead* is going to knock 'em dead!"

She laughed while opening her door, unleashing a

cacophony of noise onto the world again. "I think you're right," she said. "The show will be my moment of sanity. But we do it at your house. Otherwise, we will be knocking 'em dead with a whole lot of background noise."

"Deal. Oh, and by the way." I leaned over her and mimed coming at her face with my fist and stopping just short of skin on skin. "Frozen frank to the eye! Weapon! Boom!"

"You are so morbid," she said. She slid into the driver's seat and shut the door, then rolled down the window. "But I love it."

I watched her drive away, barely missing Wickham Birkland's dented Mercedes on her way out of the parking lot. He was fervently following the car that dented him earlier, but paused to lay on his horn. Daisy laid on hers in return. Two kids peered out the van window as she pulled past him. They stuck out their tongues.

I doubted she was telling them to stop.

# CHAPTER 3

IF YOU WERE A BURGLAR in Parkwood, Missouri, the absolute best time to get away with ripping off every house in the entire town would be during the Parkwood High School homecoming game. Because nobody was at home that evening. Instead, we were all crammed into the PHS football stadium.

There were worse places. Most high school football stadiums—at least my high school football stadium—consisted of a browning, pocked field surrounded by a few wooden bleachers. PHS's football stadium was a high-dollar behemoth of lights and sounds. The grass was manicured so evenly, there was a halfway-serious running joke that the groundsperson did it with scissors and a ruler. The aluminum bleachers were enormous, spanning the entire length of the field, and curling around partially into the end zones, and the crowd would still overflow into standing room only areas along the fence line. Even the away team's bleachers were bigger and nicer than most schools' main bleachers. There was a concession stand and indoor restrooms, VIP cushioned seats and a special fenced-off pit for the marching band. There was a "runaround" section of grass for the middle schoolers to be middle schoolers, and for the middle school principal to be threatening and get migraines. And it all surrounded a state-of-the-art digitized scoreboard with a huge screen for displaying players' most menacing game faces mixed with distressing replays of bad calls.

PHS had two cheerleading squads, a nine-time state champion dance squad, a peppy drum line, a pack of shirtless, staff-toting spirit leaders, and a googly-eyed hornet mascot with a stuffed stinger poking out of its dancing bum.

Parkwood, Missouri, took its high school football seriously. And so did every surrounding town, who brought their equally-serious teams from their equally-serious stadiums to play on our turf.

I got to the game way too late to scope out a seat, so I wandered around, waiting for the action to start, checking out the sights and the people, letting my mind wander to the *Knock 'em Dead* podcast. I wondered if Daisy would mind if I called myself the lead investigator.

For a short period in college, I'd dreamed of being an investigative reporter on television. I'd imagined myself digging deep into stories and filling in a rapt audience as my ratings soared. I was good at research. I had a nice voice. I was a journalism major with a minor in criminal justice.

But I was also 5'3", which, according to my professors and my advisor, was just entirely displeasing to watch on a television. To listen to them, my height basically made watching me on TV something akin to watching a really educated troll climb up out from under a bridge to deliver a murder report on goats. Didn't make sense to me—I was cute with dark, shoulder length hair and brown eyes that weren't troll-like at all—but in a cutthroat industry in a big city, you could just assume there was going to be something to take you out of the game. I didn't have a gargoyle second head or a honking voice or a disproportionate amount of lumps in weird places, and I wasn't dumb, but I also wasn't my perfect classmate, Kirsten Mendoza. And if you don't know who she is—trust me, you will.

So I gave up my dream of digging deep into stories on camera and regaling rapt audiences with their details. If I had to write stories about hot dogs to pay the bills, fine. That didn't mean I had to give up my passion.

Oh. Right. The hot dogs.

As soon as the ball was in the air, I went in search of a certain new hot dog roller.

The concession stand looked like it had been hit with a bomb. Nacho cheese splatters dotted the serving counter, the floor, the metal prep table, the shoes of the trio of teens who were working. Boxes of candy were toppled and scattered, some open and spilling their Hot Tamale guts onto the tables and tile. Melted chocolate had been stepped on and tracked throughout the kitchen. The soles of the kids' shoes stuck to dried, spilled soda splots and made sucking sounds when they walked.

But right in the center of the room, like a monarch atop his kingdom, sat a glistening, pristine hot dog roller, rolling its little heart out. Buns scattered the prep table next to it in various states of strewn, torn, and wadded. A serious-faced girl with mustard-smeared glasses carefully, almost reverently, laid new dogs across the back rollers, getting them going for the halftime rush.

"Hello, may I help you?" The most enthusiastic high school boy I'd ever seen grinned up at me, all dimples and energy, from the other side of the counter. His curly hair half-sprang from beneath the paper cap that was supposed to protect our food. His name tag said:

TYLER
PASSIONATE ABOUT: RPGS
SPECIFICALLY DRAGON AGE: INQUISITION BUT DRAGON AGE:
ORIGINS IS PRETTY GOOD TOO FOR WHEN I'M LIKE SICK OF PLAY-
ING INQUISITION WHICH DOESN'T HAPPEN VERY MUCH.

I held up my work badge. "I'm from the *Parkwood Chronicle Weekly*," I said. "I was wondering if I could talk to you for a minute about your new machine there."

His hand twitched near the cash register for a second and he looked disappointed, like maybe good old dragon-killing Tyler had been stuck in the back with the nacho cheese catastrophe during the pre-game rush and had been waiting for just this slow moment to shine mathematically by taking my money and making change.

"Oh. The dog roller? That's Ari's job."

The girl with nacho cheese glasses (Arielle, Passionate about: mermaid fiction) looked up. The other lens had relish stuck to it. She held one wiener in the air between two fingers. "Huh? What did I do?"

"You messed up somebody's hot dog," a boy listlessly sweeping the back said. "Way to go, brainiac."

"What? I did?" Ari looked absolutely panicked. "I messed up your hot dog?"

"No," I said. "I didn't even order one yet."

"I'm sorry. I'm new." She flicked the glob of relish from her glasses. It landed on top of a mangled bun. A fly immediately dove for it.

"No, you're not. She's not," the boy in the back said. "She's done this, like, a hundred times or something."

"I have not, Dennis," Ari shot back.

"Well, at least thirty," the boy, whose name I now knew was Dennis, said.

"You're not going to write about it in the newspaper, are you?" Tyler asked. "Because she can just make you a new one. I don't want to get in trouble. This job is going on my college résumé."

I opened my mouth to reassure them all that I was definitely not there to get anyone in trouble, but Dennis interrupted me.

"Wow, uncool, Arielle," he said. "Get everyone in trouble, why don't you? Now Tyler won't get to go to college."

"Oh! No, no," I said, patting the air. "Tyler, I'm sure you're going to go to a great coll—"

"It'll be free," Ari offered desperately. "The hot dog, I mean. I think? Yeah. I'm pretty sure Evangeline wouldn't make me charge you. Since it was my fault. I'll pay for it."

"No, you don't need to pay for anything. You didn't mess up—"

Dennis made a *pssh* noise and shook his head. "It's pretty pathetic if you ask me, to put the squeeze on somebody over a buck hot dog. They pay you at the newspaper or what?"

"I'm not putting the squeeze on—"

"Can you describe me as strong-chinned?" Tyler asked, elongating his neck. He slapped at his Adam's apple with the back of his hand. "It would be nice to have something like that in writing."

"I'm here to write a story!" I said, holding up both hands, so they could see my blank reporter's notebook in one hand and my pencil in the other. "About the hot dog roller. A good story. A nice one. No complaints. Everyone's going to college. If they want."

All three paused, blinking at me.

"What? The roller? Why?" Arielle asked.

"It's new?" I said, and then realizing I sounded as uncertain as she, repeated the words with far more enthusiasm than I felt. "It's new! And...exciting!"

"Let me get Evangeline," she said.

Dennis had already dropped the broom and disappeared through a door in the back of the concession stand. Arielle went to the same door and stood timidly by, one leg bent like a deer ready to bolt. She had nacho cheese smudged across the back of her jeans. Soon, she backed away, and Dennis came out, followed by a tall, robust redhead dressed head-to-toe in Parkwood High School spirit wear. She was carrying a giant box of plastic nacho trays. She passed it off to Dennis, who instantly dropped it, sending empty nacho trays scattering everywhere. The woman pretended not to notice, but I could see her wince as all three kids descended upon the mess, Tyler stepping in one accidentally, slipping, and crashing into the boxes of soda syrup.

"May I help you?" she asked, but her smile was posed enough for me to know that Dennis had already filled her in. That was something you learned quickly as a reporter—people get nervous when you're around and wear wooden smiles.

I stuck out a hand. "Hollis Bisbee, *Parkwood Chronicle Weekly*."

"Evangeline Crane, that's an I-N-E and Crane like the bird," she said, taking my hand and shaking it. So she'd definitely been filled in. Also, she had a crazy strong grip. Instinctively, I pulled back and wrote her name in my notebook, just so I could save myself from permanent nerve damage. "I understand you're here about the new baby." She gazed lovingly at the refilled dog roller.

I smiled through a cringe. *New baby?* "Yeah, do you mind if I ask you a few questions?"

There was the muffled sound of a football announcer, followed by a crowd roar of disapproval. Evangeline lost her smile for half a second, but quickly recovered. People around here took bad calls personally, even when they couldn't see them directly. "Certainly. We've got plenty of time before the half. Here, let me get you a dog." She hurried to the roller and expertly bunned and wrapped a hot dog.

"Great. Has it made things easier for you here in the concession stand?"

"Snack shop," she corrected, pushing the dog across the counter toward me.

"Sorry," I said, making a note and underlining it. "Snack shop. Of course."

"Common mistake," she said. "It just sounds more fun that way. More professional. And, oh goodness, yes. It is so nice not to have those pans of boiling water back here. Safer for the kids, too."

There was another—this time louder—angry roar from the crowd. We both glanced. Things were getting serious out there. I hoped Ernie was having a rare moment of consciousness, because there might actually be a story going on right under his nose. One that didn't already have a template.

"And the customers?"

She crinkled her eyebrows. "They never really had contact with the water pans."

"No, I mean—" Another roar, including the clear sound of someone yelling, *Come on, man, it's obvious!* I wondered what was so obvious.. "Have you had any feedback from the customers?"

When the roar sounded again, it rumbled like actual thunder. Angry, ready-to-mob thunder. We all stared at the concrete wall of the concession stand—snack shop—as if we could see through it and out onto the field.

"What is going on out there?" I wondered aloud.

She scowled. "Well, we are playing the River Fork Otters, you know," she said. "Known nasty players. That coach—Farkle or whatever his name is—"

"Farley," Arielle corrected.

Evangeline pointed at her with a hot dog that she seemed to produce out of nowhere. "Yeah, that's it. River Fork's notorious Coach Farley is just the worst. I don't even like him near my snack shop. River Fork doesn't have a roller like this one, though," she said, patting the new machine. "So I can see why he'd want to eat here. All they've got is his wife Wilma Louise's rickety old crock pot. She doesn't cook at all, you know. She could donate every appliance in her kitchen and it wouldn't make a difference." She pointed at my notebook. "Could you maybe not say the thing about him eating here? I don't want potential customers getting scared off by the possibility of having to eat with our rival."

A whistle blew, then was followed by another, longer whistle. I almost felt like refs were calling a time out on Evangeline's story. Too much information. All I wanted to know about was the even cook on the franks, the donors who bought the machine, and what it's done for sales. No—what it's done for school spirit. No—what it's done for the spirit of the entire town of Parkwood. A couple snappy quotes from Evangeline and the kids and I would be done.

Dennis, who'd disappeared through the snack shop back door, burst back in. "Yo! Dudes! Field fight!"

Tyler and Arielle were out the door so fast they were practically laying cheese skidmarks on the floor, leaving Evangeline and I standing there, staring at each other and the rolling hot dogs. The machine had a squeak already.

"Shouldn't you be out there with your pen and paper?" she asked.

I glanced at the small spiral pad in my hand. True, covering a fight sounded so much more interesting than what I was doing. But that was Ernie's story to get.

If he was awake.

Which he was probably not.

It was entirely possible that nobody would get the story if I wasn't out there to get it. I felt twitchy. *Never let a potential scoop pass you by* was seared into my soul. "Maybe I should—"

"Well, I've got to see," Evangeline said, and scurried out the back door behind the kids.

"Can I quote you about the crock pot?" I hollered at her back, but she didn't respond. She didn't even slow down. I grabbed the hot dog and navigated my way toward the commotion as well.

Dennis wasn't kidding about the field fight. There was an all-out brawl going on right in the center of the football field. Fullbacks were punching halfbacks. Tight ends were kicking kickers. Coaches were swinging at coaches. The refs were blowing their whistles wildly and trying to pry guys apart without getting their own blocks knocked off. Most of the crowd was on its feet, jeering and pumping their fists.

I found a man sitting on the edge of a close bleacher, craning to see the happenings on the field between the standing bodies of the people in front of him. "What's going on?" I asked.

"Fight," he said.

"I can see that. I mean, what happened to start it?"

"Oh. Well, that boy there accused that man over there of stealing our plays right out from under us." He pointed at the knot of people on the field—I had no idea which boy or which man he was talking about.

"Stolen plays?" I stood on my tiptoes. "Have you seen my coworker Ernie, by chance?"

The man shook his head without even glancing at me. "Get him, Paulie!" he shouted. "Give him what-for!"

I maneuvered my way toward the fence that separated the bleachers from the field. The fight was starting to wear down as the boys and men involved began to get winded. One of the ref's field mics had gotten switched on, and the sounds of grunts and a lot of heavy breathing began to fill the stadium. Eventually, the refs were able to break it up, and one by one, fighters backed away, leaving only two people right in the center of the field, still grappling with each other. I recognized one of them right away.

Paulie Henderson, star Parkwood High School quarterback with amazing pass accuracy and notorious anger and impulse control issues—Parkwood police department's most coddled delinquent.

The police chief was also a Henderson. Coincidence? Not even a little bit.

Chief Henderson was a friend of Mary Jean's, so on Joyce's advice my first week, I'd never even tried to write a story about one of Paulie's hijinks, which seemed to range from fighting in parking lots to vandalizing his math teacher's house to spray painting his initials on an overpass bridge. Paulie was protected from bad press. Paulie was protected from a lot of things.

Paulie was also a hothead and was currently wrapped in what would have otherwise looked like a hug with a man I didn't recognize. Short and squat with salt-and-pepper hair, wearing a River Fork High School T-shirt—on the back, the word COACH. The infamously nasty Coach Farley, I presumed.

I'd seen him before. I just couldn't remember where.

Finally, the refs were able to pull the two apart. "You're

lucky, man! You're lucky!" Paulie was yelling, jabbing his finger at the coach, as two teammates dragged him away. "You hear me? You're lucky!"

Everyone heard him—the ref's field mic was still on.

"Lucky or not, I'm still winning," the coach said. He stomped on the field and twisted the toe of his shoe in the dirt, right on the nose of the painted-on Parkwood hornet. The actual mascot, standing with the cheerleaders, clapped one hand over his nose, affronted, and started towards him, but the entire cheerleading squad stepped in between, holding him back. His stuffed stinger shivered with anger and anticipation.

"Yeah? Well, if you keep stealing my plays, I will hunt you down and I will kill you. You hear me? You're a dead man!"

I gasped. I expected everyone around me to gasp, too. But they were too busy cheering and high-fiving. Hunt you down and kill you? Seemed Evangeline wasn't the only one with strong feelings about Coach Farley. Not by a long shot. But I could also see why she worried that allowing him to dine at her concession stand would keep PHS fans away— he seemed to have a full stadium of disgusted Parkwoodians.

"You're still losing, little man," Coach Farley sneered. "Talk all you want, but River Fork is going to win this game."

And they did. By a lot.

The crowd was much less energetic as they filed out of the stadium. There was still plenty of grumbling, some soda cans thrown at the River Fork players as they left the field. But nobody had the heart to put any muscle behind their throw, and the River Fork players caught the cans and flung them back. They clattered around on the emptying bleachers, nobody even giving them so much as a glance.

The Homecoming Queen was led out in sobs of crushed school spirit, consoled by her King. Which caused another girl to be led out in sobs, as the king was technically her date. She was being consoled by a passel of scowling girls who all talked loudly about *just skipping the dance if that's the way he's going to be, because you're worth more than that and you're way better than her and everybody knows it, Martha.* And the football team slunk in and out of the field house locker rooms in record time, their cheeks rosy from what they would all claim was a very hot and rigorous shower scrubbing and not, absolutely not, tears.

I sat on the top bleacher, eating the surprisingly delicious hot dog Evangeline had given me and idly writing my story while watching the stadium clear out. Eventually, I saw a slumped figure down in the bottom corner of the bleachers. I sighed, gobbled the rest of the frank, and clunked my way down.

"Hey, Ernie," I said. I jostled his shoulder and he woke with a snort.

"What? Huh?" He blinked at the scoreboard. "Aw, rats. I'll have to change all the *wons* to *losts* again." He shook his head. "Inconsistent team."

"I'm sure they would rather you didn't have to change anything. So what did you make of the big halftime show?"

Yes, this was a test. Yes, he failed it. He cleared his throat, thumbed through a timeworn reporter's notebook, and said, "I would say the girls have a good chance at the state competition this year. That, uh, number in the middle, that, uh, was something else."

Something else. Like nonexistent. "You're talking about the…" I trailed off to let him finish.

"The cheerleaders, of course."

"I thought it was the dance team that did the halftime shows," I said.

He rubbed one eye with his finger and yawned. "That's what I meant. They look like cheerleaders." This, of course, I couldn't argue. It was true.

"Ernie," I said. "You mean to tell me you missed the fight?"

He looked confused. "The girls had a fight?"

"The girls never got to come out. The teams had a fight. Don't worry, I've got you covered. I got the story. With quotes." I opened my own notebook and flipped through the pages, even though I didn't really need to. "The boys fighting were—"

A screech of tires, a revving engine, and a long, loud scream from the lower parking lot interrupted me.

Ernie and I glanced at each other and then took off toward it.

Well, I took off toward it. Ernie was staggering around behind me, cursing about his leg being asleep after sitting in one position for all that time and why didn't they spring for cushioned seats for the press already. I raced down the rest of the bleachers and out the stadium gate toward the scream, which died off and then started up again.

By the time I reached the source of the shriek, there was a crowd. They seemed to be circled around something—reminding me of the field brawl.

"It just came out of nowhere and...*thump-thump*...and was gone," a woman's voice said. She hiccupped twice and burst into loud tears. "And I can't feel a heartbe-e-eat."

"Excuse me," I said, pushing and prodding my way

through the crowd, my Chicago reporter instincts kicking in. "Excuse me, I—oh."

In the center of the crowd, at the feet of the crying woman, was an unmoving, crumpled body, facedown, his head turned to the side, his eyes open.

The back of his T-shirt read COACH.

The body was definitely Coach Farley's.

And he was definitely dead.

# CHAPTER 4

CHIEF HENDERSON, WEARING PARKWOOD HIGH School spirit wear, was first on the scene, his entire face a tanned wrinkle of concentration. He immediately began waving everyone away.

"Move back, folks," he said, flailing his arms around. "Give me some space to work. Get out—now, Stella Jensen, I heard that and I am not having a power trip, this is police business, and you're standing in the way. Get back, get back. We've got to make room for the ambulance. Get on, now."

We all shuffled backward, making a wide semi-circle around the coach, which only served to make him look even deader somehow. It had been a while since I'd reported on something like this, and I'd forgotten how the sight of a deceased person brought about so many conflicting feelings. Excitement, because I was about to get a story. But also sadness that made me wonder who out there loved the victim, maybe called them son or husband or wife or daughter. Or mom. Or dad. Was Coach Farley someone's dad? Was a wife's life about to be turned upside down forever? I couldn't help thinking those things. Yet, at the same time, I knew what this meant. I was the first reporter on the scene of an accident, and someone had died. I had a job to do. A job I loved and believed in.

I felt my heartbeat quicken with anticipation. I pulled out my notebook and pencil, ready to take notes.

We were standing in what was called the lower lot, which was a hastily-paved and largely ignored parking lot that had been added on when the new stadium crowds strained the capacity of the upper lot. Those who arrived last-minute were forced to park there, and most chose to park on the lawn surrounding the upper lot—much to the principal's chagrin—rather than walk up the hill to their seats.

The lower lot was small and shadowy, blocked from view of the stadium by a row of evergreen trees. Two of the three lamps had burnt out and nobody had bothered to fix them, making the area even darker than usual. Adding a dead body only made the scene all the creepier.

"I was walking to my car and heard a noise behind me," the crying woman was repeating. "It was over so quick. Just *thump-thump* and when I looked over, there he was, on the ground like a p-p-pancake."

The crowd made a collective *ew* sound and shuffled back another step.

"Did she say pancake?" someone behind me whispered.

"I wish she'd stop saying *thump-thump*," someone else whispered back. "It's starting to give me the heebie-jeebies."

Sirens started up in the distance, and the chief got to work inspecting the scene.

"Can you describe the car that hit him, ma'am?" I heard him ask.

The woman squeezed her eyes shut and balled her fists in concentration. "It was blue. Dark blue. Or black. Or silver. Or maybe white. I'm not sure what color it was. Kind of square in the front. Or maybe more oval-shaped." Her eyes popped open wide. "The headlights were circles. I'm sure of it."

*Round headlights?* I wrote on my pad. *BMW? VW Beetle? Mercedes? Something vintage—Mustang or Volvo?*

"And could you see who was driving it?"

She shook her head. "By the time I heard the thumps and looked over, it was speeding away."

"Think hard, now. Did you happen to catch a look at the license plate?"

"No, sir. It was dark."

He sighed. "Okay. Thank you for your statement. We'll be in touch if we need more from you."

I stopped scribbling in my pad, my eyes bugged out. That was the whole statement? He was done? But he hadn't asked anything at all. I questioned witnesses harder than that about simple misdemeanor assaults. This wasn't a fist-fight; this was a dead man at the most crowded Parkwood event of the year. Was it an accident, or was it purposeful? If it was the latter, we could all be in danger. His family would want answers. The community would want answers. I wanted answers, and we deserved them.

I watched—hoping he was simply done for now and would be calling her in later for a lengthier questioning—as he dismissed the witness and went back to the body. The sirens got louder and then stopped. A police cruiser rolled up next to Chief Henderson's car and an officer spilled out.

"Ambulance is on its way," the officer said. "It got caught up outside the Hibiscus. Someone with chest pains."

*Probably* too many giblets in a 24-hour period, I thought, feeling a little heartburny myself. My grandma always said too much of a good thing was a bad thing.

Chief Henderson crouched next to the coach's body. "Tell 'em not to hurry," he said. "This one's not going anywhere." He gestured at us haphazardly. "You're on crowd control."

The officer gazed at us, and I was reminded that I'd already seen him earlier that day, directing traffic. I was pretty sure his nametag had said his name was Hopkins. He'd had no statement to share about the giblets gravy. Other than irritation at being asked, that is.

He walked toward us, waving his arms around similarly to how he'd been waving them while directing traffic. "Okay, folks, you've seen all there is to see here. You should head on home now."

There was a bit of grumbling, until someone said, "Wonder if Esther's got any gravy left?" And then the grumbling turned into a more positive sound as several people headed off for the Hibiscus.

I stayed rooted in my spot, watching as River Fork school buses rumbled to life in the upper lot and then slowly rolled away. The fact that the coach was down here while his players—and their buses—were up there only made things more curious. What was Coach Farley doing down here, anyway? This lot was for stragglers. Had he been late to the game?

"Did they see who did it?" Evangeline had sidled up next to me and was looking down at the coach with a pained expression.

"I don't think so." I scanned what was left of the dissipating crowd, an uneasy feeling creeping over me. Most everyone was leaving, except for Wickham Birkland, who looked sweaty and disapproving as he gazed at the action around the coach's body.

Chief Henderson called to the officer, tearing my attention back to the scene. "You got an evidence bag in your car?"

The officer jogged to the chief, crouched beside him over the body, then stood up and jogged to his cruiser. I tried not to notice that he was a really good jogger. Trace was not a good jogger. He was all flailing arms and visual pain. Trace was more of a good walking-through-the-shopping-district-er. And why was I thinking of Trace all of a sudden?

*There's a dead man here, Hollis. Get your head in the game.*

I tore my eyes away from the officer and refocused on the crime scene, trying to take in every detail. Loose pompon strands, bits of trash blown up against the curb, a wadded and discarded take out menu from Mister Wok's. Aside from the coach, it was a standard, ordinary high school football stadium parking lot.

The officer came back from the cruiser with a handful of evidence bags and some latex gloves. The chief snapped on the gloves and opened a bag. I watched as he leaned over and carefully plucked something out of the coach's hand. He held it up and examined it in better light before dropping it into the bag, which he sealed shut.

It was a hood ornament.

A Mercedes hood ornament.

I only knew of one Parkwoodian who drove a Mercedes. And it dawned on me that, yes, I had actually seen the coach before. He'd been the one who'd hit Wickham earlier that day. The one Wickham had been following into the Hibiscus.

Esther's voice popped into my head. *That Wickham's been looking for trouble since the day he was born, and one of these days, he's going to actually find it. You mark my words about that.*

I glanced toward the back of the crowd, but Wickham had already gone. I scanned the entire lot and the hill leading back up toward the stadium; he was nowhere to be found. Weird. He was just there a second ago. He was like a ghost—coming and going without so much as a whisper of sound.

*It came out of nowhere...*

Evangeline had turned with me. "What? You see something?" she asked.

"No," I said after a pause. "No, I didn't see anything." Did I?

"Y'all can go on home now."

I jumped. Officer Hopkins was right in front of me. The top button of his uniform shirt was unbuttoned, revealing a very white T-shirt beneath. Interesting. Officer Hopkins was apparently fastidious with his laundry.

"I'm the press," I said without thinking. I held up my notebook and pencil.

He pushed them back down, as if I was brandishing a camera in his face. "There's nothing to report on."

"Nothing to report on? There's a dead body right there!"

"People die every day. We've got to investigate this. It could be as simple as a heart attack. His family doesn't even know yet. You should report on the new hot dog contraption they've got in concessions instead. That's a story people want to read about."

He couldn't be serious. I tried to imagine myself telling my old editor in Chicago that nobody cared about a murder victim when there was a new frankfurter machine in town. If I'd ever done something like that, she might've actually called U of C and asked for them to revoke my diploma. And I wouldn't have blamed her. I might've given it back willingly.

"So he had a heart attack and then someone ran over him? There's a murder here," I said. "Or at the very least a manslaughter."

Quick panic raced across his face and disappeared, like a lightning strike. "Or an accident."

"He accidentally fell under someone's tires?"

"Nobody saw what happened."

"Not true." I pointed with my notebook at the witness, who was shuffling away in the arms of two friends, still sniffling. "She saw what happened. *Thump-thump* happened!"

He gazed at me for a long time, and then he shrugged. "From what I understand, Mary Jean wouldn't let you print it, anyway."

"Yes she—" I slumped. He was right. She wouldn't.

Unless...I was persistent.

For the first time since coming to Parkwood, I was interested in a story. Maybe I could talk Mary Jean into it. I could be very persuasive when I wanted to be. If I took really good notes, she might just be tempted to let me run with it.

I took a defiant side step so I could see around Officer Hopkins and surveyed the scene again. There was something off. Something in plain sight that I wasn't seeing.

Chief Henderson had gotten out a camera and was taking up-close photos of the coach's body. I wondered if I should suggest he take photos of Wickham's car, just in case. Who else around here drove a car with round headlights and a motive to mur—

And that was when it occurred to me.

Paulie.

Paulie Henderson drove an old, beat up Jeep. He was known for always taking it off-road to places it shouldn't go, like over curbs and through front yards...and...

Across the chest of a man he'd just an hour before very heatedly and very publicly vowed to kill?

Could that be why the chief wanted everyone out of

there so badly? Could that be why Officer Hopkins' job seemed to be to usher me away?

Well, no. The coach was holding a Mercedes hood ornament. I'd seen that with my own eyes. And I would have been willing to bet dollars to donuts that Wickham's hood ornament was currently missing.

But still. Paulie had actually told him he was a dead man. That had to be taken into account.

"So if you could just move along now…" Officer Hopkins said, stepping in my way again and making little go-away motions with his hands, like he was shooing a stray off of his porch. He was really starting to annoy me with this wanting-me-to-leave thing he had going on.

"Will you be considering Paulie Henderson for this hit-and-run?" I asked.

Officer Hopkins flinched and lowered his voice. "Shhh, you can't just go around asking those kind of questions."

I balked. "Did you just shush me? You can't shush the press, sir. We have constitutional rules about that. And I absolutely can ask those kind of questions. In fact, I think I have a duty to ask them. I owe it to the public and to this man's family to ask those questions. And I'm not going anywhere, so you might as well save your energy trying to get me out of here."

He sighed, resigned. "Fine. You want to stay? Stay. But stay right here—don't move—and don't bother me or the chief with any questions. There are no constitutional rules about that."

"You sure about that?" I asked, drawing myself up boldly.

"Obstruction of justice," he said, matching my confidence. If I didn't know better, I would think deep down he was enjoying this. And I couldn't help noticing the little jolt of electricity between us, which was definitely not what I wanted at a time like this. Or at any time. "You can't write the story if you're sitting in the back of my car with hand-cuffs on until I can get around to writing the report. And I am really slow at writing reports. Really slow. Are you catching my drift?"

I nodded. He went back to waving the crowd away, but kept half an eye on me the entire time. The chief put away his camera and began pacing the perimeter of the scene. As tempting as it was to take a giant step out of the spot the officer had ordered me to stay in just to spite him—and kind of to get him to come back within electricity-zapping range to prove to myself that I hadn't imagined it—I was there to do a job and I had to focus.

"Chief," I called out. "Would you mind if I asked you some questions? Could a Mercedes run over someone like that, or is that more the work of an off-road vehicle? Like maybe a Jeep?"

Chief Henderson flicked me an irritated glance, then aimed an even more irritated one at Hopkins, who instantly stormed back to me.

"I just told you not to bother the chief while he works the accident scene. You said you were catching my drift."

"And I told you this was no accident," I replied coolly. "Someone hit this man with a car and left the scene."

His lips pursed in a way that I could only take to be frustrated acquiescence.

"What'd I miss?"

Ernie sidled up beside me, out of breath and red-cheeked, jostling me with his shoulder. His eyes landed on Coach Farley and his entire face fell with disappointment.

"Oh, jeez. I'm going to have to change the whole article, aren't I?"

# CHAPTER 5

DAISY OPENED HER DOOR MID-SCREAM.

"I told you all to quiet that game down right now or I'll—oh, hey, Hollis." She stepped aside, tripping over a toy truck and nearly falling. She snatched it up and waved it in the air. "Lucas, guess what you no longer own? I've told you to pick it up a thousand times and now it is mine, young man. I love trucks. This is the best truck I've ever owned. I can't believe you just gave me such an awesome truck. Come on in, Hollis. I've got lemon bars. You won't believe the curd in these. Straight from heaven, I tell you. I'm late, aren't I?" She checked the time on the grandfather clock in the entryway, then sighed. "Late. I'm sorry."

"I thought maybe you'd chickened out," I said.

"Are you kidding me? I have been mentally preparing myself for this all day. I am ready."

"Good, because I was prepared to drag you over by your hair if I had to."

Two boys whizzed through the entryway, knocking into me, one on each side, then disappeared into the kitchen. I heard the sliding glass door rumble open and shut again. The music of an abandoned video game blared from the living room.

"You might have to drag me back in. Let's escape while we can."

"Where's Mike?" I asked.

She disappeared into the sweet-smelling kitchen, baby Willow toddling after her. There was the sound of drawers opening and closing. I rounded the corner to find Daisy covering a pan of lemon bars with plastic wrap one-handed, her other hand supporting Willow on her hip. The plastic wrap stretched flat and perfect. This was one reason I was pretty sure I would never be a mother—I couldn't get plastic wrap to look like that with two hands, a blueprint, and ninety spare minutes of silent prayer.

"Out back with the guys," she said. "They have boxes and the kids wanted forts. It turned into a whole thing out there."

Our eyes met briefly. I knew what that meant—something epic was happening outside. I shuffled to the sliding glass door and peered out. The backyard was a field of cardboard boxes, stacked and piled into forts. Daisy's husband Mike—the world's biggest child at heart— was inside one of them, aiming the barrel of a foam dart gun through a crack. Five-year-old Brant sat on the grass behind him, methodically emptying a bag of marshmallows into his mouth, his hair so sticky it shot up in spikes around his forehead like a cartoon character's. Seven-year-old Jake stood next to his dad, peering through a tiny crack he'd made lower in the box tower. Across the lawn, two similar forts hid Mike's buddies: Ed and Mudd in one, Spencer in the other. Lucas, who had been just moments before tearing past me was now standing on a box next to Spencer.

"Dart war?" I asked.

She sighed. "They tried to do it in here. I made them take it outside. The kids are going nuts."

As if to punctuate her mom's statement, Willow ripped the pacifier out of her mouth and tossed it. It bounced off the plastic wrap—the woman had the pan wrapped so tightly things bounced off of it, and I felt the need to bow to her in appreciation—and clattered to the floor, rolling under the refrigerator. Willow watched it, then threw her head back and let out a wail. Without missing a beat, Daisy opened a drawer, pulled out another pacifier, and popped it into Willow's open, wailing mouth.

A master, I tell you.

Daisy came around the counter, bumped me out of the way with her free hip, opened the door, and yelled. "Mike! I'm going! Come get your daughter!"

"Truce!" Mike popped up, flashing a "T" with his hands. Instantly, he was pelted with a dozen darts. Lucas giggled maniacally from inside his fort. "Truce! Truce! I said truce, you guys!" Mike called, covering his head and running up the deck stairs. "Fine!" He fired his gun randomly as he ran, yelling unintelligible sounds like he was in an action movie. "Hey, babe," he said breathlessly when he reached us. "Hey, Hollis. Have fun."

He kissed Daisy on the temple, then grabbed the baby and held her over his head. "Hostage!" he hollered, rushing back toward his fort. "Hold your fire!"

Mudd popped up out of his fort, took aim, and rapid-fire nailed Mike in the gut with a rain of foam darts, expertly missing the baby. Willow giggled and kicked her legs. "Release the innocents!" Mudd yelled.

"Does Mike have his face painted?" I asked, squinting at him.

Daisy rolled her eyes. "I don't even ask anymore. What he won't do for those kids. Should we go? Our listeners are waiting."

"Our listeners don't even know we exist yet."

She held up one finger as she grabbed her lemon bars and hustled to the front door. "Not true. I've told my mom, which means everyone who ever even thought about going to The Stray Hair knows by now. We've got some high expectations to live up to." She brushed past me. "No pressure, of course."

I felt my stomach tighten with nervous anticipation. "Of course."

"Testing, one, two," I said into one of the new microphones I'd set up on the desk in my tiny living room. I tapped it a few times and was pleased by the muffled thumps in my headphones. So far that was the extent of my knowledge in making podcasts, and the manual to my new equipment was longer than some of the novels I'd had to read in high school. We had so much to learn. "You hear me, Dais?"

She nodded, trying to shoo my cat, King, off the table and out of the food.

I'd grief-adopted King after moving to Parkwood, thinking that what I needed was a distraction to get my mind off of Trace and Tink. His name was actually Archie, but he was full of quirks that made it obvious that he fancied himself the ruler of the house, so I added what seemed like the most appropriate title: King.

King Archie required his dinner be served to him in a people bowl rather than a cat dish. He snubbed any drink other than the clear, cold stream of a lightly-running bathroom faucet, or anything I poured for myself and left unattended for longer than thirty seconds. King assumed every bowl of cereal, deli sandwich, PopTart, or can of tuna was his and his alone, as was the bottom quarter of the bed, all the way across. He refused to so much as lick a cat treat, flicking his paws disgustedly at the mere sight of one, but instead demand-meowed at the refrigerator door when he felt like snacking. And King Archie *always* felt like snacking. Which was why he was pushing twenty pounds. But he was twenty pounds of pure pomp and circumstance, and I loved him.

"I thought you said this cat was on a diet," Daisy said, waving in his general direction.

"He is, but mum's the word," I said, covering his little kitty ears. "He doesn't know it. I'm easing him into it slowly." I picked him up and set him on the floor.

"Mm-hmm, so slowly I think he's actually gained weight," she said. "I'm pretty sure he's thinking you don't know yet that he diets for no one. Come to think of it, that's a philosophy I could get behind."

"Should we get started?" I asked, changing the subject.

"Sure. Let's do this. Hey, there, fellow fans of crime!" she said into the microphone.

"Wait! I have to turn it on."

"Oh. I thought you were just testing it."

"I was, but I wasn't recording."

She peered at the computer. "How do you know if you're recording?"

I peered along with her. "I actually don't. I kind of thought you would be the tech person."

She gave me a have-you-lost-your-mind look. "What made you think that?"

I considered it. "I don't know. You're always fixing the kids' stuff. I just assumed."

"There's a big difference between replacing the batteries on a talking piece of plastic and this," she said. "My vast technical knowledge is 'blow on it, and if that doesn't work, try distraction with Popsicles while you throw it away and pretend it got lost.' You're the technical person." She pushed the pan of lemon bars toward me. "I'm the recipe person."

"Nice try, but you are not just a recipe person. This is a true crime podcast."

"No, it's a true crime and baked goods podcast. Remember, you said, 'We should record a podcast together,' and I said, 'Lucas, get out of those brownies,' and you said, 'Murder, mayhem, blah-blah-blah, oh, those brownies do look good,' and I said, 'Girl, I barely have time to listen to podcasts, what makes you think I have time to research for one? They're my secret recipe brownies, here, have one,' and you said—and I quote—" She puffed her cheeks out in a disturbingly-good impression of me talking around a mouthful of food. "'You just bring the brownies and I will take care of everything else.' So I brought the brownies—in the form of lemon bars."

Oh. Right. The brownie conversation.

In my defense, Daisy's brownies could make people say and do just about anything. They could cause out-of-body experiences. They could be the source of blissed-out blackouts. Forget the insanity defense—not guilty by reason of browniebrain was more like it. They were that good.

"Okay, fine," I said. "I'll do the editing. Let's just…try not to mess up a lot because I don't really know what I'm doing yet."

"What do those lines mean right there?" she asked, pointing to the screen.

I squinted at the lines, then flipped through the manual. "I think it means we just recorded this whole conversation. I guess it was on after all."

"Oh!" she said brightly. "Hey, world!"

"No, we can't open our podcast with, 'Hey, world.' We need something snappier."

"Well, what should I say?" She adopted a serious newscaster voice. "Welcome to K-DEAD, ladies and gentlemen, here's a first look at today's headlines. Local podcaster, Hollis Bisbee, is kind of a control freak. Let's go live with King Archie Bisbee for more." She scooted her microphone toward King, who had reappeared at the dessert plate. He meowed, pawed at the plastic stretched over the lemon bars a few times, then hopped down from the table indignantly and headed for the fridge. "Well said, King."

"Very funny," I said. I thought it over for a second. "How about this?" I leaned toward the microphone. "Welcome to the *Knock 'em Dead* podcast, where crime and passion meet. I'm Hollis and…"

Daisy bit her lip. "I don't know what I think about that."

"About what?"

"That 'where crime and passion meet' thing you're saying. It sounds too fancy romancey."

I sighed. "Fine. Let's do it again with a different—*less romantic*—tagline."

"I have one!" she said jubilantly. "Let me! You do the welcome and then I'll do the tagline."

"Okay," I said. "Great. Let's do this." I cleared my throat and leaned in again. "Welcome to the *Knock 'em Dead* podcast."

"Where murder and muffins meet!" Daisy chirped. She held up her pan of lemon bars, as if we had an audience who could see it.

"Murder and muffins?"

She nodded. "Isn't it cute?"

Cute. Granted, I hadn't exactly crafted a mission statement for our podcast, but I was thinking more along the lines of cutting-edge, engaging, hard-hitting. Definitely not cute. Nights in school flashed before my eyes—cramming for finals, swigging coffee and living off of Milky Way bars, my eyes packing bags like they were headed for a month in Europe. I did all that for cute?

*Let it go, Hollis. This is what having a partner is all about. Fifty-fifty, remember?*

"Adorable," I said. "Let's keep it." I took a deep breath, cleared my throat again, and leaned in. "Welcome to the *Knock 'em Dead* podcast."

"Where murder and muffins meet!"

"I'm Hollis."

"And I'm Daisy."

"And we're passionate about true crime." If she could have her *muffins* in the tagline, I could have my fancy romancey *passion*. "Today marks the first episode in our first series, so I want to make sure we start off with a bang."

"Ooh, bombs?" Daisy asked.

"Poisonings."

"Poison bombs?"

"No, not a literal bang. Although I suppose I can hear that mistake now." Mary Jean admonished me in my head: *Read aloud, dear.* "I just meant, you know, a metaphorical bang. Something that will make the listener feel…" I made an explosion sound and fanned my hands out by my temples. "Mind-blown by our amazing reporting. Like the history of murder by poisonings. According to an FBI Supplemental Homicide Report, women are more likely to kill by poisoning than men. So I thought it would be exciting to talk about women who have poisoned—and who have been poisoned—throughout history."

"Well, I've got something exciting," Daisy said. Again

she held the pan toward the computer screen. "Lemon bars. They are to die for." She cracked up, snorting right into the microphone. "Did you hear what I did there? To die for?" She reached down and produced a knife and two paper plates from her enormous purse slash diaper bag then began expertly cutting squares. "Now there are a couple secrets to making a good lemon curd," she said. "First of all, you should always add your eggs one at a time. Add, beat, add, beat, and so on. Make sure you strain the curd after it's done cooking so you can get all that lumpy zest out. And here's my little secret, Hollis. I add just the tiniest bit of orange juice to make it sweeter. Give it a try."

"I can't eat while—" She shoved a lemon bar into my hand. "Okay, sure, I'll take one. Should we start by diving right into the history of poisonings, or should we start with news—like the coach case?"

"Coach case? Oh, the guy who got hit after the homecoming game." She'd already heard the Hibiscus version of what had happened, of course. Daisy was as plugged into Parkwood gossip as Esther. Seemed the key to everyone's secrets—er, heart—in this town was food. She gestured at the lemon bar that was dusting my lap with powdered sugar. "Eat that."

"I'm sort of in the middle of—oh, fine." I took the tiniest bite and let out a groan. "That is so good, Daisy. You've outdone yourself."

"It's the orange juice," she said. "Secret ingredient not so secret anymore. Oh, wait, maybe that's not a good idea. I forget I have a business now. Can you just edit everything out and we can start over from Welcome?"

My eyes bugged out. "No way!"

"But my secret ingredient—"

"Is secret no more. Moving on. Yes, I'm talking about

the hit-and-run at last night's football game. I happened to be on the scene. There were clues. I just have to get them."

She waved her hand at me. "I have faith in you. The River Fork team is going to be lost without their head coach. His assistant sure has big, winning shoes to fill. He's either going to be a hero or a town punching bag. Now, let me tell you about how you add the butter into this curd…"

She kept going, but I had tuned her out completely. *His assistant sure has big, winning shoes to fill.*

Daisy was right. Coach Farley was a winning coach, and someone taking his spot could be in a lot of game trouble without him.

Or that someone could be a hero for stepping in and keeping the winning streak going, despite the blow to the team.

Would an assistant be willing to kill a guy just to get that chance?

I wasn't sure about this case, and it had been quite a while since I last investigated a murder, but I knew one thing.

I had to get out to River Fork and talk to the assistant football coach.

I also needed another lemon bar. Curse her and her orange juice.

# CHAPTER 6

W E WEREN'T DONE RECORDING YET, but Mike arrived, looking panicked. He was covered with suds and carrying a towel-wrapped Willow. Bath time in the Mueller house was not a job for one person, and especially if that person was a guy wearing an aluminum foil crown.

"I kept my fort up the longest, so I won the kingdom," he said in all seriousness, pointing at the crown with a sudsy finger. "But Spencer's a sore loser, so I expect an assassination attempt within the week."

"As one would," I said. My stomach hurt. I'd eaten four lemon bars while Daisy went on about how to get the perfect crisp-yet-gooey shortbread crust. Still, I felt good. Like maybe this was exactly what I had needed to finally put everything behind me and start over anew.

"So we get into the poisonings tomorrow?" I asked as Daisy hefted Willow onto her hip. The little girl struggled to get down, but Daisy had an amazing grip when it came to those kids. "And then I'll try to figure out how to edit and post."

"I just don't know how poisonings reflect on my lemon bars," she said. "But I suppose we'll make it work."

"It's a *true crime* podcast," I reminded her for the hundredth time. "Arsenic is going to become your jam. Get it?

Jam? Because you're a baker?" I nudged her until she smiled and slapped at my shoulder playfully.

"I hope not," Mike mumbled, following Daisy down the front walk and across the lawn. "The husband's always first to go."

"You have nothing to worry about," Daisy said, stopping to kiss his cheek. "I need you to rule the kingdom when I'm gone. See you tomorrow, Hollis. I'm thinking lemon tarts. A whole lemon theme. I've got loads of recipes."

She had loads of recipes and I had a whole folder of poisonings. Women who'd poisoned for insurance money, women who'd poisoned for revenge after an affair, and a slew of very disturbing stories from the 1800s, when it seemed like women were just poisoning everyone, willy-nilly-style.

Women who poisoned. It was a great start to the season and I was pumped.

Daisy and Mike had no sooner left when my phone rang. I checked the caller ID while I headed over to spruce up the podcast corner. Daisy and I had disagreed over the appropriate name for our recording space. I wanted to call it *the control center*, or perhaps *the anchor desk*. She wanted to call it a warm and welcoming *nook*, but was willing to settle for *podcast pad*, because of the retro-sounding alliteration, of course. In the end, we called it a *corner*, which was neither creative nor authoritative, and now I had another whole fifty-fifty-partners discussion to edit out of our episode.

I answered the phone on the third ring. "Hey, Mom. Hey, Aunt Ruta."

They were too busy carrying on their own conversation with each other to hear me. As always.

"Hey, Mom. Hey, Aunt Ruta," I repeated.

One of them said something about outdoor chair

cushions. One aggressively stirred sugar into iced tea. One complained that tea had splashed onto the clean tablecloth and there was no need to get so snippy about cushions. One countered that there was no need to get so snippy about tablecloths. I was convinced that Mom and Aunt Ruta had come into this world arguing—but we could never know who started it, because they couldn't even agree on who was born first. And my grandma never told, because she was afraid of one of them getting a superiority complex over the other.

"Ma! Aunt Ruta!" I shouted.

"Oh, mercy, no need to shout," Mom said. "Guess someone's having a bad day, Rut."

"Eh, she was born having a bad day. A bad hair day." They both cracked up with their signature twin cackle.

"Very nice," I said. "Did you call specifically to insult me, or…"

"Oh, now, don't get your Tootsie Rolls in a twist," Aunt Ruta said. "We were just teasing you."

"She doesn't care for teasing, Rut. Never has. Serious all the time. Good thing she was an only."

"What are you talking about? I am not serious all the time. And I'm not an only," I said. "What did Betsy and Harlowe do now?"

Betsy and Harlowe. My sisters. One thinks she's still in college and the other thinks she's the First Lady. They both live walking distance from Mom and Aunt Ruta but neither of them ever walks over, unless they need money (Betsy) or a sitter for their herd of nervous Pomeranians (Harlowe) or a chocolate stash to raid when their significant other is being annoying (both). And they were constantly getting themselves "disowned" by Mom and Aunt Ruta for various and sundry real and imagined offenses. And to Mom and Ruta, "disowned" was a very transient state of being. You could be "disowned" on a Thursday and invited over for sandwiches on Saturday. And then disowned again on Sunday for having previous plans that prevented you from showing up for said Saturday sandwiches.

"Oh, nothing important," Mom said. "We weren't calling about them. Even if we haven't seen hide nor hair of either of them in two full months, so they obviously don't care about two little old ladies. We could have fallen and been lying here waiting for sweet death to take us out of our misery and into the light of the Great Beyond, and would either of those girls have even known?"

Another favorite in the Mom and Ruta conversation repertoire: mortal injury.

"I mean, the chances that you would both fall at the same time are pretty low…"

"It's bad enough that you moved seven hours and thirty-six minutes away, but you would think after a lifetime of sacrifice, someone would stop in and call 9-1-1."

"But you're not—"

"You would think someone would care enough to pick poor old Ruta here up off the floor, especially since I'm dead and gone. Save one of us, you know. If not your sisters, then your ungrateful cousin, Bart. Now, there's a conversation."

I massaged the bridge of my nose. Ungrateful Cousin Bart was a subject that would last for hours, and I had zero ice cream in the house to distract me from it.

"That would be a long conversation," Ruta yelled, confirming my need for ice cream, and causing my ear to ring from the volume of her voice. I winced, pulling the phone away from my ear.

"Aunt Ruta, you're on speaker phone, you don't have to

yell. I can hear you just fine. Well, could. Now I kind of only hear ringing."

"Don't be dramatic, Hollis," she replied. "Your ears are fine."

"She always did have sensitive ears," Mom said. "You did. You always had sensitive ears. This is why you never got them pierced."

"I got them pierced in eighth grade, Mom."

"How long are we going to talk about your ears?" Aunt Ruta shouted.

"You're right, Rut. We didn't call about ears," Mom said. "Even though you clearly got them pierced without my knowing. You never did mind breaking your mother's heart."

"What did you call about?" I asked, trying my hardest not to get frustrated. And also wondering if she was right about my ears being too sensitive.

"We called to tell you that we saw Trace," Aunt Ruta yelled.

I forced nonchalance, or at least my best version of it, although my voice sounded a little strangled. "Oh? That's nice."

"We agreed we were going to break the news to her gently," Mom said.

"What wasn't gentle about that? We saw Trace. It's not like I told her that you invited him for Thanksgiving."

"You what?" I yelped, nonchalance completely out the window. My stomach had fallen to my feet.

"Christmas, too," Aunt Ruta chirped. "Not for the whole day, of course. Just a stop by kind of thing."

"You were supposed to leave it to me to tell her," Mom said, and they launched into another of their squabbles.

"Mom—" I tried. "Aunt Ru—you guys—hello, I'm still here—Mother!"

"Yes?" Mom asked, her innocence as fake as my nonchalance had been.

"Please tell me I heard Aunt Ruta wrong."

"What did you hear?"

"I heard that you invited my ex-boyfriend—emphasis on the *ex*—to celebrate the holidays with us."

"Oh, well, yes, then, you heard that correctly."

It had broken my heart to leave Trace, and I wasn't over it yet. Part of me thought I would never be over it. My best hope and strategy had been to never lay eyes on him again. And here I would be, eating, drinking, and making merry with him in just over a month.

I lightly pounded my forehead on the desk and groaned.

By the time I got to work Monday morning, I was in no mood for…pretty much anything. I'd spent the greater portion of the night stress-dreaming about Ungrateful Cousin Bart and Trace pelting me with cold, half-eaten dinner rolls with Betsy and Harlowe noshing on chocolate while I tried to save a very-loudly-fallen-and-waiting-for-death-under-the-Christmas-tree Mom and Aunt Ruta. As I was having an extremely bad hair day. And Officer Hopkins was jogging, a half-excited gleam in his eye while I tried to question him about what had happened to Mom and Aunt Ruta. I woke up exhausted and sweaty and hoping it was April and I'd somehow slept through "the festivities." Was it possible to schedule a stomach flu?

I was going to have to call Trace and uninvite him.

Nicely. Which meant talking to him. Ugh. I'd put that one off as long as I possibly could.

Ernie was sitting at Mary Jean's desk, an open box of doughnuts between them while she bent over his article with red pen in hand. I tried not to notice she was making very few marks on his article. Ernie must have already read his work aloud.

"Oh, hey, Hollis," Joyce said when I walked in. "Gosh, you look exhausted."

"Thanks," I said. "Long weekend."

"I heard," she said. "Ernie's writing a whole story about it."

"A whole story about what?"

"About how that coach dropped dead right in the high school stadium's parking lot Friday night."

I blinked. "Dropped dead?"

She nodded. "Chief Henderson stopped by this morning and told us all about it. Sad situation, really, when you think about it. Dying on enemy turf like that. Would have been much better to die in his own stadium. More apropos or something. Anyway, did you try the hot dogs?"

"He didn't just—it was a hit and—they're not investigating—" Once again, I was reduced to partial sentencing. I took a breath, trying to make sense of what I was hearing. Maybe Joyce had it wrong. I about-faced and gave her a smile. "The hot dogs were great. I should get to writing about them now while the taste is still fresh in my mind."

Ernie had finished up and was headed to his cubicle with his article in one hand, and three doughnuts balanced in a stack in his other hand. He was so worried about dropping the doughnuts, he nearly crashed into me as I headed to Mary Jean's desk.

"Oh, it's you!" I was ninety-nine percent sure Ernie

called me *It's you* because he couldn't remember my actual name. "Mary Jean's got breakfast."

"Great," I said. I pointed at the paper he was carrying. "Your piece about the homecoming game?"

He studied the paper as if he didn't realize what it was or why it was in his hand. "Yep."

"It was quite a loss."

He nodded sagely. "Nothing too exciting to publish about a game like that."

A mid-field fight with an open death threat, followed by the recipient of that threat actually ending up dead an hour later with the sole witness giving a description of headlights that just happened to match the headlights on the vehicle of the person who issued the threat? Nope. I couldn't see any story potential there.

"I hear you're writing about Coach Farley," I said. "The coach who...dropped dead?" A corner of my mouth twitched as it tried to dip down. *Smile, Hollis, just smile.*

"Yeah, I'll get to that later."

He took a giant bite of a doughnut, mumbled something that vaguely resembled a farewell, and shuffled toward his desk, happily chewing. I watched in shock.

He would get to that later? *Later?*

Well, maybe he could put it off until later, but I couldn't.

I dropped my bag on my chair and marched straight to Mary Jean's office. I was trained to chase down big stories. To not let anything get in the way of reporting crucial news. To use my reporter's notebook as a shield and my pen as a dagger. A weapon of truth and justice!

Okay...maybe I was taking that last bit a little far. But I wanted to get to the bottom of what happened to Coach Farley. Because if the police chief was calling it natural causes, he was wrong. And I wanted to set it right. The people deserved to know what really happened. Coach Farley's widow deserved to know what really happened. The River Fork Otters deserved to know what really happened.

"Hollis! Good morning! How were the hot dogs?"

I planted my hands on my hips to channel the fearlessness I was trying to convince myself I had. "I want the Farley hit-and-run story."

"Hit-and-run?" She never lost her pleasant expression. "There was no hit-and-run. He just died in an unfortunate location."

"That's not true. There was a witness. She said he *thump-thumped.*"

She took off her cheaters and dropped them onto the desk. "That witness was Agnes Tellerman. She's one of those professional witnesses. Always the one to see something strange or scary or illegal. A bit of a fibber, just trying to get attention. Loves to see her name in the paper, I would suspect. She's forever calling the police for one thing or another. You can't go off of what she said."

*Yes,* I thought. *Yes, I actually can. She was the only witness. She saw a hit-and-run. She was sure of it.* "She was crying really hard."

Mary Jean waved her hand at me, then slipped her cheaters back on and turned to her computer, dismissing me. "She cries all the time. She likes the drama. It's a ruse."

"Not this time. This was no accident and no natural death. This was a manslaughter at the very least. Maybe a murder. There was a car involved, and a witness saw it. And we owe it to the public to report on what actually happened."

Her mouth turned down in pitiful concern, as if she were feeling sorry for me. She took off her glasses and carefully placed them on the desk. "Did you see it happen?"

"No."

"Did you hit the man yourself?"

"Of course not. But I was on the scene immediately afterwards."

"But you weren't there to see him actually die."

"No."

"And did you talk to the witness yourself?"

I paused, realizing that she had me. "No."

"Charlie, however, did talk to that witness, and he did look over the body, and he's reporting it as a plain, old, natural death."

"Charlie?"

"Chief Henderson," Joyce called from her desk. "He and Mary Jean go way back."

Well. That was concerning. The police chief, whose delinquent son was always skating out of trouble, and the newspaper editor, whose job was to report on delinquency, were old pals.

Mary Jean flicked a glance at Joyce, then leveled her eyes at me. "My friendship with Charlie has nothing to do with this. We can only go on what the chief has reported to us."

"That's not true," I said. "That's precisely what we can't do. We can't mislead the public, or give them partial facts. It's our job to seek out the whole story."

"But if you didn't witness it, didn't talk to any witnesses, and didn't even investigate the body up close, you're making assumptions, and *that* is precisely what we can't do. We're not medical examiners. We report on facts, not on suspicions. You know this, Hollis."

"But if I talked to Agnes—"

"You would be wasting your time. She's an unreliable source, and nobody in this town would take us seriously if we were to quote her in our paper. Again."

"So I can't even just interview her? Find out what she saw?"

"No. I'm ordering you to stay away from her and focus on your assigned stories."

My mouth dropped open, incredulous. "Ordering me to—"

"We have to report reality, and the reality is I know Charlie very well and I trust him."

The reality was I might have an actual heart attack if she kept talking like that. I was stumped. I had no rebuttal for such an unbalanced system. The sad part was, I was pretty sure Mary Jean truly believed in her system. She had no idea it was all kinds of wrong. It was our job to dig for the truth. To talk to every witness. To view the story from every angle.

But wasn't that the chief's job, too? Yet he was shutting down the case before even opening it. Why? Surely Paulie's privileges didn't extend this far. Mary Jean was trustworthy, and I didn't believe she would ever be part of something unethical on purpose. But she was also very trusting, and I couldn't say for sure that the chief wouldn't do something unethical—not when it came to protecting his son.

Mary Jean patted my hand and gave me a soft, motherly smile. "I know it's hard for you, coming from your old newspaper to this one, but we do things a little differently here. It's what our cu—"

"I know," I said, resigning. "It's what our customers expect."

"You'll get used to it," she said. "Give it time. So tell me about the new roller."

"We got interrupted during my interview, so I don't have much." I shrugged. "It's a hot dog roller. Not sure what else there is to say." *You can find one at any gas station on I-70,* I didn't add.

"That's okay. There's a youth football game going on out there this afternoon," she said. "You can go back and get a quote or two. That way Evangeline's mom can see her daughter's name in the paper. She'll love that."

"With all due respect, Mary Jean, I just don't think this is the best use of my time. Surely there are other stories…"

"Evangeline's family will be expecting it, so we can't back out now. Her mother is ninety-eight years old. She doesn't have many more years to wait for her daughter to end up in the paper. We'll keep it short. Consider it a human interest piece."

Except I couldn't think of a human who would be interested.

"Okay."

"See if you can get it to me by tomorrow morning. And there's a soft opening today of the new housewares store. I'd like you to get that. And grab some obits and ads from Joyce. You can do those and this week's events calendar from home again. Just email it when you're done." She checked her watch, grabbed the doughnut box and shook it at me. "Feel free."

"No, thanks," I said. "I'm not hungry."

She dropped the box on her desk and resumed working, dismissing me. Defeated, I started back toward my desk. "And Hollis?" She didn't look up from the paper she was writing on.

"Yes?"

"I'd better not find out that you went anywhere near Agnes Tellerman."

And in a town like Parkwood, I had no doubt that if I tried, she would find out. I gritted my teeth. "Understood." She didn't seem to have any more to say, so I continued my trudge toward my work station.

Back to the hot dog roller, and now a housewares store,

a handful of ads and obits, an events calendar, and the big old kibosh on the only exciting story Parkwood had seen since I arrived.

There weren't enough doughnuts in the world to make swallowing all of that any easier.

By "soft opening," they must have meant "whenever the owner decides to show up," because there was nobody to be found when I arrived at Vacuumulate, even though the rest of the stores in the strip mall it was anchoring had been open for at least an hour. I jotted down the name of the store with about a hundred question marks. I didn't get it. Was the name to suggest people want to collect vacuum cleaners? Or that their vacuum cleaners *were* the collectors, specifically of the dust and dirt in their homes? I suspected it was just the only cute way they could make vacuum cleaners not sound like...well, like vacuum cleaners, and housewares not sound like housewares. And I supposed if their goal was to get people thinking while waiting for them to open, it was effective.

The weather was nice, with a mild breeze knocking the last leaves off their branches, so I decided to wait outside the store. I found a bench and sat, waiting, people watching, trying to scribble out enough hot dog story to warrant my not having to go back to the stadium.

*Suit up, Parkwood football fans, there's a new player on the roster. ~~His name is Frank and he is delicious.~~*

*~~His name is Frank and he is the current MVP. Most Valuable Protein, that is.~~*

*~~A new player has rolled into town, and frankly, we couldn't be happier.~~*

I wasn't having much success.

A shadow fell over me, darkening my pad, and I began to gather my belongings. Finally, I could get some housewares action and get on with my day. If I managed my time wisely, I could maybe even get out to River Fork and do some light investigating and just work on the obits in the evening.

"I'm so glad you're here," I said, stuffing my pad into my bag and tucking my pencil behind my ear. "I'm from the *Parkwood Chronicle Weekly* and I was wondering if I could talk to you for a few minutes about—"

I stood up to find myself face to face with Officer Hopkins.

"You're not the owner of Vacuumulate," I said, with a little hope that maybe he was, as a side job, since he wasn't in his uniform. He was casual, in a pair of jeans and flannel shirt, the sleeves rolled up to show muscular forearms.

"Nope," Officer Hopkins said. "I just happen to be..." He trailed off, his eyes darting around the strip mall, as he seemed to be at a loss for exactly what he happened to be.

"Shopping?" I supplied.

He looked sheepish. "Guilty."

"Unsuccessfully, huh?"

"Huh?"

I pointed at his empty hands. "You're not carrying any bags, so I'm guessing your shopping hasn't been successful."

"Oh," he said, staring at his hands as if he hadn't ever seen them before. "Right. No, I haven't been—I need a toaster." He gestured toward Vacuumulate, and then tucked his thumbs into his pockets, a little too nonchalantly to actually be nonchalant.

I raised my eyebrows. Was he blushing? About a toaster? Was he embarrassed for me to know he liked toast? "Well,

I would say you came to the right place, but…" We both looked at the CLOSED sign on the Vacuumulate door. I plopped back down on the bench.

"I guess I could just sit with you while we wait," he said, then proceeded to perch as far away from me as he could, barely touching the bench with his backside. I stifled a giggle. Perhaps he felt that weird electricity bouncing around between us, just like I had.

"You need a toaster, too?" he asked, grinning. "Or are you more in the market for a spaghetti strainer?"

I held up my hands like I was posting a headline. "Breaking news story. New housewares store in Parkwood."

"Ah. I see."

"But now that you mention it, I could use a spaghetti strainer."

"Do you make a lot of spaghetti?"

"Not unless you count the kind that comes in a can."

"I don't think you're supposed to strain that."

"So that's what I've been doing wrong." I smacked my forehead lightly.

We chuckled, then sat awkwardly for a few minutes in silence, during which I caught myself assessing the ringless nature of his left hand. Was he new to Parkwood and single, just like me?

The question that followed that thought popped out without consulting my brain at all, and in the dorkiest way possible. "So do you do all the toasting at your house or is your girlfriend into crispy bread, too?" Seriously, Hollis? Crispy bread? I wanted Vacuumulate to open its doors and swallow me whole.

His brow furrowed while he put together the puzzle of my ridiculous question. "Toast for one, I'm afraid," he said, and my mortification was temporarily assuaged by relief that there was no toast-eating girlfriend in the picture, even though I wasn't sure why exactly I was so happy about that. "What about you?"

"Oh," I said. "Single toaster at my house, too. But I like that I get to use both slots."

I dug out my notebook and pencil. "So, since we have some time, I'm wondering if I could ask you a few questions."

He looked wary. "About what?"

"I'm told Coach Farley had a natural death."

"Ah. About that." He nodded. "Chief Henderson did say there was no evidence of foul play."

"And the witness—"

"Unreliable, trust me," he said.

"So she was just making up the thing about the car with the round headlights and the *thump-thump* and the pancake?"

"Agnes? Most definitely."

"But why would she do that? What does she have to gain? It doesn't even make sense."

"It does if you know Agnes Tellerman. She's had us out to her house four times this month for suspicious noises or shadows or some such. She's a crier. My neighbor went to school with her older brother, Tommy, and says he's a crier, too. Well, I mean, maybe not anymore. He's some big deal up on Wall Street now. Not sure they'd put up with a lot of crying on Wall Street."

"He probably just chugs antacids now," I said. "That's crying in adult form."

"It's your stomach crying," he said, and we both chuckled.

I liked that Officer Hopkins shared my sense of humor, and there was something so easy about the way we laughed together, but I didn't want to be lured away from the subject at hand. I steered the conversation back on track.

"No, but seriously. You saw the scene. That was no natural death. What am I missing here?"

He scooted a little closer, tented his hands between his knees, and thought it over. "Are we off the record?"

*I didn't want to be, but...* "Sure."

"You have to understand Parkwood."

I waited for more, but he only sat there nodding at his own statement, as if it had been some sort of wise advice. "That's it?"

"Yeah."

I sensed my temperature rise, making my ears hot. He was toying with me. This was a joke to him. My job was a joke. It felt like I was being mocked, and my mouth did the thing it always did when I was embarrassed or irritated— started moving ninety miles a minute. "You're saying I don't know what a murder looks like because I'm from somewhere else?"

"No, I'm just saying—"

"But aren't you new to Parkwood, too? Newer than I am, actually?"

"It doesn't matter how new you—"

"Which actually makes you less qualified to say you know Parkwood, right? It would stand to reason that someone who's been here a year would know the town better than someone who's been here a month."

"You're getting upset," he said.

"No, I'm not." But I was definitely getting frustrated. Especially after I'd pointed out—aloud—that I'd been here a year. I'd always sort of considered this a temporary assignment, and that I would be back in Chicago before I knew it. But I would be re-signing my lease soon, and that meant I would be locked in for another year. And I wasn't even conflicted about it. I had obviously become used to the idea, and when the heck did that happen? I'd never felt more homesick in my life than I did right then and there, sitting outside Vacuumulate with an adorable, single police officer who got my jokes and smelled amazing, but was not Trace. "But you're being condescending about what I do and don't know about this town."

He separated his hands and lifted them, palms up. "Parkwood isn't Chicago." He knew where I was from. Weird. What else did he know?

"I know that Parkwood isn't Chicago." I stood. "But surprisingly enough, murder looks the same no matter what state you're living in. Unless, of course, the state you're living in is denial. Now if you'll excuse me, I have other interviews to do."

I hurried back to my car.

I would get the housewares story later.

Right now, River Fork seemed like the best place to find the truth. The truth I was willing to find, anyway.

# CHAPTER 7

"YOU MUST HAVE SEEN MY smoke signals. Thanks for the S.O.S." Daisy extracted Willow from her legs, expertly shoving a Popsicle into one tiny hand and a sticky teddy bear into the other while ushering the little girl toward her grandmother. Mike was at a rare meeting in the office, so Daisy's mom had been called in as second string. She looked more than a little terrified. I didn't blame her.

"Let's go. Be back in a couple hours, Ma," Daisy said as we hustled to the front door before any of the other kids noticed she was leaving. Willow began to wail, and we crouch-ran to my car and dove in like we were under fire. "Where we headed?"

"River Fork."

She raised her eyebrows. "You got the assignment? What changed? I thought you said Mary Jean shut you down and gave it to Ernie." On the phone, I'd given her a quick run-down on Mary Jean's refusal to let me follow up on the case.

"I gave the assignment to myself."

"And she's not going to notice that you're missing?"

"She's letting me work from home today. I'll do it tonight."

She nodded, chewing her lip, thinking. "And in River Fork we're going to do what exactly?"

"Interview whoever we can interview and see if we can get into Farley's office. How are you with River Fork gossip?"

Her phone rang. "Hang on. Hello? Lucas, honey, that's why Grandma is there. Well, tell him I said to stop licking you." She held the phone away from her ear as kid-noise amplified loud enough for me to hear across the front seat. There was the faraway sound of a crash. "Mommy's gotta go," Daisy yelled into the phone, and hung up. "My mother is a saint. What were we talking about?"

"River Fork gossip," I reminded her.

"Oh. Yeah. That. I've got nothing. Except I know that the high school football coach recently suffered a mysterious death."

"Thanks, I'd gathered that much myself."

She grinned and half-turned in her seat so she was facing me. "But I did hear some Parkwood gossip."

I raised my eyebrows at her. "Spill. About what?"

"About you and that cute new police officer," she said. "The one with the blue eyes and the muscles for days."

I felt a jolt that I wasn't expecting—something similar to the charge I felt when I was around him, only now it was tinged with irritation over our conversation outside Vacuumulate. Great. Now I was going to get all swoony when he wasn't even around? "What about him?" I asked, trying to play it cool. "What have you heard?"

"I heard that you two were flirting on the bench outside Vacuumulate this morning."

How could that have gotten around so quickly? I hadn't seen anyone watching us. "What? People think we were flirting? There was no flirting. I do not flirt. I was reporting. And he was being condescending. And I don't flirt."

"You said that already." Her grin spread wider. "You're rambling. Are you nervous? You seem nervous."

"I am not. I'm also not flirting with Officer Blue Eyes." Ugh, that sounded personal. "That officer with the blue—with the eyes. I'm not flirting with him. See? I don't even know his name. Where did you hear such a ridiculous thing? Besides, the fact that you heard anything is creepy. I saw nobody out there. I would have interviewed them if I did. Because I was working, not flirting."

"Brooks," she said. "His name is Brooks Hopkins. He's 32, lives alone in that sweet little rental on Nightingale—the one with the old-fashioned window boxes?—and he used to be a police officer up in Kansas City. Rumor is he left KCPD not on the best terms, but nobody seems to know exactly what happened. Some people are saying he punched out his captain, but I don't believe it. Never married, but was engaged once, no kids, no pets. Takes good care of his mother. Listens to classic rock on actual vinyl. Has a motorcycle that he only takes out on really nice weekends." She looked thoughtful. "He has this sort of naughty and nice thing going—drives a bike, but likes his mom. It's sweet."

My mouth dropped open. How did Daisy find out all of this? "What, you don't know his middle name?"

"Adam," she said definitively. "After his grandfather on his mother's side. God rest his soul." She crossed herself. I'm sure the look on my face was somewhere between disturbed and awed. "What? He likes my cherry chocolate chunk muffins. We talked over breakfast."

"You're creepy."

"Says the woman who's obsessed with poisonings and who literally tried to kill me with a frozen hot dog."

"Not true," I said, turning onto the highway. "It was an imaginary hot dog, so it couldn't have literally killed you. Besides, I'm not obsessed; I'm intrigued. And not just with poisonings, but with murder, in general. I'm interested in stabbings and strangulations and blunt force traumas, too."

"And hit-and-runs?"

"Only one."

"You caught the part where he's single, right?"

"The coach?"

"No, Officer Blue Eyes." She nudged my shoulder with each word.

"New subject, please."

Her phone rang again. River Fork was a fifteen-minute drive at best, during which she mediated half a dozen fights, directed someone to the Band-Aids, and calmed a crier. By the time we reached the River Fork exit, I was exhausted, and they weren't even my kids. But Daisy didn't even seem to notice that her life was all about putting out fires.

The surprisingly large River Fork high school was just about a quarter mile south of the exit and visible from the highway. It was 3:00 and they had just dismissed for the day. We waited for the parking lot to clear before we pulled in.

"Why are we doing this again?" The woman who was unperturbed by a zillion child emergencies suddenly looked intimidated.

"You mentioned that Farley's assistant had big, winning shoes to fill, and that made me think we should probably interview that person to see what their relationship was like. Or, you know, maybe get into Farley's office and see what we can find."

Daisy's phone went off again—she picked it up on the first ring. "Mommy can't talk right now. What?" A sigh. "Put Brant on the phone." A pause. "Let your sister join your game so she'll stop crying. Well, you might not care if she's crying, but I'm sure Grandma does.—I don't know why

Jake smells, just move away from him until I get home. Yes, I'm sure I don't need to talk to anyone. Just show Grandma where the Tylenol is and tell her I'll be home in an hour or so." She hung up. "So you're saying I'm the brains behind this mission," she said, as if we had never been interrupted. Again.

"I actually don't think I said that." I found a spot near the back of the lot and parked.

"But I was the one who gave you the idea to come here. You definitely said that, right?"

I pushed open the car door. "Does it really matter?"

"You know who says that?" she asked, following me. "The person who didn't have the idea."

"You're impossible," I said, although the truth was Daisy was one hundred percent as much brains behind this operation as I was, even if she continually tried to convince everyone that all she contributed to the podcast was baking tips. Daisy was super smart, and her improvisational skills were off the charts. "Now shush and just follow my lead so we don't get found out."

I had prepared a whole speech to talk my way past the front office, but it turned out that someone had propped the activities complex door open with a football helmet, so I motioned for Daisy to follow me and walked straight into the activities complex without so much as a word. Rule #1 of investigative journalism: Sometimes getting what you wanted was just a matter of acting like it was yours to begin with.

Actually, that may have been an Aunt Ruta Life Rule. I couldn't quite remember. All I knew was it worked.

Coach Farley's office was positioned between the girls' and boys' locker rooms and had three large windows that looked out into the gymnasium. The blinds were open, so I could see that it was unoccupied. Perfect.

I made a beeline for it, slipped inside, and closed the door after Daisy.

"Get the blinds," I said.

"Me? Why?" Daisy yelped. "My job is to give the ideas. You do the executing."

"When did we delineate these jobs? I don't remember doing that."

The boys' locker room door banged open and a boy all padded up for practice came out, flanked by the man I recognized from football games as assistant head coach. He seemed occupied with instructing the boy.

"Down!" I whispered, and we both dropped to the floor. My mind scrambled for an excuse why we would be in the office if he were to come in. Correction—why we would be in the office *on the floor*? We'd probably have looked less fishy if we'd stayed standing. Rule #2 of investigative journalism: To look less suspicious, always try to blend in. Especially while doing something suspicious.

Wait. That one I was sure was an Aunt Ruta Life Rule.

Daisy's phone rang and we both winced. She answered in a whisper. "Hello? What? Uh...we're in the library. Doing research. Yes, tell Grandma she can give Willow a cheese sandwich. No, I don't know where cactuses get their prickles from. No, cactuses are not dead witches. Well, tell Lucas he's wrong. I've gotta go, honey!" She hung up and bit her lip, her eyes rolling upward as if she could see out the windows. Mine did the same. All I saw was field house ceiling, which, of course, featured three stuck dodge balls, just like every other school gym ceiling in all of America.

We held our breath and listened as the assistant coach's

voice got louder, and louder still, and then let our breath out as the voice got softer until it was gone.

"The blinds," I mouthed.

"Won't it look suspicious if they suddenly close with nobody in here?" Daisy whispered.

"I don't care, just close them!"

She inched over toward one window, reached up, and twisted the blinds closed while I closed the blinds on another. Then she inched over to the third window and did the same. Finally protected from view, we stood, brushing off our clothes.

"That was really close," she said.

"Too close. Let's just get this done and get out of here."

"Okay." She paused. "What is it we're trying to get done?"

We both stood in the center of the office and gazed around for a long minute. There was so much junk and paperwork and equipment and old food cartons, and I hadn't really had a plan beyond *get into the office*. I had no idea what we were looking for. Or where to even start. In retrospect, it might have been a better move to just ask the assistant if I could have a moment of his time.

Daisy picked up a Taco Bell bag between two fingers and dropped it into the trash. Then moved on to an empty milkshake cup and did the same.

"What are you doing?"

"They're going to get bugs if they leave this stuff out."

"We're here to get evidence!"

"Well, just in case that evidence is hiding under the garbage, I'll deposit this Diet Coke can into the recycling."

I turned a slow circle. Two desks, two bookshelves, two file drawers. One great, big disaster-style mess. I eenie-meanied and chose the desk that looked most official. And by *official*, I meant *the one with the coiled whistle-on-a-string* sitting *on it.*

I sifted through take-out menus and used napkins and newspaper clippings and memos and printed emails—from students, from parents, from local media, from the principal. The *River Fork Tribune* wanted a photo of RFHS's new phenom freshman quarterback. They were hoping for an interview about the upcoming season. The phenom freshman quarterback's mom wanted to make sure Farley knew where the best lighting was for said photo, since the clipping was going to be pasted into the phenom freshman's baby book. Another mom wondered if her kid's seasonal allergy list was on file, and did the school own an EpiPen by chance? There were multiple copies of the article about River Fork's state win last year, with various congratulatory Post-its stuck on them. A few students' health class tests over bones and muscles—nobody scored above a C, by the way. I kept sifting. Farley loved pizza, but didn't care for coupons, apparently. And of course, there was...whoa. Wait a minute.

I pulled out a printed email. The signature line indicated it had come from River Fork's principal. It was brief.

> *Gerry,*
>
> *We should discuss before I reach out to the parents of this student. Give me a list of your available times and we'll devise a statement.*
>
> *Phil*

Below that was a forwarded email from none other than Paulie Henderson. Dated last year.

Sheesh, the man couldn't even clean off his desk once a year? Gross.

> *Principal Yost,*
>
> *Your coach stole my playbook. We all know it. It was here and then you guys came and now it's gone so*

*either he took it himself or one of his players took it for him. We deserved that win but because he cheats we didn't get it. But you know what? I don't need that old playbook, because I've got my brain and my brain's got millions maybe thousands of plays in it. But next year is my senior year and I swear he better not try to steal my plays again. I will come out there if I have to. It's good to know my plays are winning plays tho.*

*Signed,*

*Unanimous*

Someone had handwritten across the bottom:
*Henderson Mon 3:30 (816) 555-9292*

"Daisy, look at this," I said.

She came over and peered at the note. "Unanimous?"

"I think he meant *Anonymous,* but we both know that was Paulie Henderson."

"He threatened him. In writing. From his school email account. Not very smart." She picked up an empty box of crackers and tucked it under one arm. "Not that it was super smart to threaten him over a live mic at a football game, either."

"And look at the date. This was last year. The feud between Paulie and the coach has been going on for a long time. No wonder he jumped him at the homecoming game."

"What do you think happened during that 3:30 phone call?" she asked.

"I know what didn't happen," I said. "They didn't patch up their differences and become friends." *Especially considering that Coach Farley is in a morgue right now.*

"Should we look for the playbook?" she asked, dropping the box into the trash.

"Why?"

"I don't know." She picked up a can. "To see if he was guilty?"

Even if we found the playbook and proved that Coach Farley was, in fact, guilty of stealing the Parkwood team's plays, it would be circumstantial evidence at best, and I doubt anyone would be wowed by it. But when working an investigative report, any information is good information, because you never know where it might lead.

"Do you really think he would still be hanging onto last year's playbook?"

She held up the box that had been under her arm. "The sell-by on this is 2015."

"Point taken," I said. "I'll go through these drawers and you go through those." I began pawing through the papers in earnest, then moved to his desk drawers and began pawing through those as well.

"Hey, Hollis?" Daisy asked.

"You found it?"

"No. I was just wondering...what do you suppose a playbook looks like?"

I stared at the mishmash of folders in the drawer I'd currently been rummaging through. "I don't really know. I guess a notebook of some kind."

"I picture the cover red, don't you?"

"I was thinking black."

"But black is so serious. Red would be much more team spirit-y." She waved around jazz hands.

I went back to digging. "But red isn't one of the team colors, so how spirit-y would that really be? Plus, it's flashy. Easy to steal." I closed the drawer and moved on to the next.

"Well, it did get stolen, after all," Daisy said.

Turned out we were both wrong. The notebook was buried under a pile of yearbooks in the bottom drawer. It had a blue cover and Parkwood High School's hornet right on the front cover.

"Got it," I said triumphantly, just as the door opened and a man's shadow filled the doorway.

"What are you doing in my desk?" he asked.

# CHAPTER 8

F OR THE TINIEST MOMENT, I thought we had encoun-
tered the ghost of Coach Farley. I could tell Daisy was
thinking the same, because her mouth was open and her
shoulders scrunched up high as if she were preparing to
scream.

*Don't scream, don't scream. Okay, maybe scream a little.
If you scream, I am definitely screaming. I'm screaming like
nobody's business.*

Instead of screaming, Daisy slowly slid a drawer closed
with her knee, catching the shadow's attention. I used the
moment of distraction to shove the email printout and the
playbook into my bag.

The shadow took a step inside and it became obvious
that he wasn't a ghost or Coach Farley at all. Instead, he
was the slight man with the buzz cut I had taken to be the
assistant coach earlier.

"Um," I said. *Smooth, Hollis. Really eloquent. Did they
teach you the Um Technique in journalism school?*

"We're from Maid 4 U," Daisy said, sounding so much
more confident than *Um*. "The district sent us to clean out
Mr. Farley's desk."

"Already?" He looked skeptical. "The police haven't even
been through here."

*Really? Interesting.* Maybe that meant we were onto something they hadn't thought of yet. Or maybe we were completely off-track and this wasn't a lead at all. *Or maybe it's because the police chief's son is the one who wrote the email.* But wouldn't that make them want to find it before anyone else could?

"The police don't believe foul play was involved," Daisy said. "They told the district to go ahead and hire us."

His eyebrows shot up. They would have disappeared into his hairline if his hair hadn't been buzzed to his scalp. "Really? No foul play? Well, that is surprising."

Daisy cocked her head to one side. "Why are you so surprised? Do you know something?" She was as subtle as a jackhammer.

"We should get back to work," I said, and I began gathering up handfuls of papers into neat stacks, trying to figure out how exactly we were going to make a graceful exit before we ended up with mop buckets.

"Whoa, now, wait just a minute. That's my desk," he said, coming at me fast, pointing at a nameplate that had been camouflaged by a small mountain of wadded sandwich wrappers.

*Kermit Hoopsick, P.E.*

Kermit Hoopsick? Sounded like a basketball-playing Muppet.

I stared at the papers in my hand uncomprehendingly. This was his desk? Did that mean Kermit was the one who called Paulie Henderson last year to talk about playbook theft? Did it mean he was the one who stole the playbook to begin with? Or had he just been covering for Farley?

He snatched the papers from my hand.

"I'm sorry," I said. "Has this always been your desk?"

"If you're judging my tidiness, I've been busy," he said.


86

"And I know where everything is. Well, knew. Who knows where you moved stuff. Did you throw away my Diet Coke? You threw away my Diet Coke. Those aren't free, you know. If you don't mind…" He stared at me pointedly until I got the hint and sidestepped away from the desk. Satisfied, he sat and rolled around in his chair a little bit, as if to see if I'd somehow messed it up with my meddling.

"Were you and the coach close?" I asked.

"Excuse me?" He picked up a random pencil and began fidgeting with it. His knee bounced up and down nervously. "Who did you say you were with? Why do you want to know?"

I busied myself stacking and arranging the papers on the other desk, my mind trying to absorb everything it could. A framed photo of three happy-looking, interchangeable blond women. A lot of losing lottery tickets. Some junk mail. A few *Rich & Famous* magazines stuffed full with inserts about diamond watches, expensive cars, and fancy vacations. I made a quick mental note of Farley's address. When I stepped back and viewed everything on his desk together, it was kind of pathetic.

How sad to die wishing you were someone else.

I had a brief moment wondering what the still life of my desk would say about me. Would it say I was wishing I was still the person I once was? Or would it say I had happily moved on with my life?

"We're with Maid 4 U," I said. "I can't imagine how I would get along if my coworker here suddenly was gone, that's all." This was the truth, and I knew if I glanced at Daisy, we would share a look of appreciation for each other and totally blow our covers for sure.

"We were colleagues," he said. *Twitch twitch.* "He was too busy for victory beers."

Okay, that was an odd thing to say.

"I'll bet you two were good friends, though. Working this close together, you probably had lots of great laughs over the years," Daisy said. "You must be really sad."

"Farley didn't have friends," he said. "He had servants and staff, and I was both."

I was starting to think Kermit wouldn't exactly be giving Farley's eulogy.

"I'm sure you were closer than you remember," I said.

"Don't count on it." He squinted at me. "Wait a minute. Do I know you?"

I shook my head, feeling my face burn. "Nope, I don't think so."

"Sure I do!" He pointed at me. "You're that reporter over at the Parkwood paper. I've seen you around at the games. You're always carrying a little notebook."

"I have a sister," I said quickly. "Common mistake. She's the smart one. She pretty much writes a whole newspaper, and I can barely read the directions on a bottle of bleach." I forced a giggle. It sounded like wood breaking in the back of my throat.

"Yeah, speaking of bleach," he said, his brow crinkling. "Where are your cleaning supplies? I don't even see a broom or a mop. Come to think of it, you don't really seem to be cleaning anything. You're just taking stuff. Nah, I don't believe you. You're undercover or something."

Oh, no. He was onto us.

"We didn't bring our cleaning supplies out of the van yet," Daisy said. "We're waiting on boxes, so we can get all this stuff boxed up and make room for...you know. The next coach." She acted contrite, but I knew she was just trying to stall for time. She was made for this job.

His eyebrows shot up again, only this time he looked

88

eager, sort of the way King Archie looked when I got out his catnip and sprinkled it on a patch of sunlight on the living room floor. "They're hiring a replacement? Already?"

"Oh, we wouldn't know," I said. "Seeing as we don't even work here."

"No, you work at the Parkwood newspaper," he said. "I don't believe you have a sister."

I forced another laugh. "You're so funny."

"I'm also right." He whipped out his phone, pulled up to the Parkwood Chronicle Weekly's staff bio page, which included a group photo. "That's not a sister. That's you."

"Fine," I said, exasperated. And also caught. "If I'm a reporter, then let me ask you some questions. Did Coach Farley have any enemies that you know of?"

I could see his desire to savor his victory battle with his desire to suck his words back into his mouth at the realization that I was now going to question him. "None," he said meekly.

"Really? Not even Paulie Henderson? Because it seems to me that Paulie Henderson would have a very different answer to that question."

"The Henderson kid was all hot air," he said, waving his hand.

"Did Coach Farley ever talk about being worried that someone might come after him?"

"Absolutely not. He was a big guy. He could take care of himself against anybody."

"Apparently not against a car, though. Or maybe a Jeep?"

"It was a Jeep?"

"I don't know, was it?" We locked eyes. "Were you there that night? What do you drive?"

He sat back, steely. "I was putting away the equipment. I was nowhere near him. I just wanted to get out of there."

"Why?" I asked. "You guys won. You didn't want to savor your victory?"

"We couldn't ever savor victories at Parkwood. That Henderson kid was unhinged. Every time we went out there, he followed us, threw food on our cars, that kind of thing. He punched out my taillights once. I can't prove it, but I know it was him. Gerry wouldn't even let Wilma Louise go with him to the Parkwood games. He didn't want her to get upset."

"You just said he didn't have any enemies. Sounds to me like Paulie was an enemy."

"An arch-nemesis," Daisy added.

He crossed his arms. "Miss, you don't understand teenagers. When you work in a high school, you get used to kids doing things like that. But that doesn't make them deadly. Henderson didn't like us, that was true, but he wouldn't kill anybody. At least, I don't think so."

Daisy's phone rang, startling all three of us. She pulled it out of her pocket, examined it, and then said, "Oh! It's corporate. I should take this."

"He knows we're not maids, Daisy."

She marched over, the phone still trilling, grabbed my arm, and began pulling. "We should both take this."

"Wait, so you're not going to clean out his desk?" Kermit asked. "But it's the better desk. I'd kind of like to have it."

"We're not maids," I repeated, as Daisy pulled me out of the office. "As you said, I'm a reporter."

He stood, looking panicked. "You don't have my permission to use my name in any article."

"Bye, now," Daisy said, shoved me out into the field house and shut the office door. She answered her phone, said, "Mommy doesn't have time right now," and hung up. "Let's go."

"Why did you do that? I was getting somewhere."

"Let's go," she repeated, and once again started dragging me. I argued the whole way.

When I finally gave up and let her deposit me into the car, I sat in the driver's seat sullenly. "I was finally getting to the bottom of Paulie Henderson's major grudge against Farley, and you literally drag me away. Why?"

She leaned over, pulled two folded pieces of paper out of her back pocket, unfolded them, and handed them to me. "This is why."

It took me a minute to understand what I was looking at. "A resume and cover letter? So?"

"So…look whose it is."

I scanned to the top of the paper. Kermit Hoopsick. "The assistant coach. Okay. He clearly wasn't Farley's biggest fan, so it's not surprising to me that he might be looking around for something better. But still. The timing is interesting. What does the letter say?"

"I haven't had a chance to read it yet." Daisy took the paper and read aloud. "'Dear Superintendent Jacobson, I am writing to you to express my interest in the recently vacated position of Head Football Coach at River Fork High School. I've been working with—'"

"Wait, stop," I said. "Read that again."

"'Dear Superintendent Jacobson.'"

"Not that part—the first line of the letter." I took the paper from her and read it myself. "'I am writing to you to express my interest in the *recently vacated* position of Head Football Coach.'"

"So? Oh." She took the letter back from me. "Recently

vacated? He wrote this today? Talk about not even letting the body get cold."

"That's the thing," I said. "Look at the date." I pointed to the date he'd typed in the left corner.

"It's post-dated for a month from now."

I nodded. "But his footer auto-dated it." I pointed to the tiny printing at the bottom of the paper, which was stamped with the date the letter had been written.

Her mouth dropped open. "Five days ago."

I nodded again. "He printed this out the day *before* the coach died."

# CHAPTER 9

T HINGS WERE MUCH CALMER AT the PHS stadium during the youth football game than they had been during the high school homecoming game, but the concession stand was still hopping. Evangeline was working alone this time.

"The kids all called in," she said. "Apparently strep is going around." She made air quotes around the word *strep*. "I'm sure there was something much more exciting going on this afternoon. Oh, to be young again. Can't say I blame them. But my feet are killing me. Something about standing on this hard concrete floor for hours." She snagged a hot dog from the roller, slipped it into a bun, and handed it over to a little girl who'd been waiting at the counter when I arrived. "What can I do for you? Dog? It's on the house." She grabbed another hot dog with her tongs and wiggled it in the air.

"Actually, I'm here on official business," I said, pulling out my pad and pencil.

She dropped the frank back on its roller and pushed her hair net off of her forehead, leaving a red elastic imprint in her skin. "The hit-and-run?"

My fingers went numb around the pencil. I wanted to jump up and down and point at my nose, as if she'd gotten a charade correct. Instead, I played it cool. Well, as cool as I could, leaning over the counter and stage-whispering, "So they didn't get to you," as if we were in the grips of some sort of espionage.

"Who didn't get to me?"

"The chief is saying there was no hit-and-run. And it seems everyone in Parkwood is just willing to go along with that. They're all trying to say that he just dropped dead."

"Oh," she said. "Well, that's probably because he didn't have a lot of fans here."

"Was he really that bad?" I asked.

"People around here take their football very seriously," she answered. "For some of these kids, it's their only ticket to college."

"Including Paulie Henderson?"

Her eyes darkened as if I'd just trod on some dangerous ground. She hustled to the nacho cheese warmer, pulled off the lid, and stirred vigorously. "I don't know anything about Paulie Henderson, except that he very kindly volunteers his time to officiate these youth games. The parents out here just love that boy."

"That boy threatened the coach the very night of the hit-and-run. I know I wasn't the only one to hear that, but everyone is acting as if I was."

"But what about Wickham Birkland? He had a beef with him earlier that day," she said. "They had a run-in at the four-way stop."

"True. But Wickham has a beef with everyone everyday."

"You should still look long and hard at him."

I thought it odd that she was trying to point the finger at Wickham. Did she have some sort of grudge against him, or was she trying to focus the investigation away from Paulie? Or did she actually believe Wickham could have done it? I made a mental note to tread lightly around her when it came to both Paulie and Wickham. "I'm planning to talk to Wickham, too. But first, I think I should at least consider the kid who threatened to kill him. That just seems like the most obvious place to start."

She stopped what she was doing, came back to me, and leaned over the counter, pressing her fists against the plastic countertop. Her muscles looked tight. "Listen, Hollis. I know we just met, but I like you, so I'm going to tell you something you may not want to hear. Leave this story alone. When you lie and cheat, you gain enemies, and Gerald Farley learned that the hard way. Some enemies are willing to go farther than others, so you should just let this go. Entirely." We locked eyes for a long moment. If I didn't know better, I would think Evangeline Crane knew something about Coach Farley's hit-and-run. She released her fists and smiled. "You should really have one of our hot dogs. The new roller keeps them so plump and juicy."

I was going to gain a hundred pounds working in this town.

I got my story. New roller donated by The Glove and Handbag Club, hot dogs plump and juicy, no more greasy hot dog water, franks flying off the shelves, the snack shop making more money than ever, et cetera, et cetera. Nothing more than I had to begin with, except I got a few quotes from Evangeline, from some kids who happened to belly up to the bar, and from a couple moms in the stands. Everyone seemed to be in agreement—the hot dog roller was the best thing to happen to that stadium since they went two-ply in the restrooms.

Yet I couldn't keep my mind off of the real story at the stadium, and only went through the motions of jotting notes and names and getting photo permission slips signed while my mind mulled over the Coach Farley situation. I still had questions. Like if Wickham was always sparring with someone, why would this one lead him to murder? Why would the coach be in the lower lot in the first place? And how dangerous was Paulie Henderson, really? If everyone was willing to overlook the death threat at the game, what else were they willing to overlook?

I would just have to save those questions for someone else. Maybe—hopefully—Paulie himself.

After I'd closed my notebook, I decided to take a detour on my way to my car. If Paulie officiated these games, then surely he was here and available for questions. And if he was here, maybe his Jeep was, too. If it wasn't…well, then that would beg some more questions, wouldn't it?

The lower lot was empty—the youth football crowd kept all their tailgating to the upper lot—and there was nothing left of the crime scene. I wasn't sure what I had been expecting—police tape, a Coach Farley-shaped chalk line drawn on the pavement, discarded rubber gloves—but there was nothing left. Had there been grill and headlight bits on the pavement around the coach that night that I hadn't seen? Had they been *in* the coach? I shuddered. I was all for murder stories, but I couldn't make myself think about the more gruesome details—not when it happened so close by.

If Paulie was at the youth football game, he wasn't parked in the lower lot.

I stood on the little hill, scanning the upper lot for round headlights until I found the Jeep. Actually, I found four. All parked in a cluster, making it that much harder to identify which one might belong to Paulie. Since when did everyone start driving Jeeps?

I headed for the upper lot, pulling out my notebook once again. There was a chance that Paulie would clam up as soon as I started asking hard questions—most people did—so I had to be ready to dive in as soon as I saw him.

Someone stepped out from between two sedans and knocked into me. The notebook flung out of my hand and slid under a car.

"*Oof*, so sorry." The person turned and reached out to keep me from reeling to the ground. When I got steadied, I found myself leaning into the arms of Officer Hopkins.

"You've got to be kidding me," I said, quickly straightening to put some distance between us. "You again?"

"We do seem to be running into each other an awful lot," he said in a friendly voice. "Such a small world."

And an even smaller town. I cocked my head to the right and planted my hands on my hips. "You expect me to believe that this was just another serendipitous meeting? In a parking lot at a youth football game?"

His feigned innocence was so transparent, it was like he didn't even try to make it seem realistic. "I don't follow."

"Actually, yes, you do. You *follow* me everywhere."

"It's Parkwood, Miss Bisbee. We're all in the same places all the time."

"Yet I never laid eyes on you before Friday afternoon." My voice cracked on the word *eyes*. Infuriating. Also, his eyes were very, very blue. I could have seen clouds float by in his very blue eyes and I wouldn't have been surprised. Trace's eyes had been dark and brooding in that Artist Who Sees the World for What It Truly Is sort of way…and why was I thinking about Trace's eyes right now? And why was

I noticing the blue in this deputy's eyes? I needed to stop thinking about eyes altogether.

He shrugged. "I guess we have similar schedules."

I shook my head, disgusted. "Unbelievable. Literally. Don't quit your day job for a career in acting." I started to go past him, but he moved to block my way again. I side-stepped, and so did he.

He chuckled. "Want to dance?"

I gave him my best *No, I Don't Want to Do Anything But Solve This Murder* look, but the amused expression never left him. Also, I wondered if he was a good dancer. Someone who was as good at jogging as he was could probably hold his own on a dance floor. "My car is that way." I pointed past him toward the Jeeps.

"No, it's not." He pointed in the other direction, which was indeed where my car was parked. "Good thing you ran into me, huh? You would have been searching for your car in the wrong part of the lot." He raised his eyebrows and his eyes—unbelievably—darkened to an even more intense shade of blue.

"I..." But I trailed off, when I could no longer think of an excuse that would have me traveling in the exact opposite direction of my car.

"You were just headed home," he said, very matter-of-factly. "I'm sure I'll see you around, Miss Bisbee."

"I have no doubt," I said drily. I turned on my heel and walked to my car, then sat inside to wait for him to leave; he simply crossed his arms, leaned back against the hood of his cruiser, and watched me. When it became embarrassingly obvious that he wasn't going anywhere until I did, I left. He was following me on purpose. I knew that much. What I wasn't so sure of was why. Was he intentionally trying to get in my way so I stayed out of the case and out of Chief Henderson's hair?

Or was he following me because he liked me? Or was it a combination of both? And why did that thought make me smile just a little?

I drove home with a goofy grin on my face, the window cracked to let in the scent of cut grass and cool fall air with a hint of fire pit. I waved to people I knew as I passed them. I told myself I was smiling because if Chief Henderson had to send a babysitter after me, I must have been on the right track.

When I realized that I'd forgotten my dropped notepad and came back for it later that night, the upper lot was free of cars.

And my notepad was missing, too.

# CHAPTER 10

"WELCOME TO THE *KNOCK 'EM Dead* podcast," I said.

"Where murder and muffins meet!" Daisy said, holding up a gorgeous platter of dessert. "Or, in today's case, tarts! But they are not almond tarts. They're lemon tarts."

"Almond tarts?"

"Yes, Hollis," she said in a 1980s science video voice. "Cyanide smells and tastes like bitter almonds. So I thought I would point out that these are not almond tarts, so you know I'm not trying to poison you."

I paused. "…Said every person who ever tried to poison somebody."

"Well, no. If you're trying to poison somebody, it would be much less suspicious if you just handed them a bowl of almonds. Or an almondy dish." She put on the creepiest fake smile I've ever seen and pantomimed holding a platter. "Appetizer, Hollis? I made a cheese ball."

"With that look on your face, I would for sure know you were trying to poison me."

She looked crestfallen. "I thought I was being a pretty good actress. I didn't say anything at all about the almonds the cheese ball was rolled in. Or the fact that the ball was made from blue cheese and gruyere, because some bitter poisons can be masked by putting them into food with strong flavors."

We both looked at the platter—the real one, not the one with the imaginary cheese ball. "Strong flavors...like lemon?" I asked.

She brought back the creepy smile. "I don't know what you're talking about. Tart?"

"Okay, that was good."

She dipped her head in a bow. "Thank you. Head nun in *Sound of Music*, Parkwood High, circa 2004." She made a face. "Ew, 2004 gives away my age. Strike that."

"I told you, I haven't learned how to strike anything. I'm working on it." Honestly, I hadn't had much time to work on it. So far all I'd accomplished was knowing that I was having technical difficulties. "Maybe we should start with an update to the Coach Farley case."

"Oh!" She had taken a bite of lemon tart, so she had to pause to chew and swallow. "That reminds me! The visitation and funeral are tonight."

"You read my mind," I said. Everyone knew the best place to find a murderer was at the funeral of the murdered. "We should definitely be there."

"That's what I was thinking." She took another big bite, then said around it, "I'll bring dessert for the widow. Hold the almonds."

Gerald Farley may have had enemies, but he also had more than his fair share of mourners. The visitation at Bale & Sons Funeral Home was fairly scampering with community members trying to pay their respects.

One of the interchangeable *& Sons* held open the door

for us and silently gestured toward the large chapel in the back. Daisy thanked him, reached into a gift bag filled with individually wrapped lemon tarts, and handed him one. He looked startled, as though he didn't quite know what to do with it.

"Compliments of the *Knock 'em Dead* podcast, available everywhere you get your podcasts. You should listen," she said.

While I admired her devotion to marketing, I questioned her sense of timing. I gave her my best *Would You Put Those Away Before You Get Us in Trouble* glare, but she simply lowered the bag to her side and moved on.

Coach Farley lay in a steel casket, most of his face engulfed in football memorabilia brought by grievers. A woman I took to be his wife, Wilma Louise, stood nearby, gratefully greeting the long line of visitors one-by-one while dabbing at the end of her nose with a Kleenex.

"Poor thing," Daisy said softly. "She must feel like the rug got ripped out from under her. I wonder if they have kids."

"I don't see any kids," I said. "She's the only one in the receiving line."

Daisy took a breath. "That almost makes it worse. She's all alone now. Can you imagine how lonely that must feel, Hollis, to be all alone?" Her eyes grew big. "I'm so sorry. I forgot that you are alone."

"I'm not alone," I said. "I have you. And King. And my job. And the podcast." But now that she'd mentioned it… that didn't seem like enough. Was I lonely? Did Mrs. Farley and I have that in common? Would the coach pop into her memory at random, inconvenient times, like Trace popped into mine? Would those memories make her ache for him all over again?

I made a mental note to talk to Mrs. Farley. I needed to find out who Gerald Farley was when he was not on the field.

Daisy and I ducked into the back pew and observed. I pulled out my new, empty notebook and pencil and poised myself to write.

Only there was nothing, really, to write about. No matter who Farley might have been, it was hard to take in a bunch of people in various states of distress, including his crying widow, with an objective eye. It was something I always struggled with—even the dirtiest of the dirty players out there had normal people in their lives who loved them, and who were truly sad that they were gone. And it really seemed that everyone in this room fell into some version of that category.

Except for the guy standing in the corner, blending in with the potted plants, dry-eyed and scowling.

"Isn't that Wickham Birkland?" I whispered.

Daisy squinted in his direction, then gasped. "It is. What on earth do you suppose he's doing here?"

"A significant number of killers attend the funerals of their victims," I said.

"You don't suppose we should…"

"I do suppose exactly that. But play it cool."

"Of course."

We both slid out of the pew and sauntered toward Wickham. He saw us coming and disappeared into the crowd surrounding a photo display. We stopped, craning our necks trying to see where he had gone.

"Over there," Daisy finally said, peering over the crowd on her tiptoes. She was pointing toward the vestibule, where a couple more *& Sons* were congregating morosely.

We left the chapel, heads down, calm, but as soon as we

popped clear, we raced after him. He saw us coming and bolted through a door, causing an *& Son* to call out in surprise. The *& Son* followed him, and we followed the two of them through the door, down a dimly lit hallway, through an embalming room—Daisy making little, "Ew, ew, ew…" noises—past a dingy kitchen, and out the back door into the employee parking lot. *& Son* was bent over, hands on knees, panting.

"Where did he go?" I asked.

*& Son* pointed toward the front parking lot, and I took off.

We practically threw ourselves on the trunk of Wickham's car as he tried to back out of his parking space. He jerked to a stop.

"Wow," I said, breathing heavily. "He can really move."

"It's all that pent-up anger. It's like rocket fuel," Daisy said between pants.

As if on cue, Wickham got out of his car, ranting and raving about us wrecking his paint job and if there was so much as a scratch, we would pay.

"Stop, stop, *stop*," I said, holding my palms out. "We just have some questions for you."

"What in tarnation could you want to ask me on a day of grief?"

"Well, for starters, why are you here?" I resisted the urge to take out my notebook and pencil.

"Why is anyone here?" His face was red and sweaty. "This is a funeral. I'm here to pay my respects."

"Were you and Gerald Farley close?" I asked.

He jabbed a finger at the funeral parlor, where an entire flock of *& Sons* were staring us down warily from the open doorway. "Nobody in that building was close to him. He was a terrible man. And a cheat."

Again, with the cheating. It was like nobody had ever been dishonest during a high school football game before.

"His wife was close to him, I'm sure," Daisy said, and then wilted. "Oh, nuts, Hollis, I left the bag of tarts inside. You'll have to go in and get it for me."

"I'm not going back in there!"

"You have to. I can't just leave a bag of tarts lying around a funeral. It's unprofessional."

"Look at them!" I gestured toward the irately glowering *& Sons*. "I've seen friendlier faces on death row. They're not going to let me back in there."

"Well, I can't go back in there. What if I dropped it in the embalming room? If I go back in there, I might pass out. Did you notice the—" She lowered her voice. "Body?"

Thank goodness for lack of athletic ability—I was so busy trying not to trip or pass out, I never noticed a body in the embalming room. "If I go back in there, I'll notice it. And neither of us wants that."

Wickham sneered. "If you'll both get out of my way, I'll be leaving now. Have your girl fight over there." He pointed toward some bushes and started toward his open driver's door.

"Wait. No. One more question," I said. "Was that your hood ornament he was holding at the scene of the accident?"

He stopped in his tracks. "He was holding a hood ornament?"

I nodded. "A Mercedes hood ornament. I can't help noticing that your car is missing one just like it." I nodded toward his car's crumpled and unadorned hood.

"Well, I'll be! Stolen from by a dead man. Can you believe it? Stealing our plays wasn't bad enough, he went and stole my hood ornament to boot! And here I searched for it and searched for it out on that street corner. Got down on my hands and knees looking for it. Almost got run over three times, because teenagers these days are too busy with their gadgets to pay attention to what's on the street in front of them." He angrily mimed texting, back hunched, eyes half squinted, then poked a finger in the air indignantly. "I ought to march right in there and demand that widow of his buy me a new hood ornament. It's the principle of the matter! He can take the old one to the great beyond for all I c—"

"Wait," I said, interrupting him. "Are you saying the hood ornament was missing after the accident?"

He looked at me like I'd lost my marbles. "Well, yes. When did you think it went missing?"

"It's just…well, he was holding it when he died, and I guess I thought—"

He let out a bark of laughter, making Daisy and I both flinch backward. It sounded like a rusty hinge suddenly snapping in half. "You thought he reached up and grabbed my hood ornament as I ran over him? That's what you thought?"

"I mean…yeah." I felt my face burn. When he said it out loud like that, it did sound kind of ridiculous. "I guess I thought maybe he was facing the car when he got hit and grabbed at the ornament on his way down." Then it dawned on me what made that idea sound so preposterous. "Except he was facedown. Right."

Wickham hooted again.

"It's possible," I said, planting my hands on my hips. True, it may have been possible that Farley may have grabbed the ornament in the split second before the force of the hit spun him around. But plausible? That was another story. "You were so mad at him just a few hours before he died. And, by the way, I don't think the day of the funeral is the best day to put the squeeze on someone's widow over a silly hood ornament."

"Yes, I was mad. Mad enough to write a nasty letter to the editor about that stop sign being a danger to the city." He wiped his eyes. It was weird seeing Wickham Birkland smile. I didn't know he could do that. I waited for parts of his face to crack off and crumble to the ground, revealing the old, mean Wickham face beneath. "I was mad at him for running a stop sign and hitting my car. And I was mad at him for ripping off my hood ornament and throwing it on the ground in the middle of our altercation. Come to think of it, that young cop made me leave first, told me to go file a report at the police station." My stomach fluttered at the mention of Brooks. I willed the feeling away. So inconveniently timed. "Farley must have picked up my hood ornament after I left. That sneak!"

"But you didn't go to the police station," I said. "You followed him to the Hibiscus."

"Not on purpose. I went to the station later that day. I was headed to the Hisbiscus for lunch when he hit me. Apparently so was he."

"So was probably half of Parkwood, to be fair," Daisy said.

"That lunch gave me indigestion," Wickham said. He grimaced and placed his hand on his stomach with remembered pain. "I think it was those giblets Esther's been ruining her gravy with."

"So you didn't...you didn't..."

"Run over Coach Farley? I should say not." He pointed to the hood of his car. "He messed up my car enough as it is. Don't want to give him a chance to do more damage. The police can test it for DNA if they want. And If you're done wasting my time, I'd like to leave now."

Daisy and I shuffled over and Wickham got into his car and drove away.

"If you ask me, it wasn't Wickham," Daisy said.

"No, it wasn't. I agree."

"That leaves the assistant coach. Who, by the way, is not here. Is that suspicious at all?"

I frowned. "Maybe."

"But probably not as suspicious as that, huh?" she asked, nodding toward the driveway exit.

I turned just in time to see a Jeep pulling out of the driveway and screeching away.

Almost as if it had no business being there in the first place.

# CHAPTER 11

"M ARY MEAN ISN'T HERE," ONE of the middle
schoolers said as soon as I walked in early the next
morning. "She's got throat cancer or something."

I gasped.

Joyce removed an earbud. "Tonsillitis and sinusitis, not
throat cancer. Do they still have biology classes in school?"

"Either way, she's not here." The middle schooler
grabbed a bag of rolled newspapers and ambled out for his
paper route.

Actually, this was a good thing for me. With no Mary
Jean came no new assignments. I could pound out this
hot dog roller piece, put it in her inbox, and be out there
pounding my beat by lunch.

And by *pounding my beat*, I meant getting a quick story
out of Vacuumulate, then following Paulie Henderson. I
needed to get some answers from him. Starting with the
newest one—was that him at Coach Farley's funeral? And, if
so, why was he in such a hurry to leave it?

I rushed toward my desk.

"Don't worry, she left you an assignment. For after
you're done with the housewares store story, of course,"
Joyce said from behind, startling me. I turned to find her

standing at my desk, holding a sticky note, both earbuds dangling over her shoulders.

"Of course."

She held up the sticky note on her index finger. "Parkwood Community Funds."

"The bank?" I asked, taking the sticky note from her.

"Mary Jean wants you to cover the new branch going up on Highway 2. Haven't you seen it?"

"That's what they've been building there?" I had been hoping it was something exciting, like a Starbucks.

"Would you have ever imagined?" Joyce said. "Parkwood, Missouri, a two-branch town. My grandmother would be pitching a fit, God rest her soul."

I thought about how inconceivable a two-branch town would have been to someone back home as well, for the opposite reason. *There's nothing in that town, Hollis.* I could still hear Trace's words on the day of our breakup. *I can't live in a place that small.* I like having choices.

*Well, we've got two branches now, Trace.* I thought. *Look who has choices now! Draw that in your little notebook and make one of your sardonic jokes!* I sighed. He probably would. And it would be funny and win him another award.

The more I thought about it, the more I realized Trace's attitude toward Parkwood was kind of snotty. Had I been a snot, too, when I lived in Chicago? Ugh. Probably. When I first moved to Parkwood, every other sentence that came out of my mouth was, *That's not how it goes in Chicago.* Kind of a snobby thing to say, even if I hadn't meant for it to be.

And the worst part? I still missed Chicago.

Although I was finding myself missing it less and less every day.

I pushed Trace out of my mind and read the name on

the sticky note. "Francine Oglethorpe. She's the bank manager?"

"And she's expecting you."

Guess my meeting with Paulie Henderson would have to wait once again.

Francine Oglethorpe was a short, middle-aged platinum blonde, with severely-drawn, bright red lipstick, and stick-straight posture. She hurried out of her office to greet me, hand outstretched for a shake, her pantyhose swishing vigorously in the quiet lobby.

"You must be Holly," she said.

"It's Hollis, actually. Common mistake."

She gave me a curious look. "Do you ever go by Holly?"

"I'm afraid never," I said. "My grandmother called me Holly sometimes, but that's about it."

Her lips turned down from severe, red welcome to severe, red disapproval. "You should go by Holly. Hollis is a last name. It's confusing. People with two last names are confusing."

I'd never gotten critiqued on my name before, but okay. "Thanks for the advice," I said sweetly. "I'll give it some thought. I just have a few questions for you about the new branch."

"Yes, yes," she said, clasping her hands at her bosom. "But first, have a seat, and I'll tell you the history of Parkwood Community Funds."

"Oh, I read all of that on your website. Really fascinating stuff." It wasn't. "I'm all ready to start writing about the new branch." I grabbed my notebook and pencil.

"Well, the website missed some of the more amusing intricacies of the founding of our great institution. I'm certain your readers will be enthralled."

Maybe when they'd calmed down from the excitement of the hot dog roller story. Didn't want to overwhelm them with too much enthralling news all at once. "I'm sure you're right," I said.

I followed Francine into her office and took notes on the Bell family tree, dating all the way back to the founding of Parkwood by William and Sarah Bell in 1860-whatever. Mostly I was trying to figure out where I had seen Francine before. She looked so familiar, and not in the same way that everyone here looked familiar because we were all at the same places at the same time, as Brooks had been more than happy to point out. I felt like I had seen her before. Somewhere recently, and somewhere important.

"And that brings us to the new branch," she said, clapping her hands together and snapping me out of my thoughts. "What questions do you have for me?"

"Huh?" I blinked at my notebook, on which I'd written, *When* and then just a bunch of scribbles and designs. *Stellar reporting, Hollis. Once again. Did you learn it in Um class?* How would I put together a story from that? I hadn't even written down any good filler quotes. "Are you excited?"

"Yes. As I said a few moments ago." She put on a re-hearsed voice. "We here at Parkwood Community Funds are very excited for the future of our bank with this new opportunity."

I jotted some notes, but my brain was still fumbling to place where I'd seen her before. "Uh, I guess, er…um…Tell me again about the special amenities this new branch will feature? I fell a little behind in my note-taking."

She cocked her head to one side. "Are you okay, dear? You seem a little spacey."

"I'm sorry," I said. "It's just…Do I know you from somewhere?"

She fiddled with her phone, as if she was hoping it would ring. "I don't think so. You've probably seen me at the Hibiscus. That's where everyone sees everyone around here."

"Yeah, I guess that's it." That was definitely not it. "Sorry, I think I've just been a little preoccupied since the homecoming game."

I could practically feel her stiffen from across the room. It was like the air molecules themselves stiffened. It only lasted a beat before she regained her composure—so quick I half-wondered if I'd imagined it. I had murder on the brain, and I was apparently suspicious of everyone.

I willed myself back into professional reporter mode. "You were saying about the amenities?"

"Have they said what happened to that poor coach?" she asked instead, pulling herself to standing, yanking on the hem of her suit coat to straighten it.

"The police are saying there was no foul play."

She brightened. "Really? Is that so?" Why did she seem so happy about that? Was it happiness that there wasn't a murderer in Parkwood, or was it something else?

"Did you know him?"

"No, I sure didn't. I couldn't have pointed him out in a crowd of two. But I understand he had enemies. Everybody dislikes a cheater, you know."

"So I've heard."

She took a few steps toward me. "Just between you and me," she whispered, "do you think there was foul play?"

I thought about it, then decided I might as well come clean and see where this was going. "I do."

She leaned toward me, serious and eager. "Who do you think did it? Did they see the car?"

I began to have a bad feeling about Francine Oglethorpe. Maybe she was a true crime devotee like Daisy and I, but she seemed to be really, really interested in the case. Too interested. Until I could figure out where I'd seen her before and what her angle was, I thought it best to keep my mouth shut.

I held up my notebook. "I think I've got plenty for the story."

She frowned. "You're sure?"

"I think so. You've given me a lot of information."

She checked her watch. "I still have a few minutes. We can go over the floorplan."

"I would love to, but I've got to get over to Vacuumulate."

"I understand completely," she said, but she said it in a way that was not at all understanding. She sounded more suspicious—and suddenly I was acutely aware that neither of us trusted the other. Which was weird. Parkwood was a trusting town. The kind of town where you spilled your business to the person behind you in the grocery line. But I wasn't imagining these alarm bells. There was something off. "You do what you have to do. I'm hoping you'll also report on the grand opening event?"

"Absolutely. I'll be in touch," I said.

"We're even having Esther over at the Hibiscus whip us up a little buffet for it," she called after me. "Just some light snacks. Between you and me, her giblets are murder on a gut." Maybe I was crazy, but I could have sworn she put a little extra emphasis on the word *murder*. Was she trying to give me some sort of hint? A warning? I glanced back at her. She had her hands clasped in front of her and was standing still and straight as a statue. "Just deadly," she said.

The Vacuumulate interview went long. For three years during the 1990s, Tamara, the owner, had lived in Buffalo Grove, a community just 30 miles outside of Chicago. She brought out two cups of tea and we chatted about places and experiences we had in common. We didn't even start the store tour until the tea was gone. They had a nice selection of toasters, I couldn't help noticing.

Needless to say, my lunch hour was late. Which was actually fortuitous, as I found myself with idle time right at the same time that school let out.

Instead of eating lunch, I sat in my car in the pharmacy parking lot eating a bag of Twizzlers like it was my job. What I was really doing was biding my time, watching Paulie Henderson in my rearview mirror. He and his buddies had decided to go for an after-school burger at FastNHotz across the street from the pharmacy and just happened to have selected a window seat right on the other side of the Jeep, forcing me to keep a distance. My plan was to wait them out, then try to catch him for some questions on his way to his car. I'd learned the hard way that busting in on someone's lunch to ask questions was a great way to get tossed out of a restaurant, and loitering around someone's car was a great way to get them angry, so it was best to just hang around until everyone was finished eating and then have a little surprise parking lot meet-up.

Sort of like Brooks had done with me. Huh.

This was hardly my first "stake-out" for a story. But I'll be the first to admit, I wasn't great at them, mostly because everything I knew about stakeouts I got from TV. Basically you sit in your car and eat (check), you watch a car or house or business for hours (check), and at some really inopportune moment, the perp shows up and you have to scramble so hard to catch them, you spill gyro meat all over your front seat. My car was newish and I liked the way it smelled—which was to say, it didn't smell. Hence, tidy Twizzlers.

I was so lost in my own thoughts—about Buffalo Grove, about toasters, about blue eyes—I almost missed a blur of movement in the mirror. The Twizzler I'd been chewing on dropped into my lap. Paulie Henderson was high fiving his bros goodbye and getting into his Jeep. I had only moments to catch him before he left.

I flung open the door, prepared to run across the street calling Paulie's name.

Except my seatbelt was still on.

I fumbled with the release, and tumbled out just in time to see Paulie's driver's side door close. I was going to miss him.

I dove back into my car and threw my seatbelt back around me, prepared to follow Paulie to his next destination. But before I could back out of my parking space, I saw movement in my rearview mirror again. Someone was standing at my back window, waving at me.

Brooks.

"You have got to be kidding me! Not a good time, Brooks!" I made shooing motions with my hands, but he only gave me quizzical looks, turning his palms up and mouthing that he didn't understand what I was getting at. Meanwhile, Paulie's Jeep sped away and turned the corner. I released the seatbelt and got out.

"I'm so sorry," he said, coming around to the side of the car. "Were you trying to leave? I hope you weren't going anywhere in a hurry."

"Yes! Yes, I was going somewhere in a hurry." I finally

registered the knowing smirk that had spread across his face. "You were doing it on purpose. Of course you were."

"I have no idea what you're talking about."

"You're a terrible liar."

He grasped his chest. "I'm hurt that you think I'm lying."

"I don't think it. I know it."

"Okay, then I'm hurt that you're not wowed by my acting skills. I'll have you know I'm working on a very important play. It's inspired by Shakespeare." He raised one palm and looked to the sky dramatically. "To harass the chief's son...or not to harass the chief's son...that is the question. And the answer is to not." He turned back to me, one eyebrow raised. "You like it?"

"No. And I'm not harassing anyone."

"What do you call staking out someone with the intention of interrogating them?"

It dawned on me that, while he was describing exactly what I was doing, wasn't he also staking me out? It sure felt like he was. I crossed my arms. "I call it reporting. Besides, you're harassing me, have you ever thought about that?"

"I'm protecting you."

"I can protect myself, thank you very much. I'm not scared of Paulie Henderson. Do you think I survived life in Chicago by accident?" Actually, I'd sometimes survived by walking a very mean-looking creampuff bulldog named Tink, whose greatest threat to this world was a very wet doggy kiss to the face. "I dare someone to take me on. I'm trained in self-defense, you know." I wasn't. But I probably should have been. I made a mental note to look into that. Who knew where my new podcast would take me?

"I'm protecting you from you." He took a step closer to

me and lowered his voice. "The chief is onto you. He knows you're targeting Paulie, and he doesn't like it."

"So? Journalism never sleeps. We have an obligation to tell the truth. And if Paulie is the truth, so be it."

I could smell his aftershave. It was lemony and spicy and masculine and nice. And it seriously irritated me that I noticed.

He was whispering, so I had to lean in. My head was almost touching his cheek at this point. "I'm trying to keep you out of something you shouldn't be in. The chief wants to solve this case himself."

"You mean he wants to keep his son out of jail."

"No, that's not what I sai—"

"Wait a minute, I thought he was convinced this wasn't murder. He has us reporting that the coach died of natural causes."

"That's because he doesn't want to let the killer know what evidence we have."

This got my attention. I forgot all about being frustrated for a second. "You have evidence? What kind of evidence?"

"I can't tell you that."

"I'll tell you my evidence if you tell me yours." This seemed like a safe trade, given that I had almost nothing.

He clamped his mouth shut and looked around the parking lot, uncomfortable. I could tell he felt torn. I telepathically willed him to just play along.

"Grab a burger with me," he said.

Well, I wasn't expecting that.

"Excuse me?"

"Go to the FastNHotz with me for a burger."

I was enraged. Indignant. Kind of butterfly-ish in my stomach. But in an enraged and indignant way. It was a supremely enraged and indignant butterfly. "I don't think so."

He rolled his eyes and spoke slowly and patiently, as if he was explaining something to a two-year-old. "Grab a burger with me, and we can talk."

"Uh-huh. Grab a burger with you, and you find out everything I know and then proceed to continue keeping me off Paulie's back. Besides, it's four o'clock."

He shrugged. "Call it an early dinner, then."

"I had a late lunch."

"Do you want to know what we have or not?"

Now it was my turn to be uncomfortable. I wanted the information, that was for sure. But this guy was seriously pressing my buttons. And I wish he would stop looking at me with those gorgeous blue eyes.

"Fine," I said. "I'll go to the FastNHotz with you, but for information-sharing only. I'm not eating anything."

He shrugged. "Suit yourself."

# CHAPTER 12

I ORDERED A BURGER, LARGE ONION rings, and a chocolate milkshake. Stakeouts were hard work. I was hungry.
Plus FastNHotz's onion rings were legendary.

I was already three bites into my burger before Brooks
sat down with his tray. He'd ordered an identical meal. I
tried not to notice our similar tastes once again.

He nodded at my tray appreciatively. "The onion rings
here—"

"Yep, I know," I said, cramming a ring into my mouth.

He gazed around the dining room, taking it in. "There
was a place I used to go to in my home town. Their onion
rings were the best—super crunchy outside, soft onion
inside, fried to a perfect brown. Probably terrible for you,
and probably nowhere near as good as I remember them,
but in my mind, nobody's rings can touch theirs. You know
what I'm talking about? You have a hometown favorite that
can never be spoiled?"

"I'm from Chicago," I said. "There are more five-star
places to eat at than I could even think of."

"No, I mean someplace like this place we're in right
now."

I tried to imagine Mom and Aunt Ruta walking into a
fast food place where the floors were slick from the grease. I

almost laughed out loud. Mom and Ruta were always fret-
ting about food-borne diseases they'd seen featured on mid-
day talk shows. Not to mention, they'd have to first agree
on a place to go. Someone could starve while waiting for
that kind of war to resolve.

"Just a few hot dog places. I have to say, the people in
this town don't know how to do hot dogs. Who puts ketch-
up on a hot dog? It's just wrong." I downed another ring,
then silently vowed to myself to slow down and savor the
last three. As if. "So you're from Kansas City?"

He had picked up his shake and was in mid-sip; he
raised his eyebrows in silent surprise. He swallowed and put
down the shake. "You've done your research."

I shrugged as if it was my hard work and journalistic
grit that got me the intel and not Daisy's cherry chocolate
chunk muffins.

"I did live in Kansas City for a time, yes."

"What made you come here?"

His cheeks turned pink and he fiddled with his burger,
looking very ill at ease.

He looked so uncomfortable, I decided not to pursue
that one…for now. Mental checklist: there was a story there
for later, when this murder has been solved and the truth
revealed. Which reminded me…

"So we're here. What do you know about the Coach
Farley case?"

He seemed to take a long time chewing his burger, and
even took a long sip of milkshake before answering. I was
starting to think he was prolonging as part of his babysitting game. "He was holding a Mercedes hood ornament."

"Got that. It's Wickham Birkland's. Nothing to do with
this case, other than it was odd that he was holding it at
that moment. He took it from the accident scene earlier in

the day. I don't think it was Wickham. There's just no real motivation. If we went by who he was mad at, he'd be a serial killer. Next."

He nodded appreciatively at my logic. "The witness said the car had rounded headlights, so we're thinking—"

"BMW, Mercedes, Jeep—although you probably are staying away from that last one, for obvious reasons. Yeah, I know. What else do you have?"

"Well, if you already know everything." He seemed half-exasperated, half-impressed.

"That's it? That's everything? I figured for sure the police would find evidence that I didn't see with my naked eye right there in the parking lot in the middle of the night. Surely there's something else."

He shrugged. "That's it. That's all I know about, anyway. The hood ornament, the headlights, the hair net—"

I put down my burger, reached over, and grasped his arm. "Hold up. The hair net?"

He glanced at my hand and I jerked away, blushing. It was the first time we'd touched. And It wasn't unpleasant.

I turned it into a joke to cut the awkwardness. "Is it considered assaulting an officer to leave greasy fingerprints on his uniform sleeve?" I forced a laugh and brushed off his sleeve where my hand had been. My cheeks were burning. Really, Hollis? Assaulting an officer?

He chuckled, then cleared his throat. "There was a hair net. We didn't find it until the medical examiner cleared him and the ambulance took him away. He was lying on it."

Darn it, I knew I should have stayed longer. "And…?"

"It had a few long, red, curly hairs in it. That's all I know."

I had seen a hair net with long, red, curly hairs underneath it. On Evangeline. I tried to remember whether or not she was still wearing her hair net when she joined me at the accident site. Maybe she wasn't.

Could she have been the one who...? No way. Not her. She didn't seem like the murdering type.

Although she had issued me that weirdly severe warning about staying out of the case. And she seemed to have opinions on Coach Farley. Lots of them.

"And have you followed up on that hair net?"

He shook his head. "Chief Henderson believes it was probably already in the parking lot and the coach just fell on it. There's always all kinds of trash in that lot. The Boy Scouts only come out for clean-up once a month."

True, I remembered the litter I'd seen on the crime scene. Cigarette butts, discarded take-out menus, pompom strands. Still, beneath the dead coach seemed awfully conveniently placed. And everything—even if it was obvious trash—needed to be examined as possible evidence.

"So you haven't interviewed the concession stand kids?" I asked, trying to nibble my burger nonchalantly. Just one investigator passing the time with another investigator. Nothing to see here.

"Not yet. Chief's got some ideas about the perp. Just got to get a case together before he moves in."

I leaned forward, losing my fake nonchalance really quickly. "And that perp is...?"

He grinned, chewing, and those darn eyes actually sparkled mischievously. I also noticed one eye tooth—on the left side—was slightly, adorably, crooked. "Wouldn't you like to know?"

"Actually, yes. That's why I'm asking."

He took another large bite. So long to the shy, uncomfortable Brooks who nervously glossed over his reason for leaving Kansas City. This was the Brooks who pretended to be in the market for a toaster and who stood behind my car. Brooks the Babysitter. He looked absolutely thrilled to be having this exchange.

"Sorry, no can do."

"Excuse me?" Suddenly I didn't want those last three onion rings at all. "I thought that was the whole purpose of this meal. So we could share leads."

He shook his head. "Miss Bisbee, you're the press. You're exactly the person my boss does not want to have information about our leads. I can't tell you any more than I already have."

I wadded up my napkin. "So the reason we're having burgers is to keep me out of Chief Henderson's hair."

He turned his palms up. "I mean, not entirely. I did share with you."

I tossed my napkin at him. It bounced off his chest. "Uh-huh, not entirely. I can't believe I fell for it. I actually thought you were too decent to play me like that. Guess I was wrong." I pushed away from the table and stood.

"Come on, now, Hollis," he said. "It's not like that at all. I'm not playing you. I'm really not."

"Don't worry. I'll find out the truth on my own," I said as I walked away. "You can't mess with freedom of speech."

"You didn't share anything with me, you know," he called to my back. "Don't think I didn't notice."

*Not true*, I thought. *I gave you my trust. And look where that got me.* The thought made me pause briefly, then I pushed through the door and headed back toward the pharmacy parking lot.

# CHAPTER 13

THE NEXT MORNING, MIKE, THE kids, and a home-made ramp woke me up bright and early with the repeated warning call of, "Car!" Then the sound of boards dragging and being dropped, a soft whoosh of an automobile, the sound of boards being dragged and dropped again, and the *clunk-clunk* of various bicycles, scooters, and skateboards on said boards until, "Car!" again.

With every *clunk-clunk*, I mentally revisited the words—*thump-thump*—of the sole witness of Coach Farley's hit-and-run. Who did Mary Jean say she was? Agnes Tellerman? To hear Mary Jean tell it, Agnes was both a crier and a liar. According to Brooks, she was a chronic witness, and pretty paranoid. Either way, the narrative surrounding Agnes Tellerman was that she was not someone to be trusted with something like witnessing a crime. Plus there was the ban Mary Jean had issued against talking to her. But with Brooks and Chief Henderson doing everything they could to keep me in the dark, I wondered where and how I could get a hold of Agnes, and how I could keep Mary Jean from finding out about it. I had a feeling Agnes could be trusted with more than anyone gave her credit for. But I also had a feeling that Mary Jean would be really angry if I defied her direct order to leave Agnes alone.

Brooks had mentioned the witness during our short, disastrous meeting at FastNHotz, but I'd neglected to ask if they'd interviewed her again after the accident. I was guessing the answer was no. Or at least that was what I would be told, whether they actually had or not.

And what about Evangeline? Was the chief right about the hair net? Was it something that had just happened to be rolling around in the parking lot and found itself in the middle of a crime scene? Possibly. Probably. But what if it wasn't? Would it be worth it to visit the concession stand—snack shop—for a third time? Every lead, no matter how small, was worth following up. That was what I had been taught, anyway.

I needed to catch Daisy up on everything that had happened.

If Mike and the kids were outside playing at 7 a.m., it was certain that Daisy was out delivering muffins, so I showered, got dressed, and went to the Hibiscus.

As expected, she was already there when I arrived.

"Isn't it something that we have to leave our houses and come all the way over here to see each other?" she said when I came in and plunked myself down on the counter stool closest to the dessert case—what I liked to think of as *my stool*. Huh. Somehow, without my noticing, I'd become a regular in the town diner. "Can't get a second alone in that circus."

"Do your children ever sleep?"

"Doesn't seem like it. Muffin?" She handed me a muffin the size of a small human's head. "You'll never guess the flavor."

"Definitely looks like lemon poppyseed."

She beamed. "Ding ding ding! To go with the *Knock 'em Dead* theme of the month!" She pulled out another muffin and toasted our success by knocking it against mine. "Cheers! To murder and muffins!"

The man sitting next to me snapped his fingers and pointed at Daisy. "I knew it!"

We both jumped. I dropped my muffin and it bounced off the counter and onto the floor. Daisy frowned again, but simply proffered another.

"I'm sorry?" she asked.

He shook his finger, pointing at each of us in turn. "I've been trying to figure out where I've heard your voices before, and now I've got it. Y'all are those pod people. You have that show Esther's been telling everyone about. My wife listens."

Daisy and I glanced at each other incredulously. I had barely been sure I'd been uploading our short, ridiculous episodes successfully. It never even occurred to me to check and see if anyone was listening. Someone was listening? Someone was listening! Bless Esther!

"Tell her thank you for tuning in," I said. "Our next recording is going to be really interesting. Did you know that Jane Stanford—as in Stanford University—was poisoned by—"

He waved me off. "No, no, not you. She likes this one over here." He picked up his coffee cup and lifted it toward Daisy. "She's real excited about that lemon curd secret you told. She's gonna use it at our family reunion next month."

Daisy looked half-excited, half-alarmed. "I'm honored," she said. "Really. Tell her our next podcast will have a secret to making your muffins moist." She turned to me, and said through a smile, "You didn't edit my secret ingredient out?"

"I told you I didn't know how," I said. "I'm working on it. Every time I try to edit something out, I end up cutting something good." And, I didn't add, sometimes when

I edited out all the chatter we wanted to keep off the podcast, there was only about four minutes of actual podcast material left. First, we probably needed to learn how to edit ourselves—which wasn't going to be easy when it came to Daisy and me.

Esther poured me a coffee to go with my muffin. I stirred two sugars into it. "So, um…what does your wife think of the reporting?"

"Huh?" He sipped his coffee. "Oh, she doesn't really ever talk about that. She tunes in for the recipes."

"Recipes?" the woman sitting on the other side of him repeated. "What television show did you say this was?"

"Not television," I said. "Radio. Kind of. It's a podcast."

"My wife, she listens to all of them. Conspiracy theories, politics, cooking shows…" He gestured at Daisy.

"It's not a cooking show per say," I said. "It's more of a murder show, where she sometimes mentions food."

"All I know is my wife made lemon bars and lemon tarts that practically melted in my mouth. To me, that's a cooking show. A really good one."

"Ooh, I could use some new recipes," the woman said. "What's it called again? I'll have to listen."

"*Knock 'em Dead*," Daisy said. "Like, desserts that will knock 'em dead." She punched the air, looking pretty proud of her ad-libbed tagline.

"No. What? No, not just desserts," I said, but then the lady was talking to two ladies in a booth behind her, and Esther started buzzing about it to someone at the other end of the counter, and I realized it was pointless to fight it. And why would I want to? Everyone was talking about our podcast! Even if they were calling it a cooking show and only tuning in for good curd recipes. It was a start.

Daisy's phone rang. She whipped it out with a worried

look on her face. "Oh, sheesh, hello?" She paused. "No, I don't have any other laundry baskets. Why?" Another pause, then she shut her eyes and shook her head. "He what? Well, is he okay? Uh-huh. Yeah, all right, I'll be home in five minutes." She hung up. "Don't ask. Everyone's fine. Except my laundry basket. I just bought that one, too. Walk with me?"

I tore the top off of my muffin and took it with me, getting in a good sip of coffee on my way off the stool. "See ya, Esther," I said.

"Bye, honey!"

"So what's the scoop, Miss Reporter?" Daisy asked as soon as we were outside.

"The police either have nothing or they're just not telling me. There was this hair net—"

"No, I don't mean about the case," Daisy said. She bit down on a smile. "I mean about you and Officer McDreamy."

I felt my face flush. "What do you mean?"

"Your text said you met with him, but didn't say any more. Was there kissing?"

"Kissing? No. There were onion rings. Why would there be kissing?"

"I don't know," she said. "Because he's so dreamy and you're so single."

I frowned. "Excuse me, but maybe I'm single by choice."

"You're not."

"Maybe I'm single because I'm focusing on my career."

"You're definitely not."

"Maybe I'm single because I don't have time or energy to maintain a relationship right now, and I enjoy my own company and don't need a man to fulfill me."

"Maybe that one," she said. "But probably not. I think you're single because you're afraid to move on. You think if you start a relationship with someone, that will mean you're putting down roots here and finally saying goodbye to the ex for real."

"That's not true." It wasn't true, was it? Why did it feel at least kind of true? And how did she know that before I did?

We'd gotten to her minivan. She unlocked it and opened the door. "All I'm saying is you're single and he's cute and you two had dinner together and that's kind of the start of something."

"It was definitely not the start of something. Can I tell you about it now, or are we going to continue to write romance stories in our heads?"

She sighed. "I like romance stories. But okay. Lay it on me."

I told her about the crime scene and how the witness never had anything else to say—probably because no one ever asked her—and how they were focused on the Mercedes hood ornament. I told her about the hair net and that Chief Henderson had assigned me my own interference force.

"I've seen worse methods of interference," she said, elbowing me.

"This again?"

"No, no, you're right. I'm just teasing you anyway. And the assistant coach?"

I shook my head. "Not one word about him. Which, I hope, means we're ahead of them, and they haven't even considered him yet." Or they had, and Brooks was just keeping it from me. But I preferred my version—the version where we had the scoop.

"We should go back over there, see if we can get a better interview with him or something."

"You think he'd talk to us?"

She slid behind the wheel. "Honey, he is desperate for a promotion. We play this right, and he'd talk to us if we were spiders under his desk."

She watched me absentmindedly nibble the muffin top I was still holding, and somehow she knew what I was thinking. "Hollis. Roots are okay. Roots are a good thing. I put down roots and look how happy I am. Sweet kids, awesome hubby, nice little house with the best next-door neighbor. Who wouldn't want those roots?"

I started to respond, but was interrupted when a car came down the street and passed the Hibiscus. Wait. Not a car. A Jeep. Paulie Henderson's Jeep.

Forget roots. Who cared about roots at a time like this?

"I have to talk to Paulie," I said, practically tripping over myself in my hurry to get to my car. I fumbled out my keys and dove inside, turning the ignition before the door was even closed. "Let's record later," I yelled.

Paulie drove like his pants were on fire and he could only put them out in the river across town. I had my pedal pushed to the floor trying to keep up with him. I nearly took out Wickham Birkland's already-smashed Mercedes at the four-way stop at Tutor and Oak, causing him to lay on his horn and shout something I was glad I couldn't hear, his face contorted with righteous rage. I was guessing the path that Paulie had taken, since I couldn't see him anymore. I let my intuition—honed by years of sleuth reporting in one of the toughest cities in America—guide me. Actually, there were so few streets in Parkwood, I let the obvious lack of choices guide me, but calling it honed reporter's intuition sounded better.

My phone rang, and I dumped my entire bag on the floorboard trying to get to it. It was my mom. Why was she up so early?

"Not a good time, Mom," I said.

Her voice was way too loud over the speaker. "Are you on a date or something?"

I made a face. "Who goes on a date at seven o'clock in the morning?"

"It could be a breakfast date. And that was not a denial. I think she was on a date, Rut."

"It's about time," Ruta yelled. "Is it a good date?"

"No, it's not a date at all. I keep telling you, if I have a date, I will call you." Not necessarily true—I would probably only call if I'd had a good date— but it was what they needed to hear. They were convinced that I was lonely and needed a man to pick up my spirits. "And I've also told you, if you keep hassling me about men, I'm going to stop answering the phone." Totally not true, but they didn't believe me anyway.

"You mean to tell me if we're dying in a ditch you won't pick up just because I might mention a boy?" Aunt Ruta called from the background, her voice way louder than Mom's.

"You don't have to yell, Aunt Ruta. You're on speaker. I can hear you just fine. And if you're dying in a ditch, call the police. Why would you call me first? I'm five hundred miles away."

"To say goodbye," Mom said. "Wouldn't you want us to say goodbye? I would expect that from your sisters, but not you."

"Of course I—That's not the point." I turned onto

another side street, winding my way into town the way I thought Paulie would do. "If you called for actual help, maybe you wouldn't have to say goodbye. They could save you."

I paused at a four-way stop, unsure which direction to go, and deciding straight was still the best option.

"So, speaking of boys—" Aunt Ruta said.

"No, I'm not speaking of—you know what? Forget it. I'll answer the phone when you call, no matter what. Goodbye!"

"But you don't even know yet why we called," Mom said.

"You mean it wasn't to harass me about men?"

"Well…" Mom hesitated.

"It's about Trace," Aunt Ruta yelled. "So, yeah, kinda."

I rolled my eyes, just like I used to do when I was a teenager and they would butt into my love life. It was a habit. Mom and Aunt Ruta had almost taken my breakup harder than I had. They loved Trace. They started cutting out magazine photos of models in wedding dresses by the time we went on our third date. "Nope, it's not about Trace. We broke up. End of story."

"End of chapter, perhaps," Mom said. "Which is why we called, actual—"

"No. Mom." I adopted my best patient voice while cutting off two cars and nearly plowing into a woman on the sidewalk. "Trace and I are no longer together. And that is the end of the story. No Thanksgivings, no Christmases, no birthdays, or National Ice Cream Days, or July 4ths or Cheese Appreciation Day. We're done, and you just need to accept it."

"Before you say that, you should probably hear us out, Hol—"

"Mom," I said, trying very hard to keep the fourteen-year-old whine out of my voice. "I have to go. I'm working. I'll call you later. I love you." I raised my voice, "And I love you, too, Aunt Ruta."

"Hollis—"

"Gotta go! Bye!" I ended the call, knowing full well I would regret the decision in short order. But I had Paulie to concentrate on, and I couldn't get sidetracked by Trace.

I passed the Jeep before I realized it had stopped. And even then I only recognized it because I saw Paulie sauntering to the old, musty gas station that sat right between a used car lot and a body shop.

Wait.

I slowed, gazing in my rearview mirror. A body shop, and his Jeep was definitely parked there. Why? Did it need work? I hadn't gotten a chance to see it up close yet. Maybe this would be my chance to arm myself with information before talking to Paulie.

I rolled to the next driveway—a tattoo parlor slash independent tax service—and turned around. I parked in the used car lot and waited until Paulie had disappeared inside the gas station, then made my move.

A skinny man with a beard that reached his sternum was crouched in front of the Jeep, peering into the grill with one eye squinted shut. I couldn't help noticing that the grill was broken, one headlight cracked. Had that happened while, say, hitting a body?

"Hello?" I asked.

The man glanced at me, then went back to staring at the Jeep. I waited for him to speak, but he never did, not even when I cleared my throat awkwardly.

"I'm Hollis Bisbee. I work for the *Chron*—" I caught myself. "For *Knock 'Em Dead* podcast."

"Whatever it is you're selling, I'm not buying."

"I'm not here to sell you anything. I'm a reporter, and I'm hoping you can talk to me a little bit about this Jeep."

"What about it?"

"Has it been in an accident recently?"

He looked me up and down. "Why?"

I fought the urge to squirm, reminding myself of the time I had to ask a crime boss if he knew anything about an explosion in a mattress warehouse. This twerp made me uncomfortable, but he was nothing compared to that completely terrifying guy. *You've stared down known killers, Hollis. You've got this. You are a hardboiled reporter, and your podcast audience is depending on you to bring this story to light.*

Not exactly true—my audience was depending on lemon curd tips—but now was not the time for reality.

I swallowed, pulled myself to full height, and tilted my chin up professionally to give myself confidence. "I'm investigating a story that might feature this Jeep."

Wordlessly, he went back to peering at the grill of the Jeep.

"Sir? Excuse me?"

He grunted again. I felt like I was back at square one. I took a deep breath. When in doubt, just dive on in.

"Can you tell me why this Jeep is here? I'm reporting a story about a hit-and-run. It looks to me like this Jeep was involved in an accident recently. Do you know what happened?"

Most importantly, was there any blood on the fender? I tried to casually look, but didn't see anything. Paulie Henderson was not an idiot, and his father knew his way around crime scenes. Most likely, any blood that might have been involved had long since been wiped clean. I was sure of it.

Also, I couldn't help noticing the damage to the front of the Jeep wasn't very extensive. I made a mental note to research how much damage a hit-and-run would do to the front of a car.

The man took his toothpick out of his mouth and used it to point to the grill. "Looks to me like he hit a bird."

"A bird?" Not the response I'd thought I would get.

"Happens pretty often out on the country roads. Birds get a little too big for their britches, end up getting blown up by the front end of a car."

I studied the grill a little harder. The damage seemed like a little too much to have been made by a bird. Unless it was a giant bird like...an emu.

Were there wild emu in Parkwood?

"So you don't think this damage could have come from, say, hitting a man in a parking lot?"

He studied me intensely. "Who did you say you are again?"

The air around us began to feel weighty, uncomfortable. "Hollis Bisbee." I took a breath and tried to add some confident conviction behind it. "I'm with the *Knock 'em Dead* podcast." I pulled out my notebook and pencil.

"Uh-huh," he said. "I heard about you. You're that fancy big city reporter. I haven't got anything to say."

Stonewalled again. It was harder to get this town talking than that time I had to get a story on a murder inside a monastery.

"I—I'm not—if you don't mind just telling me—"

He pointed to the side of his head with one finger, the way Mary Jean did when she told me to read my work aloud and listen for too many giblets. "Can't you hear? I said I'm not talking."

"Can you at least tell me if the Jeep has been here before today for any other body work—"

"Nope."

"Especially in the past week or so—"

"Nope."

"Fine." I crammed my notebook and pencil back into my bag. "Are you the only body shop in Parkwood?"

He thought this one over, then peered at the ceiling. "Yep," he finally said.

"Thanks for your time." I turned on my heel and walked away.

And nearly tripped over a pair of big feet in shiny black shoes. I stopped short, started to apologize, then realized who I'd tripped over. Brooks was standing just outside the bay doors, his arms crossed, his legs splayed confidently. He was in uniform.

"You have got to be kidding me. Not right now, okay?"

"I just happened to be driving by and saw your car. Thought I'd stop in to make sure everything's okay." He looked over my shoulder. "Hey, Mark."

"Hey, Brooks," the mechanic said.

"Everything's fine," I said. "Thanks for your concern." I was so frustrated at this point, I almost didn't notice how it felt kind of nice to see him. Almost.

"I know what you're worried about, and I haven't said one word to Paulie Henderson," I said.

"Not for lack of trying."

Well...that was true. Which reminded me... "Please step aside, Officer, I need to get to that gas station."

He didn't step aside. "Why?"

It was my turn to cross my arms. We looked like two children having a pouting stand-off. Which would have made me smile if it weren't for my extreme frustration with everything that ever had to do with Brooks and Chief Henderson and Mark the tight-lipped mechanic and the whole impossible system. "I don't need to divulge that to you."

"No, you're correct, you don't need to. But you might want to."

"Why on earth would I want to?" I pointed at him.

"You know, I'm starting to think you're actually a spy."

"Is that so? Why would I be spying?"

"You're as eager to find out what I know as I am to find out what you know."

"That's ridiculous," he said, but something about the way he set his jaw made me think I was closer to the truth than I realized.

"But you're planning on talking to Paulie," he said. A smirk pulled up one corner of his mouth. "Which is gonna be hard to do."

"And why is that?"

"Because of that." I followed his nod toward the gas station. Paulie Henderson had emerged with a girl, each of them holding packages of mini doughnuts and bottles of chocolate milk. A before-school breakfast. The two of them were getting into her car.

"No!" I said, starting to walk faster, but it was useless. The car had started up and pulled away before I could even get out of the body shop lot.

"I'm sorry," Brooks said, and something about the way he said it—or maybe the crease in his forehead—made me believe that he really was sorry. But that didn't make the situation any better. "I'm just doing my job, Hollis, and protecting the investigation. Not to mention Chief Henderson is my boss. And I'm trying to keep you out of his sights, too. He knows you're after his son. It's not just your life he can make miserable. It's mine, too. And I have to work for the guy."

"Ah," I said. "So this is about you."

"It's about letting the chief do his job."

"It's also about letting me do mine." I didn't wait for him to respond—just walked to my car, not even bothering to look at him again until he was in my rearview mirror.

# CHAPTER 14

"WELCOME TO THE *KNOCK 'EM Dead* podcast."

"Where murder and muffins meet!"

"I'm Hollis."

"And I've got cake," Daisy said. "To celebrate!"

I eyeballed her. "What are we celebrating?"

She thought about it for a second, then brightened. "Cake! We're celebrating cake."

"So we're having cake to celebrate having cake."

She pushed her bangs out of her eyes. "Can you think of a better reason?"

Actually, no, I couldn't. And the cake was gorgeous. Bright yellow, cooked in an embellished mold, shiny with glaze, dusted with powdered sugar, and smelling sugary and warm, like sunshine on a platter. My mouth watered. "Well, slice her up, then."

She pulled out a knife and a couple of plates and began cutting the cake. "Speaking of slicing, do you have any murders for us?"

"Yes, but not the sliced kind. More like the poisoned kind. You ever hear of Jane Stanford?"

We were getting much better at this. Smoother. We still didn't sound like reporters, exactly, but I was proud of our progress. In fact, it may have been a good thing that we didn't sound like reporters. We were conversational. And at least we could get through our opener without debate now.

"Like, Stanford University?" she asked.

"Yep. Jane Stanford's death was most definitely a poisoning, but after a jury ruled it that way, another doctor came in, did an autopsy, and had the official cause of death changed to heart attack. But there was definitely strychnine in her system, and someone had tried to poison her just a few weeks before, so it was clearly a poisoning, not a heart attack. So did someone pay off the doctor to lie? Who killed Jane Stanford and why has remained a mystery ever since."

"Whoa," Daisy said. "I had no idea. Who do you think did it?"

"I'm not sure," I said. "There was only one person who was with her both times."

"Mmm-hmm, the husband. It's always the husband." Instinctively, we both leaned over to look out my front window. Mike and his buddies were running around inside giant inflatable balls, smashing into each other and knocking each other over.

"What exactly is he doing?" I whispered.

"They're calling it life-sized soccer, but it looks more like demolition derby to me. Just as long as nobody gets hurt, I don't care. They can knock themselves silly. Probably wouldn't be able to tell much difference, especially with Spencer." She leaned toward the mic. "Cut that, just in case he listens."

"You sure you don't want to be the technical department?"

Her eyes grew round. "Cake?" She pushed a plate at me. The inside looked even better than the outside. This was Daisy's entirely effective way of changing the subject.

"Jane Stanford's husband was already long gone at the time of her death," I said. "The person who was with her both times was her personal assistant, Bertha Berner. She didn't have much in the way of motive, but she definitely had the means. I'll get into a lot more details."

"Ah," Daisy said around a mouthful of cake. "When in doubt, go with the personal assistant. It's always the assistant."

"I thought you just said it was always the husband."

"Except when there's an assistant. Speaking of, when should we talk to Kermit Hoopsick again? I still think he could be the one who murdered Coach Farley."

"Cut!" I said. "You can't level an accusation like that on the show. You have to use words like 'allegedly' and 'supposed.' And tomorrow. I thought we could talk to him tomorrow."

"Good plan," she said. "This case is getting cold. We need to warm it up. It's been a week." She leaned toward her mic. "Which reminds me, I think it's time for my baking tip of the week. To make my cakes moist, I use brown sugar instead of white sugar, and I also use sour cream instead of milk, and put in two extra tablespoons of oil. Enjoy!"

I stared at my forkful of cake. "That's a lot of calories," I said.

She looked at me like I had lost my mind. "It's cake. You're expecting it to be diet friendly?"

"No, but when you spell it all out like that, it makes it seem—"

"Delicious?"

"Well, yes, definitely but—"

My front door opened, making both of us jump. "Daisy?" Mike had stuck his head inside. "We've got a situation."

Daisy yanked off her headphones and tossed them onto

the table. "Oh, cheese and crackers, one of the kids got stuck in a bubble, didn't they?"

He hesitated, seemed to weigh his words. "Yeah. I, uh— can't get him out."

We both leaned forward again, to see Lucas's feet wriggling excitedly in the air out of the top of an inflatable bubble, and Mudd, Ed, and Spencer standing by his feet, arguing about the best way to extract him. We could hear Lucas's giggles.

She sighed. "Why is it always Lucas? Press pause, Hollis."

I stared at the app. "I don't know how to press pause."

"Well, then finish the Stanford story, because I have to rescue my kid from my husband's brainiac friends."

She stormed outside while I clicked around, looking for a pause button. Instead, I just ended up stopping the recording altogether. "A minisode," I said to myself, and then followed her out.

I wasn't three steps across the lawn when I saw Brooks.

He had parked his car at the curb and was heading toward me. I groaned. "They called you?"

He looked confused, then noticed the scene in Daisy's yard. Daisy had one foot planted on the inflatable and was tugging Lucas's feet with all her might, hopping along as the only movement she could seem to get was the ball turning.

"No, it looks like they have that under control," he said.

The ball caught the downside of a little hill and took Daisy with it as it rolled to the curb. Lucas shrieked with hilarity. "I'm not so sure about that," I said.

"Regardless, I'm here to see you."

I noticed then that he was not wearing his uniform, but instead a stiff-looking pair of jeans with a pale green polo shirt. His hair was combed neatly, as if he'd paid it close attention. "What's going on?" I asked warily. "I haven't followed Paulie all day." *Because I plan to follow him tonight,* I didn't finish. There were just some things Brooks didn't need to know.

"I'm not here about that, either," he said.

"Okay. Then…why are you here?"

He scratched one bicep, and then crossed his arms, tipped his chin up. His face was flushed—was he sweating? I fought the urge to grin. Why was he so darn cute?

"I'm here to ask you to dinner. Off the record. To make up for the one at FastNHotz."

"You're asking off the record, or dinner will be off the record?"

"Uh, both, I guess," he said. He'd put product in his hair. And I was pretty sure he was wearing cologne.

"Why?"

He looked like he didn't know how to answer that, which was fair because I didn't know why I'd asked.

"What I meant to say was, where?"

"I was thinking Chinese," he said. "Unless you don't like Chinese food."

"I do." And I hadn't had it since moving to Parkwood. An egg roll sounded as good as that cake inside. "When? Now? I don't think I can—"

"No, I was thinking maybe Saturday."

I chewed my bottom lip. Daisy had extracted Lucas, who was sweaty and breathless with laughter, but now Jake had jammed himself inside one upside down and was walking himself around the yard on his hands.

"And the why is because I don't like the way we ended at FastNHotz the other day. I feel kinda like I owe you." He spread his hands across his chest. "I'm not a bad guy, Hollis. I don't like you thinking I am."

"Mike Mueller, you're in so much trouble," Daisy seethed, rushing off to stop Willow from getting into a ball.

"And this is to talk about the case?" I asked. "Off the record, like you said, of course."

He thought about it, then nodded. "Yeah, sure. If that's what you want."

Every cell in my body told me this was a bad idea. Having dinner with the enemy could only end with the enemy learning my battle plans and adjusting his troops accordingly.

At the same time, this was Brooks we were talking about—there were no battle plans to be found there. Even if the chief had some—and I doubted he did, beyond *keep her out of my hair*—Brooks was way too open to hide them from me successfully. Besides, he didn't necessarily feel like the enemy. Not anymore.

I could learn a lot about the case.

I could learn something that would help me break it wide open.

I could report that I had an anonymous source and break the case wide open and establish myself—and the *Knock 'em Dead* podcast—as a serious news outlet. A podcast to be reckoned with.

"I'll pay for myself," I said.

He looked a little crestfallen at that idea, but quickly recovered. "Okay. Seven?"

"I'll be here." And then for reasons I didn't understand, I held my hand out.

Warily, he took it and shook it.

"I'll see you on Saturday, then."

# CHAPTER 15

MARY JEAN WAS BACK IN the office the next day, and she looked horrible. She was pale and damp and her nose was red and raw. She winced every time she swallowed or yawned and kept patting her forehead with a tissue.

"Are you okay?" I asked as she suffered through the final draft of my hot dog roller story. "Maybe you should go home."

She waved a tissue at me. "I'm fine. It's just a little sore throat, and copy is due to printing by lunchtime. Can't afford to get behind."

"But you're miserable. I think you may have the flu."

"The news doesn't get the flu."

Fair point. *The news doesn't* was a mantra among my colleagues in Chicago. *The news doesn't cry. The news doesn't worry about blood. The news doesn't get himself tossed from the President's press conference for muttering unsavory nicknames loudly enough for the president to hear, Jimmy.* I was definitely not one to criticize anyone for being single-minded in their pursuit of a good story.

"This will do," she said at last. "I can tell you're listening to yourself more. Email it. Have you seen Ernie?"

Yes, I had. Out in the parking lot, asleep in his car with

a hoagie balanced on his stomach. "Nope. I think he's out on a story." *You so owe me, Ernie.*

"I don't recall assigning him a story." She scrunched her eyebrows together, then gave her head a slight shake. "I'm sure you're right. Concentration is not my strength right now." She opened her drawer, then wrestled unsuccessfully with the lid on a bottle of Tylenol.

"Looks to me like strength isn't your strength today, either," I said, taking the bottle from her and easily opening it. I shook two out onto her desk. "Really, you should go get rest. Nobody will even be here. I've got the bank grand opening to do today."

She dry-swallowed the Tylenol.

"Good. And I hope you've given up on your ridiculous obsession with the Coach Farley case. I've heard from the chief that you keep popping up in all the wrong places. You're not investigating, are you? I've told you, we're not doing a story."

*You've also told me that the man died of natural causes, so...*

"No, ma'am. No story here." Not for the newspaper, anyway.

"Well, good. One of the most important things to learn about journalism is you don't poke your nose where it doesn't belong."

I bit my lip—hard—to keep from responding that, actually, keeping your nose out of other people's business is the total opposite of one of the most important tenets of journalism.

Mary Jean burst into a long, hard, croaky-sounding cough followed by a groan of despair. I heard a distinctly aerosol noise in the direction of Joyce's cubicle—undoubtedly a fresh cloud of Lysol was hovering above her right now, and I only wished it was hovering above me, too.

"You should go home and rest. Maybe go to the doctor?" I said.

Mary Jean waved me off again. "I've got deadlines. And so do you."

"Right. I'll be off, then."

I passed Joyce's cubicle on the way out. Without looking up from her computer, she picked up the can of disinfectant spray, pointed it at me, and sprayed.

"Thanks, Joyce."

"Anytime."

"I'm so glad you called," Daisy said as she got in the car, forcing Mike to pry a wailing Willow off of her body. "Where are we going? Please say it's a spa in Bali and we have free airfare and hotel and a million dollars in spending money."

"Close," I said. "We're going back to River Fork High School."

She pooched her lips as she thought it over. "Almost as good," she said.

"And Wilma Louise Farley's house."

She raised her eyebrows. "Even better. You know where to find her?"

"I saw the address on one of the magazines on his desk. We'll just swing by and see if she's home."

"Sounds like a plan."

"What's with Willow? Everything okay?"

"Oh, you know," she said on a sigh. "Terrible Two started early."

"My aunt says Terrible Two came early with me, too, and that she'll let me know when it's over."

Daisy cracked up. The one time I'd let Daisy and Mom and Aunt Ruta have a conversation, they'd ended up staying on the phone for well over an hour. Afterward, Daisy knew more about me than I cared to contemplate. And there was no payback—Daisy's mom was quiet and polite and didn't have a single embarrassing story she was willing to share.

"Go ahead and laugh," I said. "You could be saying the same thing someday."

She patted my arm. "I would be so happy if she ended up like you."

"Thank you."

"Minus the hard-headed part." She cracked up again. "You could crack walnuts with that thing."

"I prefer to think of myself as determined. Determination is a good quality."

"Well, Willow is nothing if not determined," she said.

"Just wait until she's old enough to firmly grasp how wrapped around her little finger her daddy is," I said. "Mike is hardly the strict authoritarian with that girl. Or with anyone."

"Eh." She gazed out the window. "Mike is forever young. But that's what I love about him, you know? When we're ninety, he's going to be building blanket forts in the living room for our great-grandkids. I'd rather have someone like that than someone who's always carrying around the worries of the world. That person turns into Wickham Birkland and starts yelling at people for standing on his sidewalk too long. No thanks." She turned toward me. "What about you?"

"What about me?" I asked. "I like Mike."

"No, I mean what do you want out of a guy? You never talk about relationships. Every time I try, you clam up."

"This again? We weren't talking about relationships. We were talking about Mike."

"Who I happen to be in a relationship with. You're splitting hairs, Hollis. You can't avoid the subject forever."

"Yes, I can."

"We're supposed to be best friends, right?"

We hadn't ever "officially" defined our friendship, but, yes, Daisy was definitely my best friend here in Parkwood. I couldn't think of the last time I'd even heard from my girl posse back in Chicago, so it may just be that Daisy was my best friend, period. "Yeah."

"Best friends talk about relationships. So spill. What kind of guy gets your heart thumping?"

Immediately and without warning, Trace appeared in my mind. Not career-driven Trace who chose Chicago over me, but sweet Trace who drew me funny pictures. Clever Trace whose cartoon commentary was clipped out and posted on thousands of office walls and refrigerators. Genius Trace who could hold a conversation on socio-political relations between the U.S. and basically any other country in the world, while choosing the exact right opera—Verdi? Puccini? Mozart?—to play in the background and the exact correct wine—most definitely a Chateauneuf-du-Pape—at the exact correct temperature and the exact correct aeration to be holding while having said conversation. That Trace was amazing and wonderful and…would be someone else's someday. If he wasn't already.

"There's nothing to talk about," I said.

"Your face says otherwise."

"My face says I want to talk to Kermit Hoopsick again. I don't have time for anything else."

Her eyebrows furrowed. "That's sad."

I glanced at her out of the corner of my eye. "No, it's not. It's realistic."

"If by realistic, you mean sad. You're thirty years old, Hollis. Way too young to swear off romance. You're at the age where it's just starting to get good." She shifted her whole body so she was facing me. "What about Brooks?"

I blinked. "What about him?"

"He likes you. I can tell."

"He's assigned to me. There's a difference."

"Let's just say it's an assignment I don't think he minds too much."

"Well, I mind it!" I said. "He's frustrating and annoying and has no understanding of the role of media in a civilized society. And he does this thing where he looks down at the ground and talks to his feet when he's uncomfortable instead of meeting your eye. And he has this cowlick on the back of his head and he chews his food too long before swallowing."

She was grinning.

"What?" I asked.

"For someone who doesn't like him, you sure have paid a lot of attention to details about him."

*I'm not a bad guy, Hollis.*

"I do not pay atten—can we just focus on the issue at hand, please? How should we approach Kermit?"

Her grin widened. "You're flustered. You like him!"

"I do not! I mean, he's fine. He's a likable person. But he's in my way."

"Maybe you should just have dinner with him or something." I didn't respond. Her eyes grew wide. "You're having dinner with him? When?"

"Tomorrow night," I said, then followed quickly with, "It's to talk about the case off the record."

"Uh-huh," she said. "How far off?"

"Not as far off as you're trying to make it sound right now." I pulled into the River Fork High School parking lot. "Now can we please focus on how we're going to approach Kermit?"

Her shoulders sagged. "You're no fun." She thought about it. "I say we go old school. Like, old, old school." She adopted a gangster voice. "Listen up, you. We know you did it, see. Tell us where the goods are or else you'll end up in the big house, see.. "

I watched her struggle and fail to hold back giggles.

"I'm starting to think I should have left you at home with your circus," I said. She laughed harder. "You're losing it." Harder still. So hard, she was wiping tears from the corners of her eyes. "I think Mike and those little terrors have finally cracked you. Let's go."

She giggled behind me all the way to the field house door, which again had been left propped open, even though school was still in session. Total safety violation, but it was working for me. I would save breaking that story for another day.

Kermit was in his office eating a tuna sandwich. The blood rushed from his face when he saw us walking toward him. He half-stood when we opened the office door and burst inside like we owned the place.

"You again," he said. "I already told the police, I don't have any information." So Chief Henderson and Brooks had finally gotten around to Kermit.

"We think you do, see," Daisy said in her gangster voice, but turned her lips in when she saw the warning glare I gave her. "Sorry," she mumbled.

"You've talked to the police?" I asked.

He nodded. "The chief came here and questioned me right in the middle of my first hour bowling unit. You guys are starting to make me look really bad. This is harassment. I could turn you in, you know."

I glanced at the other desk in the room. It had been mostly cleared off. All that was left was the framed photo, some coupons, and a long-dead potted plant. "They took evidence," I said, more to myself than to him.

"I told them, and I'll tell you. You're going to have to arrest me to make me talk."

"We're not the police," I said.

"We're podcasters," Daisy said, and when he gave a blank look, added, "*Knock 'em Dead* podcast? It's about murders."

I wasn't sure which one of us was giving her the more alarmed look.

"*Old* murders," I amended. "Like, from a long, long time ago."

"Now I really have nothing to say," he said, coming toward us, waving his arms in "shoo" motion.

"And muffins! It's about muffins, too," she added, but the damage had already been done.

"Out!" He backed us to the door.

"I can give you my secret to a creamy lemon pie," she said.

"You can talk to my lawyer! Move it!" He shuffled us along.

"Wait, wait! I can help you," I said, pulling up just short of the door. "Yes, we're podcasters. But that only means we want to get the full story. Objective and fair." He looked like he might be open to buying it, so I continued. "We're your chance to get your side of the story out there. Because,

I mean, you have to admit, it looks a little weird that you had the information about stealing plays and you had the playbook. You can clear the air about that." I neglected to mention that Daisy and I currently had possession of those things, so the police hadn't been able to get their hands on them.

"And you wanted his job. And you printed out a resume and a cover letter talking about the vacancy the day before he died. You should probably explain that, too, because it is way fishy," Daisy added.

Alarm flashed on his face and he started shooing us again.

"We will approach this from the perspective of an unbiased third party. I promise." What I wasn't promising was that we wouldn't turn him over to the police if we figured out he was the killer. Kermit looked like he was considering it. "Several people wanted him dead," I said. "It's not like you're the only—or even the most likely—suspect. What was your relationship like, exactly? You said he was too busy for beers. I assume that means you didn't hang out a lot after work."

His shoulders sagged. "He was mean. You try sharing an office with a cranky boss. I couldn't even eat my tuna fish in peace because he thought it smelled bad. Everything I did, he criticized. I hated him. Well, actually, we hated each other. Everyone knew it."

Daisy gave me *I-told-you-so* eyebrows; I gave my head a tiny *don't-you-dare-say-it* shake. We were finally getting somewhere. The last thing we needed was for him to get spooked and shut down again.

"Yes, I was trying to get his job," Kermit said. "I was meeting with the superintendent the following day to turn him in."

"Turn him in?"

"He was a cheater," Kermit said. "Paulie Henderson was right. And I had proof. I found the playbook in his desk drawer when he was out for one of his long lunches."

"Long lunches?" Daisy asked. "The Coach?"

"He called them 'meetings' so Wilma wouldn't start asking questions. He went over to Parkwood so she couldn't just stop by." He nodded toward the photos on the coach's desk—three blonde women standing on a beach with their arms wrapped around each other. One of the women I now recognized as the widow I'd seen at the visitation—Coach Farley's wife, Wilma Louise.

Curious. I had never seen Coach Farley lunching in Parkwood anywhere. There were only so many choices. Where was he really going?

"I was planning to turn him in and then show the superintendent that I was ready and able to step into the job. I need the raise. My wife's cat's about to have another litter. Expensive little buggers."

A litter of King Archies would put me in the poorhouse in food bills alone.

"But you never made it to the superintendent because Farley got killed the night before."

He nodded miserably. "And now I can't ask for his job or I'll look guilty. Someone else will get it and I'll have to stop bringing my tuna fish again." I had never seen anyone look so forlorn about canned fish in my life.

"What kind of car do you drive?" I asked, switching gears.

"It's a 1969 Mustang, why?"

The 1969 Mustang was a sweet muscle car with rounded headlights, that was why. This theory was starting to have more and more promise every minute.

"But I can prove I'm innocent," he said quickly. "I have video."

My mouth dropped open and I felt the insta-buzz I always got when I received a huge lead on a story. "You have video of the hit-and-run?"

He shook his head, dashing my excitement. "It's a video of me packing up the equipment. I have a friend in district security. I got him to let me look at the footage from the stadium cameras once I realized people could be suspicious about me. I thought maybe you could see me on one of the cameras and it would prove I didn't do it. And I was right. My friend could get fired, but he owed me, so he sent me this as long as I don't use his name."

He pulled out his phone and hunted around on it, then turned the screen toward us. The video showed a man wearing a baseball cap scooping footballs and helmets into bags. With the cap on, it was impossible to tell who it was. Could have been Kermit, but it also could have been just about any other man in Parkwood. It was thin proof at best.

"Wait, is that your car?" Daisy pointed to a tiny speck in the background, way off in the upper parking lot. A red muscle car with rounded headlights.

He nodded. "I had to carry those bags all the way out there by myself, as you'll see in the recording. It's at the eighteen minute mark."

I checked the time stamp on the video. "How long is this recording?"

"Twenty-two minutes. I had a hard time getting one of the helmets in."

He touched the bottom of the screen and slid his finger slowly to the right. We watched as sped-up Kermit—at one point he turned and scratched his head in consternation, revealing his face to the camera—packed up for eighteen minutes, then hauled the bag up the hill toward the upper lot. I did a little mental math. His story checked out. If he was packing and loading materials for twenty-two minutes, there was no way he could have been driving through the parking lot where Coach Farley was killed.

"Will your friend send me that?" I asked, thinking I could possibly turn up other useful clues if I got a good, hard look at it on my own time. Maybe the real killer was in the background somewhere.

He blanched and turned the phone screen to his chest, as if we hadn't just been watching it. "No way. He wants his name kept out of this, remember?"

"I won't bring it in. He can send it to me anonymously."

"Or you could leak it."

"She wouldn't do that," Daisy said, and in that moment I loved her for her loyalty.

He seemed to think about it, then changed his mind and shook his head, backing away from us. "No."

"And you don't think the police will want to see it?"

"They probably already have. If not, they can write up a warrant for it. I'm not getting my friend fired."

"Even if that means you might be sitting on a clue that could solve the crime?" Daisy asked. "Like a video of the killer's car driving away? You'd let one friend's murder go unsolved to protect another friend's job?"

He swallowed nervously. "I already told you. Gerald Farley and I were not friends."

"Thank you for your time," I said quietly. I turned to Daisy. "You ready?"

By the indignant look on her face, I could tell she clearly hadn't caught on yet. "But he has all kinds of motive. And round headlights."

"I thought you were going to be unbiased," Kermit said.

"We're done here. Get out." And there was something in his voice that told me this time he meant it.

But I was ready to go, anyway.

There was video proof: Kermit Hoopsick was not our guy.

We were silent in the car on the way to Wilma Louise's house. I was pretty sure we were thinking the same thing—if it wasn't Wickham or Kermit, we had two swings and two misses. So far all we'd managed to prove was who didn't kill Coach Farley. If we were going to solve the crime by process of elimination of everyone who might have had a grudge against the coach, this was going to take a while.

"We still need to talk to Paulie," I finally said, breaking the silence. "That may be the conversation that blows this whole story wide open. You never know."

"Yeah," she said, staring out her window. "I guess."

"What do you mean, you guess?"

"I just...Don't get mad at me, Hollis, okay?"

"What?" I asked, my voice low and wary.

She squirmed for a second more. "It's just...Don't you think it would be pretty dumb to kill a guy right after you told everyone you were going to kill that guy?"

"Nobody ever said Paulie Henderson was a genius. He signed an email Unanimous, remember?"

She nodded her head. "True. But he's not stupid, either. He could have followed Farley to somewhere much less public and run him over there. Or strangled him. Or...or killed him with a frozen hot dog. Whatever. The point is, doing it somewhere else would have been a much better plan."

"Maybe it was a heat-of-the-moment kind of thing. Maybe Paulie was mad because they lost, he had this huge grudge on this guy, he saw him walking in the shadows of the lower lot, and took his chance. Bam. Done. No more stolen plays."

"Yeah, I guess," she said. But she said it in that same doubtful way.

"It's entirely possible," I said. "And right now it's all we've got."

She chewed her lip. "But here's the other thing. Even if you think Chief Henderson would cover for Paulie." She put her hand out as if to hold me from talking. "And I totally see how you'd think that, given how many times Paulie has magically skated out of charges, and I agree that's super sketchy. But...well...do you think Brooks would be complicit in that?"

I opened my mouth to tell her, yes, that was exactly what I thought. But something stopped me. She was right. Brooks didn't seem like the kind of guy who would cover for a murderer. He was genuine, and sweet, and probably felt really sorry for Farley's widow. But more than that, he was honest. That was not the kind of guy who would go along with a cover-up.

Unless, of course, he didn't know about it.

"We still need to talk to Paulie," I said, pulling into the Farley driveway. "If nothing else, just to cover all of our bases."

"You haven't had much luck getting to him," she said.

"The football team has to practice, right?"

"Yeah...?"

"And they have to finish practice at some point, too."

"I don't know if that's the best idea," she said.

"Daisy, do you trust me?"

"Of course."

"Then don't worry about Paulie. Everything will be fine. Here's the house."

I parked at the curb. Daisy and I looked at the front of the Farley house, and then at each other.

"I'm nervous," she said.

"Why? You'll be fine."

"I've never questioned a widow before. It seems invasive or something. Like it's the last thing she needs. And I don't have any food to offer."

I unhooked my seatbelt nonchalantly, even though on the inside I was feeling exactly what Daisy was feeling. Questioning someone in new, raw grief was always difficult. "If it makes you feel better, most people want to talk," I said. "They want to know who killed their loved one. We're helping her."

"I wish I'd brought some muffins," Daisy said. "You're supposed to feed the grieving."

She took a deep breath and wrapped her hand around the door handle. "Let's go."

Nobody answered the door, and all the shades were pulled. The house was buttoned up tight. So much for finding out more about Farley's home life.

"She's not there." We turned to find a neighbor coming across the lawn toward us, rake in hand.

"Any idea when she'll get home?" I asked.

The neighbor shook her head. "I haven't seen her much since the funeral. Really sad what happened, isn't it?"

"Definitely sad," Daisy said. "You don't happen to know where she went, do you?"

The neighbor cocked her head, giving us a curious look. "Who are you, anyway? I don't think I've ever seen you around here before."

"We're podcasters," Daisy said brightly. "The *Knock 'Em Dead* podcast. Where murder and muffins meet." I was pretty sure that in our job delineations, Daisy was the PR department.

The woman brightened. "Oh, yeah, I've heard about you. They say your recipes are to die for."

"That is so on brand," Daisy said. "I really need to start using that more consistently."

"We're reporters," I said. "We were just hoping to find out a little bit more about Mr. Farley's life. What did he like to do with his spare time? Where did he go? Did he have any enemies?"

She waved her hand. "I never really had anything to do with him, so I don't know what his personal life was like. He never bothered me and I never bothered him. I thought he died of natural causes. Some sort of heart attack or something."

"That's definitely what they're saying," I said, busily jotting down notes.

"What about Wilma Louise?" Daisy asked. "Are you close?"

The neighbor wrinkled her nose. "We chat every now and again. But we don't have a lot in common, so it's usually pleasantries. Neighbor stuff. What do you think of this heat? Did you get to the HOA meeting? That kind of thing."

"How's she holding up, though?" Daisy asked. "Does she need muffins?"

The woman shrugged, nearly losing her rake in the process. "I have no idea. She hasn't said a peep."

"What do you mean?" I asked.

"She comes and goes all day long, but never stops to chat. I even called out to her and she kept going. A couple other ladies brought her a casserole and we all saw the curtains flutter when they knocked, but she never answered. They ended up leaving the food on her porch, and in the morning, it was still there. Stayed there until one of them came back and picked it up. I figure she's just grieving. Everybody does it differently." True, but the idea of poor Wilma Louise grieving all alone in that closed-up house, not answering the door or even eating, was just too sad to think about.

"Probably," I said. "One more thing. Have you seen anyone unusual hanging around?"

"Only you two," she said. "This is a really quiet neighborhood."

We thanked her for her time and headed back to the car.

"Oh, come to think of it, there was someone else hanging around." We stopped and let the neighbor get a little closer. "Earlier today. I can't believe I forgot about it. A police officer was sitting out here for a while. Told me he was just patrolling the neighborhood. Making sure nobody from the press was bothering Mrs. Farley. But I think he meant TV cameras and such. Not you two."

Daisy and I exchanged *I wouldn't be so sure about that* glances.

"Did you catch his name?" Daisy asked.

The neighbor shook her head. "No, but he was really handsome. Young guy. Dark hair, lots of muscles, really blue eyes. I think he's new around here."

"Is that so?" Daisy asked, turning slowly to me. She was grinning like the cat that ate the canary, one eyebrow raised. I could see her inner matchmaker stirring once again.

"I wonder who that could have been?" she asked. But neither of us needed to say it aloud.

# CHAPTER 16

I DROPPED DAISY OFF AT HER house, where Mike and Mudd were sitting on a blanket in the grass, having a tea party with little Willow. They all wore big, floppy wicker bonnets and held tiny plastic teacups with their pinkies out.

"We recording tomorrow?" Daisy asked, opening the car door.

"I have plans."

"Oh, that's right. Your dinner date with the adorable deputy." She fluttered her eyelashes. "The one who was waiting for you at the Farley house."

"It's not a date. It's a make-up information-sharing meeting. And he wasn't waiting so much as stalking."

"Uh-huh. Don't forget to bring along some breath mints. In case your information gets…close." She made kissing faces, so I leaned over and shut her door. "Bye."

I wished I had time to just think about dinner—it wasn't a date, was it?—but I had an assignment to take care of first. Today was the new bank's grand opening. I drove toward the new branch, thinking about Kermit the whole way.

Had the police gotten as much out of him as I had? Did he show them the video? If so, what did they make of it? And what exactly had they taken from Farley's desk? I wished with everything I had that I'd been the one to go through the things on his desk instead of mistakenly going through Kermit's and then just blindly grabbing stuff off of Farley's. Yes, Kermit had the playbook, but now that I'd heard his explanation, that didn't seem like much of a find.

Daisy was the one who had found Kermit's letter of intent, which had seemed huge at the moment, but now seemed like it could be just a coincidence after all. Either Kermit was innocent, or he was a good liar. And an excellent video editor. Maybe I could ask him how to cut things from our podcast.

I pulled into the bank parking lot and went inside.

Francine Oglethorpe was pacing in front of her office, waiting for me. She was wearing a blue power suit this time, her blonde hair yanked into a tight bun.

"Oh, good, you're here. Let's go," she said, plucking a purse out of the air and nearly hip checking me into a rack of wilted brochures in her haste to get out the door. "I'll drive myself."

"I thought we could ride tog—" But she was already halfway to her car before I could finish. "Okay."

I followed her through town. She nearly bumped Wickham Birkland's car at the corner of Tutor and Oak, leaving him shaking both fists in the air. Soon we got to the site of the new bank building. A large ribbon had been strung across the front entrance and the mayor was standing next to it, checking his watch. Several customers came in and out of the bank, and were having to duck under the ribbon, looking annoyed.

"Why haven't you cut the ribbon?" I asked as we approached the building.

"We were waiting for you," she said. "I wanted the photo to look authentic."

"What photo?" I asked, but before she could answer, a man came out of the bank, looking at his phone, and plowed right through the ribbon, knocking the mayor off balance. The mayor grabbed a sconce to keep himself from falling to the ground, and accidentally ripped it off the wall.

"Watch where you're going!" Francine snapped, and the man sulked away to his car. "Okay, okay, let's do this. Where's your camera guy?"

"I don't have a camera guy," I said. "I have a phone." I rummaged through my bag, searching for it.

"Well, then," the mayor said, before I could even pull up the camera app. He put down the sconce, grabbed a giant pair of scissors that had been lying on the ground next to him, snipped the ribbon in two, and walked away wordlessly.

Francine pulled out a confetti popper that looked left over from July 4th out of her purse and pulled the string. A small amount of confetti and a few paper ribbons flew out and landed on my shoe. I shook them off.

I pulled out my notepad and pencil, trying to look as official as possible.

Francine's face brightened as a woman got out of her car and walked toward us. "Oh, look! A customer! You can interview her. Hello, customer! Thank you for your business. Maybe you'd be interested in talking to this lovely reporter here."

The woman skirted us warily and disappeared into the bank wordlessly.

Francine's shoulders slumped. "I would say business has been surprisingly good," she said. "You even got to meet a customer. You can write that down."

"Oookay," I said and took notes. "What would you like to point out that makes this branch special?"

"It's on the other side of town from the original bank," she said.

I paused, waiting for her to say more, but she didn't. I wrote down *nothing special—it's a bank.*

"And, as bank manager, will you be moving your office here, or staying at the flagship branch?" I asked.

"I'll have an office at both," she said. "Win-win!" She flung her arms wide, and in that instant, I felt once again like I had seen her before.

"I'm sorry," I said. "But I'm just sure I know you from somewhere."

A smile struggled to stay on her face. "From the bank, silly. Did you get enough material?"

"Well, I would kind of like to go inside," I said. She was definitely trying to get rid of me. Had I trod on sensitive territory with that question?

"It's a bank," she said. Either I was crazy or her voice was shaking. "What is there to see? A counter, a few desks, a vault, the usual."

"But I could take photos," I said, holding up my phone.

She waved her hand. "We've got enough of those."

"I didn't get any."

She waved again. "We don't need to be flashy." She laughed, shrill and nervous. "See what I did there? Flashy. It was nice seeing you again. I'll be looking forward to the article."

"Okay," I said. "If you're sure."

"I am," she said. "Bye, now. You just call if you need anything else. Save your gas."

But as I walked to my car, I kept looking back at her, studying her. She hadn't convinced me. I was sure I had seen her somewhere else. Somewhere other than the bank. I just couldn't remember where.

# CHAPTER 17

I WAS NOT WHAT ANYONE WOULD describe as an undercover reporter. I could be as in-your-face as a boot camp drill sergeant when I was tracking down a good lead. Everyone—including my partner—had made it clear that being in-your-face on this case wasn't the best plan. But I was running out of ideas, and every minute that ticked by, the case got colder. And I knew that if you let a case get cold enough and it was nearly impossible to solve. Plus, I wanted to report something important on the podcast, too. Something that would make listeners stop and...well, listen.

As I suspected, the PHS football team was in the middle of practice. They were on a water break when I arrived at the school, having taken another late lunch. They had all taken a knee on the sidelines and were listening to their coach as they gulped from paper cups. All except Paulie, who stood impatiently by, hands on his hips with his helmet dangling from two fingers. He looked intense. And for the first time it really struck me that...he looked scary. And it was as much that scariness rattling around in the back of my mind that kept me pursuing him as a suspect as anything. I felt jittery and anxious. It didn't happen often, but it happened. And usually when it did, it was because I was talking to someone bad.

Paulie Henderson was a big guy. At least 6'3" and well over two hundred pounds, he could have crushed Coach Farley with his bare hands without even breaking a sweat. So why didn't he do that? Why use a car to kill him?

Because it would make it that much harder for his father to cover up the crime if he literally had his hands in it? Especially if he did it on the field in front of all of Parkwood? Maybe. I wasn't sure. Paulie—Mr. "Unanimous" himself—didn't strike me as the kind of guy to think things like that through. And Parkwood didn't strike me as the kind of town to mind that Gerald Farley suddenly was gone from their lives. Maybe the only thing keeping Paulie from tearing Farley limb from limb right there on the field was the presence of the officials pulling them off of each other.

I sat in my car and assessed the current situation. The team was on the sidelines. The cheerleaders were practicing cheers in one end zone. The dance team had taken the center of the field for their rehearsal.

I needed to get Paulie alone so I could ask him some questions. If I waited by his Jeep, I ran the risk of Brooks blocking me again. If I approached the field, I ran the risk of getting the police called on me. I had to catch him in an unnoticeable place at just the right time.

I fumbled together a stack of books and random papers from my back seat and waited until I saw someone heading into the school. It didn't take long. A car pulled up and a pouting teenage boy got out, dragging an instrument case that looked heavy and bulky enough to be housing a dead body, and headed for the school. I got out of my car and speed-walked to catch up to him.

"Hold the door!" I said when he started to go inside. I gasped as if I was out of breath and acted like I might drop all of those books at any moment. Which wasn't really acting. I had gone overboard with my props and they were heavy.

The teen stepped aside and held the door open for me.

Rule #3 of investigative journalism: Ask people to let you in, and they usually will.

"Thank you so much," I said. "You're a lifesaver."

He let me in the second set of doors and then disappeared toward the cacophonous sounds of a marching band warming up. I kept going, trying to look as if I knew exactly where I was headed. Look uncertain, and someone—most likely an administrator cranky about working late—is going to stop you.

My phone buzzed. Groaning inwardly, I ducked into a ladies room and dropped my books on the counter to answer.

"Hey, where are you?" asked Daisy. "You never came home."

"I'm at the school."

"What school? Didn't we just leave a school?"

I peered under each stall door. I was alone in the restroom. Good.

"I'm at Parkwood High School," I said. "I'm going to talk to Paulie Henderson."

"He agreed to talk to you?" Her voice was a squawk.

"Kind of."

"What does that mean, kind of?" I could hear water running and dishes rattling in the background.

"I haven't exactly tried yet."

"And how are you going to do it? Just show up and say, 'Hi, there, I'm a reporter and I'm convinced you're a murderer, so you should probably tell me everything so we can all go home for dinner?' I know I'm not a journalist, but I'm thinking that tactic is unlikely to work."

"No, that's not my plan." It was kind of my plan.

I heard the water shut off. "You're totally going to do some sort of reporter ambush on him, aren't you?"

"I wouldn't have put it into those words, but yes."

"You need backup. Wait for me."

"What? No, I don't need backup." The door squeaked open and two girls in marching band uniforms came in. I lowered my voice. "I can't wait for you. The timing has to be perfect for this."

"I live four minutes away." I heard the jangle of car keys.

"What about the kids?"

"At the pizza arcade with Mike."

Another girl came in, her polyester uniform unzipped down to her navel, a crumpled and sweaty PHS Hornets T-shirt beneath. Her face was beet red and she had rings of sweat around her temples and forehead. She went straight for the sink and plunged her head under the running water. You'd think she'd just run ninety yards for a touchdown, from the looks of her.

"I'm running out of time," I said.

"Four minutes!" Daisy cried. I heard her car door shut and the phone went dead.

I took my stack of books and hid in a stall, secretly very glad that Daisy was coming to back me up, and trying not to think about what Trace—or anyone at my old paper— would say about me needing backup in the first place. Maybe I wasn't the reporter I thought I was. Maybe I'd gone soft. Maybe hot dog roller was my speed now.

I heard whispering, and peeked through the stall crack. The girls who had come in together were murmuring and pointing toward my stall. Great. I was creeping people out—Step one in a Quick and Easy Plan to Get Yourself Arrested at a High School. *Hurry up, Daisy.*

I sat there for what seemed like forty days and forty

nights, and was most assuredly longer than four minutes, and was just about to abort the whole mission when my phone buzzed again. I picked it up.

"Where are you?" she asked before I could even say anything.

"I'm in the restroom. Meet me by the band room. Follow the noise."

"I hear it. See you there."

I left my books in the bathroom stall and took off, scaring the heck out of the marching band girls who were still whispering, only outside of the restroom now.

"Excuse me," I said as I pushed past them.

"There she is," one band girl said to another, who had not been in the restroom with us. "She does that podcast Mrs. Bunch had us listen to."

I stopped so quickly, my shoes squeaked on the floor. I turned back, my winning smile in place. "Did you say something?" I asked.

She shrank back, suddenly shy. "I recognized your voice in there. You do that podcast."

"Yes, I do. Wow, you have great auditory recall."

She nodded excitedly. "Our culinary arts teacher makes us listen to it." She turned to her friend. "She's amazing. She bakes all these cakes and stuff. We used her tip for a flaky tart crust last weekend for the bake sale and it was perfect."

My smile fell. Figured.

I ran into Daisy just outside the band room. "Found it," she said, then put her hand on my shoulder. "What's the matter with you?"

"Nothing," I grouched. "Because of your podcast baking tips, you have fans in marching band."

She beamed, her hand going to her heart. "I do? Well, how cool is that? I'm popular in high school. Finally!"

"So very, very cool," I said, and even though I meant it, I couldn't make my voice sound that way.

"Don't worry," she said, patting my back. "You have fans, too. They're just less vocal."

"Because they don't have vocal cords. Because they don't exist. Let's go."

"Where to?" she asked.

"Wherever Paulie is sure to go," I said.

"Maybe we wait in the hallway outside the gym? I mean, they have to go back into the locker room after practice, right?"

"Right."

We sought out a bench outside the gym, on the side where the men's locker room was. It felt very public, and like maybe we should have waited by his Jeep after all. Every time someone walked by, I wanted to re-route. But the parking lots were big, and wrapped around the school, and I had no idea where he was parked, which would give Brooks—who I just knew had to be out there somewhere— ample time to intercept me. And if I kept changing my mind, Paulie would be home and I would once again be without an interview.

"Try to look like a mom," Daisy whispered.

"I can't," I said.

"Why not? Just look…tired. Check your watch a lot."

"I don't wear a watch."

"Well, how do you know what time it is?"

"My cell phone, Fred Flintstone."

"You should get a watch," she said, studying hers. Mike had given it to her for their anniversary and she wore it always. It had a rose-gold colored band and little sparkly gems around the face.

"Why?"

"So you can check it!" she said.

"I'll tell you what. You be a mom. I'll be an older sister." I adopted a too-cool-for-this slouch, while fiddling with my cell phone. "A not-that-much-older sister. I could get mistaken for a student here, you know." We caught each other's eyes, then both cracked up.

She abruptly stopped giggling. "Shhh! Do I hear people talking?"

I listened. Voices. Male voices. And several of them. They were coming our way.

"The team," I said, jumping to my feet and instantly losing every ounce of cool I might have had.

A handful of boys loudly plowed through the doors, not even noticing we were there, and headed for the locker room, their heads sweaty.

And then Paulie Henderson loped inside.

"Hey, Paulie," I said, my heart pounding in my throat. Daisy had jumped up beside me. I could feel her shoulder so close to mine they were almost touching. Feeling her there, literally backing me up, bolstered me.

"Yeah?" He looked wary. And he was tall. Very tall. Had I thought 6'3" before? He was definitely closer to Paul Bunyan size. Actually, if we'd run into him at the top of a beanstalk, I wouldn't have been surprised.

"I was wondering if you have a minute." My lips were numb. Did my lips always get numb when I was nervous? I didn't remember ever having numb lips in Chicago. Maybe I didn't get nervous back then. No, that wasn't possible. Why would I not be nervous there, but be nervous here? Maybe it wasn't nerves; maybe it was excitement for having finally caught up with Paulie. Yeah, excitement. I was going to go with it.

"What for?" he asked. "Who are you?"

"I'm Hollis Bisbee," I said. "I'd like to talk to you about the hit-and-run that occurred here last weekend." He looked unsure, his face darkening, so I dove in, trying to get back into my rhythm. Don't give them time to think—only time to answer. "Do you know anything about what happened? Where were you when the coach was hit in the lower parking lot? Did you see anything?"

I could see the realization begin to dawn on him. "You're reporters?"

"Yes. The *Knock 'em Dead* podcast," Daisy said.

"I knew it! You're the muffin lady," someone said from the back. "She has amazing chocolate cherry muffins at the Hibiscus. My mom gets them every Saturday morning. She also listens to that podcast. She fast-forwards all the murder stuff to get to the baking tips."

"Thank you!" Daisy said excitedly, at the same time that I said, "Seriously? It's a *murder* podcast."

"Murder?" Paulie started to look panicked while at the same time very, very angry. "What about murder? Are you accusing me of something?"

"No, I'm the press," I said. "I'm neutral. I'm just asking questions." I tried to look a nonthreatening and peaceful as possible. I was pretty sure if Paulie Henderson thought I was trying to bust him for something, he was going to bolt. And I was one hundred percent positive that if Paulie ran, I wouldn't be able to catch him.

Instead of running, though, he whipped out a cell phone and frantically punched in a phone number.

"Dad? You should get here. That reporter lady you were

telling me about is here asking questions and is going to call me a murderer on her baking podcast or something."

"What? No! That's not at all what I'm going to do. And it's a *murder* podcast," I said, reaching for the phone, which only caused him to freak out even more.

"You gotta come." He paused. "Yeah, we'll keep her here."

He shoved his phone back into his pocket and crossed his arms, stepping toward us so that we inched backwards until our legs were touching the bench. If he was trying to make himself look less murdery, I wasn't sure this was the most effective approach.

"Guess you're gonna have to talk to my dad. He's the police chief, you know. And he doesn't take lightly to attacks."

I balked. "I wasn't attacking you."

"We'll see who he believes, I guess."

There was commotion, and I realized that a crowd had begun to form. A cheerleader popped into the center and grabbed onto Paulie's arm.

"What's going on?" she asked. She laid her head against his arm. He ignored her.

This had definitely not gone as I'd hoped it would. And I knew once the chief was there, my chance to interview Paulie was over. Probably for good. I had to make use of what little time I had. "How come your Jeep was at the body shop, Paulie?" I asked coolly.

"Oil change."

"I thought a bird hit the grill."

"That too."

Sketchy. I reached for my notepad and pencil, but remembered I left them in the restroom. Drat!

"And where were you when the coach was hit in the lower parking lot?"

His eyes were black dots. I could see a little bit of discomfort there. "I was in the locker room. Changing."

The sirens got louder. His jaw pulsed. Anger? Nerves? I couldn't tell.

The sirens got really loud, and then stopped. I heard car doors slam and boots grind into pavement furiously. The crowd bustled and parted and Chief Henderson himself was standing in front of me. He, too, was bigger than he looked from a distance. A lot bigger. And his face was a lot meaner in the daylight. And more mustachey than I remembered it being.

"We got some trespassers here?" he said, addressing Paulie but keeping his eyes locked on me.

I swallowed. "I'm Hollis Bisbee with the *Knock 'em Dead* podcast. I was just hoping to ask Paulie some questions about the hit-and-run here last w—"

"I know who you are, and I already told Mary Jean it was no hit-and-run. It was just the man's time. Lucky he died doing what he loved best."

"Walking across a parking lot?" Daisy asked. "Seems like an odd thing to love best." The chief shot her a look.

"I'm sorry, Chief," I said. "But this was not a natural death. You had a witness."

"Agnes isn't a witness, she's a hassle. She witnesses stuff all the time, and funny thing is there's never anyone else around to corroborate her story. Consider your source, Miss Big City Reporter. Time to move along." He motioned at the crowd and they shuffled again, making an opening for us to leave.

"You have a suspect," I said, the words popping out before I could think it through. "Sounds to me like you don't really believe the natural cause thing, either."

"How would you know what I have?" he asked, his

eyebrows drawing together. Which, by the way, wasn't a denial. Also, I felt a pang of guilt because if he believed that I really knew about his suspect, he would probably be able to guess where the information came from. I didn't like the idea of throwing Brooks under the bus, even accidentally. And I wasn't sure, given our...uncertain...relationship, that Brooks would believe me that it was unintentional. The crowd closed in again, rapt with attention.

"It was just a guess," I said. "And you didn't deny it."

"I don't have to confirm or deny anything with you. And nobody gave you permission to be in here asking questions in the first place. Move along."

There was more jostling of the crowd and Brooks appeared by the chief's side. He looked physically sick to see me there.

"True, you don't have to. But with all due respect, sir," I said to the chief. "Free speech allows me to ask questions."

"And trespassing allows you to get arrested."

A murmur rippled through the crowd. A couple of giggles. Paulie looked smug. His girlfriend held up a phone, recording everything. Daisy stuck out her tongue at the camera. The girl curled one lip and zoomed in.

I swallowed, gathering my courage. It wasn't often that asking questions was this uncomfortable, but if I believed in getting answers—and I did—I had to do it. "I'm sorry, but the public deserves to know the truth about what happened." I flicked a look pointedly at the cheerleader's phone, then turned to Paulie. "You made a threat on Coach Farley's life during halftime. Can you tell us what that was about?"

"It was about you going to jail, you nosy trout!" Paulie snarled.

"Did he just call you a trout?" Daisy asked. "Trouts don't even have noses, do they?"

The chief's eyes narrowed to slits. I could feel the anger radiating off of him. I might have been better off in jail, actually.

But, no. I wasn't going to jail. Not for trying to do my job. Even if, technically, my job was to write a six-hundred-word piece on a bank grand opening right now. Okay, fine, I was trying to do my hobby. No, wait, seeking truth and justice wasn't a job or a hobby—it was a calling. A calling that I, and a great many journalists before me, couldn't ignore.

"Paulie, were you alone in the locker room, or were your teammates with y—"

"Okay!" Chief Henderson said. "I warned you."

But before he could follow that thought, Brooks lunged between us.

"Wait, wait, wait," Brooks said, spreading out his arms to protect me. "If you arrest her, you could have a problem on your hands." The chief seemed to be thinking, suspicious. "This whole thing got recorded," Brooks whispered, indicating with his head Paulie's girlfriend's phone. "Hollis isn't Mary Jean. Her podcast has potential worldwide reach, and you know what the media does with stuff like that. She can spin it however she wants, and if just one news outlet picks it up, that video could end up everywhere by the end of the day. She could make it look very bad for Parkwood PD."

"Put that thing away!" the chief snapped. The girl squeaked and whisked her phone behind her back.

"Just—let me take care of it," Brooks said. "You and Paulie let it go. You don't want to give her any ammunition. Just go your separate ways and I'll get her out of here."

While I was appreciative of Brooks diffusing the situation, this was starting to feel like a damsel in distress situation—exactly what I'd told him I didn't need from him. And right when I seemed to have Paulie on the verge of talking. "Excuse me? That's very nice of you, Officer Hopkins, but do I have any say about when and how I'll leave?"

"No," Chief Henderson, Paulie, and Brooks said at the same time.

The chief thought about it for another maddening minute, burning holes through me with his stare. Then slowly, he turned toward the crowd.

"Get out of here, son," he growled. "Everybody get going, now. Go on! Shower and go home."

The crowd dispersed into the locker rooms. I could hear their voices through the door, going over the excitement of my near-arrest.

The chief turned to face me again. He pointed a finger at my nose. "If I catch you near my son again, you'll wish for jail. You understand me?"

After the chief left, all three of us let out a sigh of relief. Well, mine was part-relief, part-frustration, because I still hadn't gotten any information.

"Thanks, Brooks," I said. "I don't want to sound unappreciative, but next time could you not do that? I had him. He was so close to answering."

He gave me an irritated look. "What are you doing here? I thought I told you to leave it alone."

"I'm not going to leave it alone, Brooks," I said. "I literally can't. You have to understand. You have a calling, too, right?" I touched my finger to his badge. He softened immediately.

"Well, I can't be saving your behind every time you get it in your head that you need to go poking the chief and his son."

"I don't expect you to."

"And you owe me one."

I held out my hand to shake, this time feeling a little less weird and awkward than the last time. "I'll pay for both of our dinners tomorrow, then. Deal?"

He tried to maintain his exasperation, but a grin prevailed. "Deal," he said and shook. "I'll pick you up at seven."

"It's a date," I said.

"I told you so!" Daisy cried, hopping on her toes. "It's a date! I knew it!"

# CHAPTER 18

D
AISY SAT ON MY BED amidst what was basically every scrap of clothing I owned. Willow happily dove in and out of the pile, while her boys entertained themselves with the gaming system Trace had bought during his "techno-hip" phase—a phase that ended the minute he got bored. I didn't even realize I'd inherited the system until I was unpacking a box in my new house in Parkwood, only to find it tossed in with the bath sheets and washcloths. I'd sat on the hallway floor right in front of the open closet door, hugging the console to my chest and crying over the complete U-turn my life had taken. I was hardly a gamer, but I couldn't bring myself to part with it. Now it was a dust-collector and I never even thought about it until I needed something to entertain Daisy's kids.

"I think I've gained weight," I said, trying to button my cutest denim skirt. I finally got it, then grimaced when I let out my breath and the waistband actually rolled under a layer of flab. "I blame you."

"Me? Why me?" she asked.

"All those cakes and pies and brownies."

"Well, you don't have to eat them."

I flung the skirt away and reached for a roomier dress.

"Okay, sure. I'm just going to pass up the world's most famous baking podcaster's food."

She chuckled. "Famous. Okay, Miss Hyperbole. Someone sounds bitter."

"Well, why are they all skipping over me and listening to you?" I asked, exasperated. The dress slipped down over my form easily. I sighed with relief. Except I looked like a box. A box with flowers on it. "Poisoning is interesting."

"True," she said. "But maybe not to everyone." Willow crawled toward the edge of the bed— Daisy grabbed her and slid her back into place, whipped a toy out of nowhere, and handed it to her. "Have you noticed that once one person started listening to our podcast, suddenly everyone was listening? That's the way it works in Parkwood. We want local. I'm local. They can listen to my recipes and then ask me about them at the Hibiscus. They can buy my muffins there. It makes them feel like they're part of something greater."

"They could ask me about poisonings when they see me at the Hibiscus," I said, but even I knew that wasn't ideal.

Maybe I needed to rethink my plan. We'd mentioned the coach's death here and there, but we'd never really presented the story. Maybe if I gave the mystery more focus, play up the "local" aspect of it, listeners would want to ask questions when they saw me around town. Maybe they would stop ignoring my part of the podcast if it was talking about something more directly related to their lives.

No. Our lives. Because I was local now, too. And this story mattered to me for different reasons than the stories I covered in Chicago. It wasn't only that a murder happened, but that a murder happened on my turf. There was a feeling of connectedness in Parkwood that I'd never felt before. Not just that I had connected to the town, but that we were all connected to each other. The objectivity that used to be so easy to me wasn't easy anymore, because I had changed. Because Parkwood had changed me.

"Do you have a belt for that?" Daisy asked, her nose wrinkled.

I grunted and whipped off the dress, tossing it right over Willow's head. She giggled and pawed at it, falling over backwards into her mother's lap. "I have no idea what to wear to this…this…whatever it is."

"I think the word you're looking for is 'date,'" Daisy said. She uncovered Willow, said, "Boo!" and covered her back up to more giggles.

"It's not a date date," I said for the thousandth time since I'd accidentally called it one in front of her. "That was a figure of speech. You know, like 'Have your people call my people.'"

"Uh-huh, I'm not sure that's what he was thinking. Your handshake may have been, 'Have your people call my people,' but his handshake was definitely, 'Let's fall in love and get married and have babies.'" She uncovered Willow again and blew a raspberry on her cheek.

"His handshake said no such thing!" I said, but in the back of my mind I was afraid she may have been right. There was definitely something a little…more…in that handshake. I had been ignoring it. It was difficult to tell whether Brooks's intentions were to keep me out of trouble or if they were about something else. And it was even more difficult to tell what my intentions were. Brooks was…confusing. "We're information-sharing. I want to know what he knows about the Farley case. And I'm sure he wants the same."

"Okay, sure," Daisy said. "I would say those capris are perfect. You should go with them."

I picked up the black silk capris with the long tassel belt that I'd bought for a journalism conference two years ago. I'd worn them with a pink top and black kitten heels and had felt so very cosmopolitan and international and important. Trace had worn a tie that matched my shirt, and the pink reflected off of his olive skin beautifully. We'd shared a glass of wine that night and talked about possibly getting married someday after our careers had settled. I felt a tug in my heart for the past. The outfit was full of memories.

But the capris also had an elastic waistband, so Daisy was a genius.

An hour later, I emerged from the bedroom ready to go.

Daisy looked up from the recipe book she was flipping through. "Very nice," she said. "That's an outfit that just screams for impersonal information-sharing about perps and forensic evidence."

I picked up a pillow and threw it at her. "You're going to be fired as my personal dresser."

"Promise? But the pay was so good," she teased, catching the pillow and tossing it back. She stood and smoothed a wayward wave on the back of my head. "Seriously, Hollis, you look awesome. He is going to be eating his heart out. Speaking of, what are you ordering at Mister Woks?"

"I have no idea," I said. "I just hope there aren't giblets involved."

There weren't giblets involved. Just egg rolls and crab Rangoon and stir-fried wonderfulness.

Brooks was wearing a crisp pair of jeans and a tight polo shirt. His hair was combed neatly and he smelled like soap and aftershave and leather seats.

"I hope you like Mister Wok's," he said, handing me a menu. "I didn't think to ask. We can hop over to China Steve if you don't. I just thought it might be good to get out of Parkwood for some privacy."

"No, this is great," I said. "I've never eaten here. I didn't even know it existed until recently."

To be fair, to know this place existed meant to know that there was a Highway B that led out of Parkwood the opposite direction of River Fork and that the shack almost all the way to the city of Golden Fields—population seventy-three, all one family—was, in fact, a restaurant. It hadn't occurred to me until just now that the crumpled menu I'd seen on the school parking lot had belonged to a restaurant I'd never heard of before. I had just chalked it up to my being new-ish in town.

"You'll be wowed," he said. "Get the egg drop soup. When you taste it, you'll feel like you've been transported straight to Beijing."

"Well, I've never been to Beijing, so I'll have to take your word for it," I said, and then asked myself if that had sounded snippy or flirty. And then asked myself why I even cared. And then told myself I didn't want to know the answer to that. Brooks and I weren't doing much talking yet, but I was having a heck of a conversation with me.

We placed our orders and gave the waitress our menus and then we had nothing but sweating glasses of soda to distract us from each other. I was fairly certain my hands were sweating as much as the glasses were, and I was totally speed-sipping the soda out of nervousness.

"So the Farley case..." I said, breaking the silence.

"Tell me about Hollis Bisbee," he said at the same time.

I blinked in surprise. "What?"

He shrugged. "Tell me about yourself. I don't really

know you, other than that you're a very determined reporter."

I smirked. "You have no idea how determined I can be." I blushed. Did *that* sound flirty? It definitely sounded flirty. Daisy would be loving this. I cleared my throat. "I mean, I've kind of been holding back because my boss doesn't want me working on this story."

"Probably wise of her," he said.

"Why is that?"

"I haven't been here very long, but I know that when it comes to crime, you have to be very careful about whose toes you step on. Wrong toes, miserable life."

I wondered if he was speaking from experience. I wondered if that experience had anything to do with why he left KCPD. Maybe the rumors were true. Maybe he'd stepped on some very wrong toes.

"So…?" He leaned forward, grinning, and I could swear that right in that moment, he grew a dimple that hadn't been there before. I was a sucker for a good dimple on a man, and this dinner was not going at all like I'd planned it to. It was impossible to be impersonal with a dimple sitting right across the table. "Who is Hollis Bisbee?"

The waitress brought a kettle of hot tea and two tiny round tea crocks. She poured each of us a cup and left. I picked up mine, grateful for the distraction. "Hollis Bisbee likes tea." He cocked his head to the side and crossed his arms, saying nothing. "Okay, okay. Um, let's see. I'm a reporter, obviously."

"Obviously."

"I grew up in Chicago, went to the University of Chicago—which I loved—and until I moved here had never really been outside of Chicago. My two sisters, my mom, and one aunt still live there. My dad died my freshman year of college." I blew on my tea and took a sip.

"Oh, that's too bad. I'm sorry to hear that. He probably missed out on a lot."

I shrugged. The warmth from the tea—or from him, from that darn dimple, whatever—had relaxed me a little. "Yeah, he never got to see my name in the paper. I mean, other than the school newspaper. Never got to see me graduate, or get my first apartment, or get marr—" *Oh. My. Word. Was I really about to say the M word on my first date with this man? Did I really just think of this as a date? A first date? Like the there-will-be-more-dates kind of first date? Hollis, save what dignity you have left and stop talking, woman!* I tried to quickly shift my words. "Get moved to Parkwood. He never got to see me move." *Get moved. Very eloquent.* I sipped my tea, suddenly nervous all over again. I felt a desperate need to redirect the conversation. "Enough about me. What about you? Who is Officer Brooks Hopkins?"

He spread out his hands. "What you see is what you get."

"Uh-uh. Nope. It doesn't work that way. I told you about myself, now it's your turn."

"Says who?" His eyes were actually sparkling—and did I detect a second dimple? Seriously, did the man just will dimples into existence when he wanted to be adorable? If so, it was working.

"Says me. Start talking."

"I see. Well, I'll have you know that I'm a vault, Hollis." He tapped his temple. "So much information up here that will never come out."

I laughed and then leaned forward, just as he'd been doing a moment before, and lowered my voice so that I sounded very serious. "Officer Hopkins. You forget who you're dealing with. I am a seasoned reporter. I can get you to talk."

He chuckled. "Okay, what is it you want to know?"

"Where are you from?"

"A small town in Southern Missouri. Trust me, you haven't heard of it."

"Siblings?"

"I have a brother. He still lives there. He works for my parents' business." I raised my eyebrows and waved my hand in a *go-on* motion. He rolled his eyes playfully and sighed. "Family farm."

"You grew up on a farm?" I asked, losing my hardboiled reporter decorum. There was something about this little factoid that delighted me. Something about the mental image of Brooks in jeans and a flannel shirt, sweating under a harvest sun, his muscles rippling while he baled hay or built a fence or did whatever they did on his farm. He nodded. "You were a farmer?"

"I wouldn't say that."

"Have you ever milked a cow?"

"Yes."

"Planted a vegetable?" He nodded. "Harvested anything?" He nodded again. I crossed my arms. "Farmer."

"Okay, I guess technically I farmed, but I was a kid. Being a farmer is a lot more than just planting things and milking livestock. I left for school when I was a teenager and haven't really been back a whole lot except for family gatherings."

"Fair enough. We'll go with ex-farmer. So what made you want to be a police officer?" I asked.

He glanced into his tea, which reminded me to sip mine again. He sighed, as if this was a subject he didn't want to get into. "There was this family of five brothers. The Spurck

Brothers. They were always beating people up, stealing stuff, vandalizing, causing problems. My brother was little and they bullied him—picked on him every day on the way home from school. They were total criminals, and it seemed like they always got away with it."

"Like Paulie Henderson," I said.

He paused. "Maybe. But anyway, I don't like bullies or thieves, and I didn't like that they always got away with it, so I wanted to have a job where I could do something about people like them. And here I am."

"Here you are." We locked eyes, and for the tiniest moment I swore I could feel how much his job meant to him. It wasn't just a job—it was passion, the same way mine was passion to me. And if he really felt the way he said he did, then I knew he wanted to see justice for this case, too. "So why are you here?" I asked, breaking the connection before the weight of it got too heavy.

"What do you mean?"

"I mean, you left KCPD. Why?"

"Oh." And just like that, I could feel lock the vault he'd been talking about. Connection lost. "Differences of opinion."

And in very un-Hollis-like fashion, I let it go. Changed the subject. "So about Coach Farley's case. If Paulie isn't the one—"

I was interrupted by the arrival of appetizers. The waitress gave us each a small plate, and Brooks started loading his.

"You've got to try the chicken on a stick," he said, holding up a skewer. "It's the best I've ever tasted."

He set the skewer on my plate and picked up another.

"With that endorsement, how could I pass?" I asked.

"Their dumplings are pretty good, too," he said. "Not as

good as China Steve's, but a pretty close second. And Mister Wok's Szechuan totally makes up the difference. Buries China Steve."

"How do you know so much about these places? You haven't even been here as long as I have."

He nodded. "When you spend as much time in your car as I do, you get to know where everything is."

"Hopkins! Welcome back!" A very large, pale man with red hair and freckles was coming at us, a smudged apron wrapped around most of his waist.

"Wok! Good to see you," Brooks said. He wiped his hands on his napkin, stood, and shook the other man's hand. "This is my friend, Hollis. Hollis, this is Mister Wok."

"He's being so formal. You can call me Sean," the man said. His eyes were strikingly green. *This* was Mister Wok?

"I'm Hollis," I said, and took his hand.

Brooks settled back into the booth and Mister Wok stood by, his hands on his hips, which shifted his chef shirt up just enough to see that he had freckles on his torso, too. They talked for a moment about someone's lake house, about car troubles, and about a few people I'd never heard of.

Finally, Mister Wok clapped his hands together, making me jump. "Gotta get back to the wok. Make yourselves at home, you two. Eat! Eat! I don't want to interrupt your date."

"It's not a real date," I said, at the same time that Brooks said, "Okay, good seeing you, buddy!"

We looked at each other in surprise. Mister Wok looked at both of us with uncomfortable confusion.

"You weren't interrupting," I said lightly, to try to shovel my way out of the awkward. "We were just meeting to discuss a case."

"Case?" Mister Wok asked, apparently deciding against leaving us alone.

"We were ..." Brooks tugged at one ear uneasily. It was super red. "You should have an egg roll," he said. "Wok, you've outdone yourself tonight."

But now I was feeling the heat that I could see from his ears that he was feeling, too. This was a real date to him, and I was kicking myself for questioning that. Why couldn't I just go along with it? Why did I have to be all business, all the time?

"Wait, is she a cop, too?" Mister Wok asked. "Did something happen that I should know about?"

"No," Brooks said miserably, which actually made me feel a little bad. I worked to shuck off the guilty feeling. I had a job to do, and maybe I was all business, all the time, but Brooks knew that going in.

"Yes," I said. "Actually, everyone should know about the Coach Farley hit-and-run case." I gave Brooks a pointed look. "Since there's a potential murderer in Parkwood and nobody seems to care."

Mister Wok's eyebrows shot up. "Murderer?"

"No, there is no murderer," Brooks said, giving me the same look. "It could have just been an accident and someone's scared to come forward." He touched his chest defensively. "And I care. I'm not keeping anyone from knowing anything."

"Murder or accident, it still wasn't 'natural causes.'" I made air quotes with my fingers.

"Wait. Gerry Farley is dead?" Mister Wok asked.

"You knew Coach Farley?" My fingers twitched as I willed them to not reach for my notebook and pencil.

He nodded, scooted Brooks over, and sat with us. "I've met him. His wife is a regular here. Take-out only, which she always picks up herself. I think it's just an excuse to show off her shiny Jaguar. Anyway, her order's always the same: Sweet and sour chicken for one, hold the pineapple and green pepper. He won't eat Chinese food. No idea what he eats while she's eating her sweet and sour. I mean, who doesn't eat sweet and sour? Even little kids like it. It's like chicken nuggets with barbecue sauce." He leaned across the table. I leaned in, too. Brooks sat back and sighed, tossing his napkin onto his plate of half-eaten egg roll. "

I don't really know much about him, other than he won't eat Chinese food and people say he cheats to win—cheated, I guess. I don't know if that's true or not, but I could see it."

It certainly had become a theme of the case.

"There's no hard evidence of that," Brooks said.

I looked down at my plate. No, there wasn't. Because Daisy and I had it.

"There is," I said quietly. "We found the playbook."

Brooks's eyes grew wide. "You what?"

"Daisy and I found a few things in his office, including the playbook." Brooks and I had locked eyes again, only this time all I could feel was regret.

"What playbook?" Mister Wok asked.

"Never mind," we both said at the same time. I tried to look away, but Brooks's stare lingered on me a moment longer.

Mister Wok shook his head and *tsk*'ed. "You really think it was murder?"

"Yes," I said.

"It's an ongoing investigation," Brooks said. "There are new developments all the time." This last part he said to me.

We stared each other down for far longer than was comfortable for anyone sitting at the table. Finally, Mister Wok gazed out the window and said, "Well, look at that. Speak of the devil and she arrives." He scootched out of the booth.

I turned just in time to see Wilma Louise walking through the front door, a designer purse looped over one arm. Her blonde hair was perfect—not a single strand out of place—and her dress looked like it had fallen right off the pages of a trendy catalog and onto her body. My silk capris suddenly felt like ugly old sweat pants in comparison. She had lifted one foot and was fiddling with the buckle on the side of one very high heel. I wondered if it would be poor form to excuse myself from the table to go ask her some questions. I had already made things uncomfortable enough with my admission about the playbook. I decided to leave her alone, and made a silent vow to catch up with her another time.

"Mrs. Farley," Mister Wok cried, heading toward her, arms open. "I just heard. I'm so sorry."

She stopped messing with her shoe, looked up in surprise, then burst into loud tears and unintelligible words. Everyone in the restaurant—all eight of us—stopped talking and stared. Some clucked their tongues in pity.

"Yes, yes, it was so sudden," Mister Wok said as he crammed take-out boxes into a paper sack. She garbled another sentence at him and he nodded. "Oh, I know. He was a great guy." She choked out another statement and he stopped, a fistful of fortune cookies poised over the open bag. "Heart attack?" His eyes flicked to Brooks and me and then back to her.

"You haven't even told the widow the truth?" I whispered.

Brooks shrugged. "That's Chief Henderson's duty. I thought he had."

"Apparently, you thought wrong. Just look at the poor thing. You should tell her."

"Hollis. I like having a job. I'm not going over my boss's head on this one."

"Then maybe I'll tell her myself, since you won't."

He reached over and took my arm before I could slide out of the booth. "Don't."

"She deserves to know what really happened. Just like the whole rest of the town. Only no. She deserves it *more* than the rest of the town. It was her husband. What if whoever killed him decides he wants her dead, too?"

"Just…let the police handle it, okay?"

"Ah." My stomach dropped with understanding. "The chief doesn't want her to know it was murder because she might guess that his son was the murderer."

"No."

"That's…obstruction of justice. Or evidence tampering. Or…or I don't know! I know it breaks a law, and that's all that really matters, right?"

"No, it's just…We're really narrowing in on a suspect."

I paused, surprised. "You are?"

"It's not just an idea anymore—we're starting to turn up evidence."

Mister Wok had finished loading the paper sack and consoling the watery Wilma Louise Farley. He stapled a take-out menu and receipt to the bag, and handed it over. "How about I carry this to the car for you?"

She sniffed very loudly and followed him, her back hunched and twitching with hiccups.

"It wasn't Kermit, if that's what you're thinking. He's got video proving that he was in a whole other part of the stadium when it went down. Plus, his story seems legit to me."

"You're believing someone because they seem legit to you? Not very scientific, Hollis."

Mister Wok and Wilma Louise had gone outside, but

194

that didn't stop her tears from being audible. I watched them make their way to Farley's—and now her—enormous and highly expensive white truck. I could only imagine the bells and whistles inside that thing.

"We don't think it's Kermit, anyway," Brooks said.

"I already told you it wasn't Wickham."

He waved away Wickham's name. "No, it wasn't. We never even considered him."

"Well, then who, if not Paulie?"

He looked tortured, and I almost felt bad enough to drop it and go back to our getting-to-know-you conversation. Almost. "Fine. This is completely off the record." I nodded eagerly. He licked his lips and glanced around. "Evangeline Crane."

"Evangeline?" I barked, and then when he shushed me, lowered my voice. "Why on earth would Evangeline want to kill him?"

"We're still trying to figure that out. We know that she used to work in the River Fork cafeteria, and from what we're able to glean, they did nothing but fight with each other even then. Rumor has it he cut her son from the team, and that's why she and her son moved to Parkwood."

Wow, had I ever been fooled. Even though they'd found a hairnet in the parking lot that was almost certainly hers, I never in a million years would have suspected Evangeline.

Although...she did really seem to dislike Coach Farley. And she was pretty adamant about me leaving the case alone. And she was working on the day I'd dropped my notepad in the parking lot only to later find it missing. Had she been watching? Had she seen me drop it?

"You said you thought he just fell on the hair net."

"That was before we knew the other information. He

could have fallen on it. Or it could have blown out of the car when she hit him. Or who knows?"

I narrowed my eyes. "You really think someone would commit murder over a kid being cut from a high school football team?"

He placed his napkin in his lap, smoothed it, and went back to his egg roll. "You think someone would murder over stolen plays?"

Point taken. "But at least Paulie said it out loud. He made threats, got in Farley's face. She moved to get away from the guy."

"Or she moved to give herself an alibi. We've got forensic evidence," he said. "More than just the hair net. She was on the scene. There's no doubt about it."

I thought about the witness statement. Agnes Tellerman had said nothing about anyone being on the scene. In fact, what she'd said had seemed the exact opposite—they hit and before she could even look, they were gone. She was adamant about that.

"What kind of evidence?"

He finished off his egg roll, chewed and swallowed, thinking. Outside, Mister Wok patted Louise's back sympathetically. "I can't share that with you just yet."

"Wait," I said. "She *was* on the scene. Afterwards. She was standing next to me watching the chief collect the evidence." But she hadn't been wearing a hair net. "Isn't that a problem for your case? She couldn't be standing next to me if she was driving the car, right?"

"Maybe. Or she could have just parked in the upper lot and hurried down to the scene in order to make herself look innocent. We're still working it. I'm just telling you that's where the case is going. There is literally no evidence against Paulie Henderson."

"Not true," I said. "We have a verbal threat, a threatening email, and a stolen playbook that we got out of Farley's office. And you were there when Paulie's Jeep was in the shop for 'hitting a bird.'" I made air quotes with my fingers. "But did either of us really get to see how much damage that bird caused? Was it really bird-sized damage, or was it more coach-sized?" I hadn't gotten a close look. And I had no idea how much or what kind of damage hitting a human would do to your car. I made a mental note to do some research.

"About that playbook," he said. "How did you get it?"

"That's a minor detail." He bored into me with those eyes. "I kind of stole it. But when you steal from a thief, the two thefts cancel each other out."

His mouth opened and closed, as if he didn't know what part of what I'd just said he wanted to tackle first. He shook his head lost-cause-style. "And what does the email say?"

"The same things Paulie said at the game. Basically, 'You're dead to me.' Only without the 'to me' part."

This seemed to give Brooks pause. I could see him mulling over how incriminating this was. But then he seemed to make a decision.

He went back to eating, silent and contemplative. I missed the dimples.

"So what is University of Chicago like?" he finally said. "I'll bet it's huge."

I picked up my fork. Clearly our information exchange was over and this was back to being an actual date.

I could have done worse.

He had given me something about the case. A big something. Maybe I should give him his date.

Plus, I liked him.

It was within the realm of possibility that I could enjoy this, too. I gave him a thin grin. "It's the best school," I said. "Really beautiful. You should visit it sometime."

# CHAPTER 19

B Y THE TIME BROOKS DROPPED me off at home, we were full to our eyeballs with rice and soy sauce, and were sleepy from sitting on the Cicada River Bridge watching the water slowly shift and roll. Brooks was easy to talk to. He was funny. He was smart. We had things in common. All in all, it was a nice date.

It was nice if you didn't consider all the things we couldn't talk about, that is. Paulie. Evangeline. The witness. The case in general. I was left with a whole lot of questions and zero answers and I wasn't sure how exactly I felt about that.

"So I guess I'll be seeing you around," Brooks said as we sat in his car at the curb in front of my house.

"Was this a date for you, really?" I asked. "Or was it an assignment? Or a little bit of both?"

His eyebrows knitted together. "It was a date. I told you."

"He didn't assign you at all?"

He shrugged. "I mean, I'm supposed to keep an eye on you. But this wasn't about that."

I put my hand on his shoulder. "But, for me, there will always be that doubt, you know? Does he want to be with me or was he ordered to be with me?"

"Trust me, he wants to be with you." He plucked my hand off his shoulder and briefly clasped his own around it. My pulse fluttered. "Henderson doesn't even know I'm here. And he would kill me if he knew what I've told you about the case. I'm meeting you halfway, Hollis. More than halfway, really."

"I know," I said. I managed a weak smile, because I was pretty sure that I did know—but knowing was scary. "Maybe we'll go out again after the case is over."

"Sure," he said. "Yeah. Of course."

We nodded at each other like a couple of acquaintances, and then I got out of the car.

"Goodnight, Hollis," he said through the rolled-down passenger window.

I turned. I could still see the blue in his eyes, even peering out of the dark shadows of his car. "Goodnight."

I stood in my driveway and watched Brooks pull away. I waved goodbye, then lingered for a moment, appreciating the crisp smell of nighttime while I thought about what potential we had as a couple, if that was what he was going for. We had chemistry, true, but I wasn't sure if I could really trust him. When this case was over, would we truly be free to spend time together on our own terms, or would he just be assigned to me again when I annoyed the chief on some other case? I was guessing the latter.

I slowly started up my porch steps, still thinking, and stood at the door trying to locate my keys in my bag, when I sensed movement to my left. I barely had time to process the sensation when something brushed my leg. I let out an ear-piercing scream and cocked my arms to swing my purse at whatever—or whoever—was lurking in the shadows of my porch.

"Whoa, whoa, whoa! Hollis! Don't swing! It's just Tink!"

It took my brain at least a full minute to make sense of what I was seeing. Standing in front of me, staring expectantly, was Tink. In the shadows of my porch, sitting on the rocking chair, holding out both of his hands in stop pose, was—

"Trace?" I blinked. Then blinked again. "Trace?"

He laughed. "Yeah. It's me." In seconds, he had gotten up from the chair and crossed the porch, arms out to envelop me. I stood rooted to the floorboards, disbelieving, as he wrapped me in a hug. Tink licked my knee, then went back to panting.

"Trace?" I asked again, because that was the only word my mind could seem to form. I dropped my purse on the porch, my arms trapped at my sides by his hug, then shrugged him away. "You scared the daylights out of me."

He laughed again. "I'm sorry. You are a sight for sore eyes, Hollis." Tink decided this was way too much action for him, and heavily plopped onto the creaky porch floor, instantly sighing himself to snuffly sleep, his wet muzzle on my foot.

"What are you doing here?"

He gazed at me. "Gosh, it feels like it's been forever." My cheek had smudged his glasses; he took them off and cleaned them with his shirttail, then pressed them back in place—a habit so familiar to me, I reflexively found it endearing. "You look different. Your hair is longer."

My hand traveled to my hair. "Well, it's been a year. You didn't answer me. Why are you here?"

"You didn't know? Your mom told me she would warn you that I was coming."

"She didn't."

"No wonder you seem so surprised. Well, I'm here now." He flung his arms out wide and gave me a smitten smile.

"Yes, you are," I said. "But you still haven't told me why."

"Long story short, I couldn't make it another day without seeing you."

I blinked, wondering if I'd heard that correctly. "You've gone a year without seeing me."

He shrugged. "But I've thought about you. Every single day. Isn't that right, Tink?" Tink let one eye flutter open just the slightest, then closed it again, readjusting his chin to a comfier place on the floor next to my foot. "Ah, well. He knows."

"Surely you weren't thinking about me every single day that you were dating Sophia Cranberg," I said, the comment out before I'd even had a chance to register that the anger and disappointment I'd held in for the past year was bubbling to the top.

He seemed taken aback. "You knew about that?"

"My mom knows everything. And what she doesn't know, Ruta does. And what they know, I hear about. Except you coming here, which was a somewhat major detail they kept to themselves."

He tilted his head back and gave a merry laugh. "Oh, good old Vida and Ruta. I just love it when I run into them. What a hoot those two are." He took a breath. "I dated Sophia, yes."

I held up my hand ticked off the girls my mother had told me about. "Let's see. You also dated a Pilates teacher who has a Masters in nutritional science. There was the French professor. The pilot. The model who was also a Rhodes Scholar."

"Wow, your mom really did keep you up to date."

"It's a gift. The point is, you haven't been missing me for a year. You've been dating a lot of very impressive girls." Bearings back, I bent to pick up my purse and resumed digging for my keys. "And speaking of dates, I'm just getting back from one, and I'm tired. It was nice seeing you, but you should probably call first in the future."

A fleeting look of alarm crossed his face as he glanced the direction Brooks' car had gone. But he quickly recovered, re-pasted his smile, and bent at the waist, trying to maintain eye contact. "But that is the point. I've been dating a lot of very much top-notch girlfriend candidates."

"I'm so glad to hear it," I said. I wasn't, by the way, glad to hear it. I wasn't even sure *why* I was hearing it. If I could write a list of things I didn't want to hear, the lineup of way-more-amazing-than-me girlfriends that Trace had been with over the past year while I was married to my job and spending my evenings with my cat would be in the top three, at the very least. Also, I was hardly the worst dating candidate in the world. I was cute. I was smart. I was professional. I'd done Pilates once.

At the same time, I couldn't help noticing that the guy I'd been pining over for a year was standing right here on my front porch...and I wasn't feeling much of anything more than irritation that he was here. Had I gotten completely over him? Something I thought would never happen, and here it was happening right now on my front porch?

"But none of them were you," he continued. "Every time I was with one of those girls, all I could do was compare them to you. And then I would start missing you all over again."

"But you're the one who wouldn't move to—"

He held out a hand to stop me. "Now, I'm sure you've dated plenty of scholars and whatnot, too."

Mostly the whatnot—heavy emphasis on *not*—but I wasn't going to tell Mr. Rhodes Scholar Pilot Pilates Professor that. In fact, I loved it just the teeniest bit that he'd busted in on me coming home from a date.

"But I ask you. Did you feel the connection with them that you felt with me?"

"That, I can honestly answer no."

"Exactly," he said.

"Trace, I—"

"I should have come with you," he said, interrupting me. He straightened, clasped his hands behind his back, and began pacing, giving his speech to the floor, just as I'd seen him do a million times. "I was hurt, Hollis. Hurt that you chose your career over me. But eventually I realized that you just didn't have as many opportunities available to you as I did, career-wise."

"I had opportunities," I said. "This was my opportunity. And it was a great opportunity."

"I know," he said. "The industry is shrinking and you had to leave. I get it now. And I have so many regrets about how I handled that. And the point is—no matter how many women I've dated or how secure my career is in Chicago, I can't get past it. Our breakup." He swept back to me, full of eagerness. "I want you back. I want to try again. I think we can make it."

I backed up. I had literally dreamed of this moment so many times. In my dreams, it all felt right and stomach-swoopy and there was orchestral music in the background. In my dreams, I said yes, yes, always yes. But that was not at all how I was feeling now. "I…I don't know what to say."

"You don't have to say anything." He reached for my

hand, but I dodged his advance. He acted like he didn't notice. "We'll just pick up where we left off. You can come home. Leave this..." He glanced around my porch, my house, my street. "Speck on the map."

"I like my speck," I said indignantly. For some reason, my hand drifted right to a little flower pot I'd bought at the dollar store, my thumb stroking the petunias I'd planted in it. I'd watered those flowers every day over the summer. And I'd bought that rocking chair from the thrift store and painted it myself, and, darn it, I liked that, too.

"Of course you do." He gave me the kind of smile you give a child who adorably mispronounces a word. "As you should. It's your home. You're amazing for making the best out of a bad situa—"

"Stop," I said.

He gazed at me, perplexed. "Stop what?"

"Stop doing that," I said. "Stop patronizing me. And stop acting like you were pining over me this whole time. Stop pretending that you want to somehow work this out, when we both know that working it out means me coming back to Chicago. You're not ready to change your life for me—you just want me to change mine for you. What's changed? I know what's changed. You suddenly want me back because all those other women dumped you."

He blinked in shock; I blinked in shock. I'd been so heartbroken by Trace, I hadn't realized how angry I'd been. It felt good to get it off my chest at last.

He quickly recovered, pasting the benign grin on his face again. Which told me I was right. Trace loved to argue. He wouldn't just choose a hill to die on—he would choose a hill to stuff ten tons of dynamite into and blow with him standing on top bellowing how right he was. If he didn't argue, it was because he knew he didn't have a leg to stand on. He considered what I'd said for a long moment, then nodded contemplatively. "Those relationships did not work out, you're correct. And that is exactly why I'm here. We worked, Hollis. You can't deny it."

No, I couldn't deny it. We *had* worked. And I would be lying if I said the idea of going back to our old life wasn't a little bit enticing. Dinners at Everest followed by front row seats at the Symphony Center. Tomato sandwiches and kale chips on Promontory Point, reading side-by-side—me a novel and Trace an historical biography—and listening to the sounds of the lake. It was a life. It was my life.

It was a great life.

A life I missed every single day.

Or at least I thought I was still missing it every day.

Wasn't I?

"Trace," I said, scooting away from him to give myself thinking space. "I have a job here. Remember, I left for a reason. There's nothing there for me. You said it yourself. The industry is shrinking. I can't come back to that. There would be no point. I would just have to find another job somewhere else and we'd be right back to square one."

"Oh! That reminds me." He was all excited smiles. "I talked to Tiana Gregory about you."

The name sounded familiar. "Editor of the political commentary page?"

"The one and only," he said. "She agreed to give you an interview."

"What?"

He beamed. "You're back in. As you know, I have a few strings in political. I pulled one and got you a second chance. She'll love you. The job is essentially yours."

"What?" I asked again, barely able to absorb what I was hearing. I could leave Mary Jean's ridiculously boring stories and get back to the way news was meant to be. I could honor what I was taught. I could be legitimate again.

Except…I had kind of come to see myself as legitimate here. Just a different kind of legitimate.

"So you can come home and go back to what you love doing." He snapped his fingers three times. Tink lumbered to life and wobbled over to me. He nuzzled against my leg. I reached down and stroked his head absently, still numb. "It's all going to work out," Trace said.

"I don't know if it would, Trace."

A look of concern flitted across his face, a look of rarely-seen Trace vulnerability peeking through. "Haven't you missed me?"

I squirmed, not wanting to hurt him. "Well, of course I've missed you, but—I mean, I wasn't expecting this. I have a life here. I have a job and a house and a podcast corner. I have a cat." Tink flicked an ear against my palm.

Trace jumped into motion. "I've overwhelmed you and you need time. Of course. Take all the time you need. Think it over. I'm confident that you'll come to the same conclusion I did. We're meant to be together. Come on, Tink." Tink followed Trace him down the porch steps, toward the rental car he'd parked on the street across from my house. "I'll be back in a couple days," Trace yelled over his shoulder as he got into the car. "We can talk about it again then."

"Wait, what?" I said aloud when I'd finally snapped out of my dismay. But by then he'd already gone.

# CHAPTER 20

I WAS UP BEFORE SIX THE next morning, waiting for it to be late enough to call Mom and Aunt Ruta. I called at exactly seven o'clock. They answered on the first ring, singing "Hello" in harmony.

"I think you know why I'm calling," I said icily.

Mom gasped. "You're engaged? She's engaged, Rut!"

"It's about time," Ruta yelled from the background.

"Once again, you're on speaker, you don't need to yell. I can hear you just fine. Unfortunately," I added under my breath. "And, no, I am not engaged. How could you, Mother?"

"How could I what?"

"Oh, I don't know. Encourage Trace to visit me without ever telling me anything."

"Well, he's a grown man," she said. "There wasn't exactly anything we could do to stop him. He's very motivated."

"You could have warned me," I said. "You told him you warned me."

"We tried," Ruta said.

"When? I am pretty sure I would remember if you told me Trace was going to be sitting on my front porch last night."

"When we called you and you so rudely hung up on us,"

Aunt Ruta yelled. "We were calling to warn you. You never called back."

Oh. Yeah. That.

"I didn't know that you wanted to tell me something important," I said. "You could have called again."

"Nah," said Aunt Ruta. "We decided you'd like the surprise instead. Were you surprised?"

"Uh, yeah. Very."

"We thought you would be excited to see him," Mom said.

"Excited? To see my ex-boyfriend who I've spent a year trying to get over? No. Whose side are you on, here?"

"I wasn't aware there were sides," she said.

"Two sides," Ruta yelled. "The rational side and her side. Glad to see you finally came around."

"I did not come around," I said.

"That's not what we heard," Ruta said.

"We heard there was lots of apologizing, and he's going back in a couple days after you've had a chance to think about it. And we heard there's a job interview. It will be so good to have you in the city where you belong, Hollis."

"Finally a decent driver to take me to my eye exams," Ruta yelled.

"I'm a decent driver, you old picky-pick," Mom said, and then the two of them launched into one of their trademarked arguments. I knew this one by heart and could have mouthed along if I hadn't been so angry.

"You talked to him?" I asked. "After he was here?"

"Well, we had to know how it went," Mom said.

"Why didn't you call me to ask that question? My answer would be that it went terribly. Because I was totally blindsided and I didn't know what to say to him and I didn't have time to think about anything." And because even after thinking about it all night long, I still wasn't sure what to say or do.

I had ached for my old life since the moment I'd left it. And now I could get it back.

And I was pretty sure I no longer wanted it.

"Welcome to the *Knock 'em Dead* podcast."

"Where murder and muffins meet."

"I'm Hollis."

"And I'm Daisy, the cookie lady!" Daisy had brought a beautiful tray of iced lemon sugar cookies decorated to look like slices of lemon. I'd already scarfed down two; they were amazing. "Now, most people add water to their royal icing to thin it. But I add fresh lemon juice to make it extra lemony. Tart and tasty."

"And very dangerous," I said. "Sort of like a hit-and-run on the tastebuds."

She covered her mic with her hand. "Nice tie-in. But I was thinking something more along the lines of, *So delicious, they could be poisonous.*"

"Most poisons are bitter and unpleasant to the taste," I reminded her.

"Antifreeze tastes good," she countered. "That's what makes it so dangerous."

"True," I said.

"Do you remember the band?" she asked. She grabbed a cookie, shook off the crumbs, and took a bite.

"Band?"

"Poison," she said. "'Every Rose Has It's Thorn'? 'Unskinny Bop'?"

"No," I said. "I don't remember the b—you know what?

Let's start over." I stopped recording, took a deep breath and started again. I was feeling off-kilter and grouchy. A dangerous combination.

"Why? I thought we were being charming."

"Welcome to the *Knock 'em Dead* podcast."

"Where murder and muffins and unskinny bops meet!"

I flicked a look at her, but decided to keep going. Let the listeners try to figure that one out.

"Today I have cookies," she said, and went into her spiel about royal icing again, allowing me just enough time to scarf down a third cookie while stressing about how I was going to segue into what I was planning to say to start the episode. I pushed the tray closer to her to get it away from me.

"So last time we talked about the mysterious poisonings of Jane Stanford," she said. "What poison scandal do you have for us today, Hollis?"

Perfect transition. This was why we were partners. We could set each other up without even trying.

"No poisoning just yet, but I definitely have a scandal. A local scandal. We've talked about it a few times, but I think something really sketchy is going on here. A cover-up of the Coach Farley hit-and-run, which I'm starting to suspect was purposeful. Regardless of what has been reported, the coach's death was not due to natural causes."

She gave a curious look, put her hand over the mic and whispered, "What are you doing?"

"You said people like local. I'm giving them local."

"They like local *cooking* stories. They aren't going to like this. And you're going to get yourself fired."

"They can't fire me for telling the truth. The community needs to know. Something sketchy is going on, and it started right in the parking lot of their beloved football stadium."

"That's why not," she said. "The people of the community don't want to think about there being a murderer among them. And they don't want to think their police department is crooked. It's too close to home. It scares people. They just want to watch winning football games, go to the Hibiscus for victory pie, and go home."

A look of concern fell over her face. "Is something wrong? You're not being yourself. Have a cookie. Please." She uncovered the microphone. "I have a poisoning story to talk about. It's about this woman named—"

"So, here's what we know. Coach Gerald Farley from River Fork High School was hit by a car in the parking lot of the Parkwood High School's football stadium after a contentious homecoming game," I said in my best anchor-woman voice, once again noting how it was the world's loss that I didn't have a face for TV. "It was reported as a natural death, but that did not appear to be the case forensically. A witness said she heard a car come out of nowhere, heard a *thump-thump* sound, heard the car speed off, and Coach Farley was dead. From where I sit, this doesn't look at all like a natural death. This looks like a hit-and-run, and we have just a few clues about the car that ran him down. I, personally, would love to hear more from the witness about what she saw, but the police aren't even bothering to interview her. I think there's a cover-up going on, and here's why—"

"So this woman had taken out a life insurance policy on her husband," Daisy interrupted. "And did you know, Hollis, that when someone dies of strychnine poisoning—"

"Daisy, stop." She did. "I want to start with this story."

She shook her head. "I just think you don't understand what you're doing."

"I do," I said. "I've been reporting news for a while. I understand what can happen when you report the truth. But I'm a reporter and the truth is important to me."

"It's important to me, too." She looked confused. And kind of hurt.

"Reporting that Coach Farley just dropped dead of natural causes when I know it was a hit-and-run goes against everything I've ever believed in. The people need to know, and I need to tell them. We need tips and someone must know something. Just because Parkwood is a speck on the map doesn't mean it isn't important to solve the crimes here."

"Did you just call us a speck?" she asked, pulling back, away from the microphone, uncharacteristically serious.

"I didn't. Trace did. But that's not the point."

"No, you just did. I heard you."

I let out an impatient sigh. "I was quoting Trace. And, by the way, I told him it may be a speck, but I like it here."

She pointed at me. "See? You did it again just now."

"But I said I liked it. Being a speck doesn't have to be a bad thing." Her eyes narrowed just slightly, and suddenly it felt like no matter what I said, it was going to be the wrong thing. "What? It's not like I said Parkwood is full of bumpkins or something."

She gasped. "We're bumpkins now?"

"No, I said you're not bumpkins." I put my hand on her shoulder. "Dais. Don't take it so personally. A lot of towns are specks compared to Chicago." I felt the words come out as if they were in slow motion, knowing as soon as I said them that they definitely did not come out the way I meant them to.

213

"Well, it didn't take you long to drop the old big city background on the podcast, now did it?" She shrugged away from me. "You know, I never joined in on beating up the new hoity-toity reporter, but now I'm starting to wonder if maybe everyone had a point."

"Everyone? What do you mean everyone? Hoity-toity? I am no kind of toity."

"Maybe this is just your podcast now," she said, taking off her headset and pushing away from the desk. "Since you know what to do, and all I know is baking."

"Daisy, no, I never said that. You know so much more than baking."

She worked the plastic wrap back over the plate of cookies and swept it up. "You finish with your truth. I've got to get back to my speck house and my speck life next door where my speck kids are waiting for me to remind them that they matter, even though they're just specks."

"You're putting a lot of words into my mouth," I said. "And I was only quoting Trace."

She smiled thinly. "Another reporter from the center of the universe—that big, important city of Chicago. An actual dot instead of just a speck. Whoop-dee-doo."

"No, I mean, yes, he is from Chicago, but what I'm saying is—"

"We sure do appreciate you demeaning yourself by living in our town," she said, then turned on her heel and stormed out.

I sat at the table, dumbfounded. I didn't understand how I was doing everything so wrong.

Before I could stop them, tears flooded down my cheeks. In some ways, I was crying an entire year of tears. I felt so misunderstood. By everyone. And so out of place.

All I wanted to do was solve a crime. Was that so much to ask?

King Archie abandoned the cookie crumbs he was nibbling and rubbed against my shoulder, making me cry even harder. You knew you were pathetic when King forgot about food for you.

But just five swipes in, he happily knocked over my glass, sending a cascade of water onto the floor. I laughed through my tears. I was pretty sure King was telling me to suck it up and get the job done—monarchs didn't have to be liked in order to be respected. Or something like that.

Which was good. Because right now, I was definitely not feeling very liked.

I got up, grabbed a paper towel and blew my nose, then sat back down, erased everything that had been said previously, put on my headset, and clicked RECORD.

"Welcome to the *Knock 'em Dead* podcast, where murder and muffins meet. I'm Hollis, and Daisy is on a break today. So this will be a minicast with just yours truly, and I have a very interesting local story to tell you. But first let me tell you about the amazing lemon royal icing she's making, and her trick to getting it extra lemony."

# CHAPTER 21

"I WAS GLUED TO MY COMPUTER," Joyce said when I arrived at work Monday morning. "It was so awesome. You didn't say his name, but I definitely knew you were thinking about Paulie Henderson. Let me tell you about what he did to my son in the third grade."

She continued—something about glue sticks and a stepped-on foot and a missing lunchbox—and I mostly stood there and appreciated that this was the first time I'd ever seen or heard Joyce be this animated. She was excited, and it was my podcast that had done that.

"I mean, what kind of monster does that to a third grader?"

"Another third grader?" I ventured.

She pointed at me, her freshly-manicured fingernail glistening in the morning sun that was shining warmly through the front plate glass windows. "A third grader without a conscience," she corrected.

"I don't know if stolen glue really translates to murder later in life," I said.

"It's about whole-life morality," she said sagely. "I've never liked that boy, I'm telling you. He's bad news, and his father is as crooked as the day is long. But don't you dare tell Mary Jean I said that."

Well, I could give Joyce one thing—she was the one person in all of Parkwood who was willing to say that she didn't think Paulie Henderson was an angel on earth. She was also the first person to be excited about my work on the podcast.

So why did I feel so hollow?

I knew why, and it immediately ushered in a pang of guilt over what happened with Daisy. It wasn't my podcast or her podcast. It was our podcast, and that was what made it work.

*You're not a bumpkin*, I'd texted Daisy the night before.

Two hours later, she'd texted, *I know*. I'd quickly replied, *I never thought you were*, and she'd responded, *Thanks*. So the good news was she probably didn't hate me forever. The bad news was, I wasn't exactly sure where we stood with responses like those.

"Is that Hollis?" a voice called from across the office. Mary Jean.

"I may want to interview you later," I said to Joyce.

She wiggled in her chair. "Really? I've never been interviewed for anything before. I'll be famous." Then she seemed to remember something and her eyebrows dropped seriously. "Mary Jean's been waiting for you all morning," she said in a low voice. "I don't think she's very happy."

"I'm sure she's not," I said on a sigh.

"And just as sick as ever. She's sort of like a caged bear back there." She leaned across the desk and whispered. "She even told Ernie to wake up and get to work this morning. No doughnuts."

Yikes. That was serious.

"Thanks for the heads up," I said.

"Sure. And you just let me know when you want my story."

"Will do," I said, heading toward Mary Jean's voice, which was calling out again.

She sat at her desk, surrounded by chosen, used, and forgotten readers and red pens, as usual. She glanced at me over the top of her glasses, reminding me of the stern librarian in the university library who would shush you if you turned pages too noisily.

"Good morning," I said cheerfully.

"Not good for everyone, wouldn't you say?"

"What do you mean?"

"The chief has already been by," she said. "He heard your little show."

I forced a smile. "Chief Henderson is a listener?" That didn't seem likely. But when I thought about it, it made perfect sense. He could know exactly what I was up to if he tuned in.

And did that mean Brooks listened, too?

She did not return the smile. In fact, it seemed like the wider I smiled, the deeper she frowned. "The chief is an angry member of the community who is ready to sue us for libel," she said.

"That's ridiculous. Libel has to be written down, and I wrote nothing. I spoke it, which makes it slander, but even then it had nothing to do with the newspaper. I would fight that lawsuit if I were you, Mary Jean. Fight it all the way to the Supreme Court. Besides, I didn't use anyone's names, except for Coach Farley."

She laid down her pen and took off her glasses, which she contemplatively chewed. "Hollis, do you want to work here?"

I tried not to think about Tiana Gregory and the job that potentially waited for me back in Chicago. A job offer that would come with a lifetime price tag that I wasn't sure I was willing to pay.

"Yes, of course I do."

"Then you have to abide by the rules."

"With all due respect, Mary Jean." I licked my lips nervously. "I am abiding by the rules. My podcast has nothing to do with my job here."

"In Parkwood, everything you do has to do with your job here. Everyone knows you're one of our reporters. They think I've sanctioned this hooey about that coach being murdered."

"It's not hooey," I said. "And you said nothing about moonlighting when you hired me."

"It is hooey, but I'm not going to convince you of that, am I?" She slid a pair of readers onto her face. "And I may not have said it then but I'm saying it now. If you insist on moonlighting in this way, I would just suggest to you that you tread very carefully."

"Wait. Is that some sort of threat? Are you saying I could lose my job?"

She pursed her lips and thumbed through some papers on her desk. "Did you get the bank story finished?"

Case closed. I wasn't sure what resolution we had come to, but I was pretty sure I was on the losing side of it.

But, darn it, I was right. I was not about to let it go now.

"Yes, ma'am. All that's left is to write it up."

"End of the day," she said. "And I've got a new one for you. Human interest piece on Wickham Birkland. His bird-seed store is celebrating its twentieth anniversary this week. I thought we could do a brief history of seed in Parkwood. Or maybe a brief history of birds. Or both."

The most gripping part of writing that story would be surviving Wickham's ire du jour.

"I'll get right on it," I said in my best can-do voice.

I went back to my desk, noting on the way that Ernie was sleeping again. I thumped his desk with my fist. "Rise and shine, Ernie! Got stories to do!" He snorted and jerked awake, his hand flying to his computer mouse.

"I've got it right here, Mary Jean…" He started clicking on random things. I held back a laugh and kept on.

I was four paragraphs into the bank story when Mary Jean slipped out, telling Joyce she was going to run to Leaf It to Me and get some tea to soothe her sore throat. The atmosphere in the news room lightened drastically when she left. I breathed a sigh of relief. Joyce—earbuds in place—began humming along with the song she was listening to. Ernie raided the vending machine for Donettes.

The door opened and in walked a young woman.

"Obituary? Fill out this form," Joyce said, automatically plucking the form from the file folder that sat permanently on her desk. Purchasing obituaries was really the only reason people ever came in anymore—and even that was waning after Bale & Sons began offering free webpages for their deceased. She tried to hand over the form.

"What? No. I don't think so," the woman said. She sounded kind of bewildered. She also sounded very familiar. Where had I heard her voice before?

Joyce blinked. "You don't think so?"

The woman shook her head and began to tear up. "Unless you know something I don't. Did someone call you?"

Joyce's mouth hung open in confusion, the paper still dangling between her fingernails. "I don't know," she said. "Why would someone call?"

The woman began to sob. "Because you're the news and all. Oh, no. Bad luck follows me everywhere."

And that was when I realized where I knew her from. I stood at my desk. "Agnes Tellerman?"

The woman turned to me in surprise, her knees bending as if she were about to bolt. Or faint. "Y-yes?"

I came around my desk. "You're Agnes Tellerman?"

"So someone did die? I just knew it."

"What? No. I mean, yes. Gerald Farley died. And you witnessed it, right? I was there that night. I remember your voice."

She wiped her eyes with the palms of her hands, the sleeves of her shirt pulled down over them, just like a child would do. And only then did it become obvious that Agnes Tellerman was not much older than a teenager herself. Maybe mid-twenties. She was pretty, in a droopy-eyed, downtrodden sort of way. She sniffed.

"You're that podcast lady?"

Whoa. Four listeners in one morning. I was on a roll.

Thinking of the podcast and rolls made me think of Daisy and my heart dropped again. I missed her. I was going to have to make things right, as soon as I possibly could. Also, I needed to talk her into making cinnamon rolls soon.

"I am that podcast lady." I stuck out my hand. "Hollis Bisbee."

"I came to talk to you," she said, shaking my hand with hers still covered by her shirt sleeve.

"About?"

"About what I saw that night. The night the coach died."

Over Agnes's shoulder, I could see Mary Jean come out of the tea shop, steam rising from her cup. She patted her pockets, looked alarmed, and went back inside.

Mary Jean didn't want me to seek out Agnes, but if

Agnes came to me, what was I supposed to do? Talk to her, that's what. This was my moment, and I couldn't pass it up.

I pushed Agnes toward the door. "Meet me in the library across the street in five minutes. Third floor."

"But—"

The tea shop door opened again, then kind of bobbed against Mary Jean as she talked to someone inside.

"Just go," I said. "I'll be right there." I gave her another push.

"But—"

"Go!" I started to say, but the word was out before I could form it. I whipped around and saw Joyce standing behind her desk, also pointing toward the library. Who knew I'd have such an ally right here in our receptionist?

Agnes gave us one last distrusting look, then scurried out the door and across the street. Mary Jean, finally freeing herself from the tea shop, came toward us, head down, not seeing Agnes pass on her other side.

"I'll create a diversion," Joyce said. "Get back to your desk."

I didn't have time to ask questions. I raced to my desk and slid into my chair, my heart racing. Agnes Tellerman had come to talk to me. So technically I wasn't violating Mary Jean's orders, as she had forbidden me from going to Agnes. Regardless, Agnes had information to share, and she was sharing it with me. This was the adrenaline rush I got every time I scooped a story. It had been so long, and it felt great. Like running a race.

Mary Jean came in, grumbling about the wind chill.

"It's nice outside, Mary Jean," Joyce said. "You sure you don't have a fever? You look a little flushed."

Mary Jean shivered, her tea releasing little drops through

the cap and landing on her hand. She didn't even seem to notice. "Oh, I'm fine."

"You're not fine," Joyce said. "I think you should go home. You're not going to miss any huge headlines."

"And we'll call you if something happens," I added, trying to look like I had been perfectly calmly going over my story. I didn't even glance up from the papers on my desk, I was so focused on my work.

"Well..." Mary Jean hesitated.

"Well, nothing," Joyce said. "You've already got your coat and your purse. Just go home, take some heavy duty meds, and come back tomorrow."

Mary Jean still looked unconvinced. But she was also still shaking, and I was no longer certain if Joyce was getting her out of the office on my behalf, or if she, like me, was legitimately getting worried about our feverish boss.

"Okay," Mary Jean said. "But I'm going to leave my phone on. Turned up loud, too. So if anything happens—"

"Yes, yes, I know," Joyce said, plugging her earbuds back into her ears. "We'll call you first."

Mary Jean left, and I waited approximately zero seconds after she rounded the corner to the parking lot before I was up and out of my chair, racing for my own jacket on the coat rack by the front door.

"Thank you," I said to Joyce on my way out. "I owe you."

She screwed up her face in confusion, slowly taking out one earbud. "For what?" she asked. Then she winked, and plugged her music back into her head.

I had to hand it to her—she was good.

I smiled and ran out the door, a million questions for Agnes swirling through my mind.

Agnes Tellerman was pacing in front of the library's third floor window, wringing her red hands raw. By the time I got to her, I was out of breath and felt a little like I was going to throw up. If I was going to keep gobbling baked goods, I seriously needed to get to the gym.

"I thought you weren't coming," she said, and her chin twitched into a pathetic crumple.

"I'm here, I'm here," I said, holding out one hand as if to physically hold back her tears.

"I was getting ready to leave, and then my story would never get told," she said. My efforts to hold her tears back failed. She was crying again.

I waited for her to pull it together. "Do you mean the police still haven't talked to you?"

She produced a wad of used tissue out of nowhere and scrubbed at her face. "Just that night."

"They haven't brought you in to give a statement or anything?"

"No, ma'am."

I was guessing they were definitely sure it was Evangeline if they didn't even want to talk to the sole eyewitness. Even though Brooks had told me their suspicions about Evangeline, from the way he kept changing the subject, I still thought there must be more to it. Did Evangeline have enough motivation to knock off Coach Farley?

I'd been with Evangeline just before it happened. And again just after. But at the moment of the screech and scream, I had just finished my hot dog and was talking with

Ernie. I had no idea where Evangeline was at that moment. Or at any moment between the fight and the accident scene, come to think of it.

"So what's your story?" I asked, pulling up a chair for each of us.

She hesitated, and I could tell she was trying to get herself under control before speaking. "It was really dark down there in that lower lot," she said. "It always is. It's unsafe. So I keep thinking maybe what I saw was just an accident after all. Maybe whoever hit him didn't even know he was standing there because they couldn't see anything."

"Seems unlikely," I said. "Didn't they have their headlights on?"

To my surprise, she shook her head. "That's how I noticed that they were round, because I actually looked right at them thinking they should have been on or how else was the driver going to see anything? Plus, with the lights off, I couldn't see the license plate at all."

"Did you see the color of the car?"

She shook her head. "It was so dark down there. All I saw were the shadows of a man and a lady standing in the parking lot. They seemed to be arguing. I went the long way around so I wouldn't interrupt their conversation, and as soon as I turned my back, I heard this sound. *Thump-thump.* When I turned around, the lady was running away, and there was a car there. Only it took off before I could see anything else. And it was gone."

"Could you describe the lady you saw?"

She nodded. "She was about this tall." She stood and leveled her hand a little higher than her own head. "And she was kind of round and curvy and her hair was dark, like maybe dark red. And her run was kind of different."

"Different? How so?"

"She ran like maybe her feet were hurting. Kind of like..." Agnes hobbled in place to demonstrate. It did look like the gait of someone whose feet were hurting.

So the mystery woman's hair was long and dark—maybe even dark red. And her feet were hurting.

*My feet are killing me.*

Evangeline?

Maybe Brooks and Chief Henderson were onto something with her. But how could she be in the car if she was arguing with Farley outside the car? Could it have been a set-up? Could Evangeline have been distracting the coach, keeping him in one spot, while the driver got into place? Could Agnes be remembering it wrong? Maybe I was reading into things. Surely Evangeline Crane wasn't the only redhead with bad feet in Parkwood.

We both paused as sirens blared out of nowhere and Chief Henderson's car raced past the library, then went back to our conversation.

"Did you see what kind of car it was? Was it a Jeep?" I asked, though I was starting to feel a little bit of doubt about my Paulie Henderson theory. Unless, of course, he and Evangeline were in on it together. Which seemed unlikely.

"I don't know cars," she said. "But that's like an Army car, right?"

"Kind of."

She shook her head. "No, this was just like a regular car. A nice one, though. Not a junker."

Outside, there were more sirens, and Brooks's car raced through where the chief had just gone.

"Whoa," Agnes said. "What do you suppose that's about?"

"I don't know," I said. "But I intend to find out."

Joyce was glued to the scanner, actually staring at it like it was a TV. It was behind her desk, covered with papers and dust. I honestly wasn't aware we even had one until that moment. I wondered if Mary Jean wouldn't let it be used when she was in the office. Or if she even knew about it at all. Maybe she inherited it from the previous editor.

"You'll never believe this," Joyce said as soon as I walked in. "Shoot, I'm gonna have to call Mary Jean back in."

"What's going on?"

"Accident." She pointed at the scanner with her long fingernail, then looked at me with shock on her face. "It was another hit-and-run."

# CHAPTER 22

I'D LEFT MY JACKET AT the library, but I didn't care. I
didn't even feel the air as I dove into my car.

An ambulance roared past me just as I was pulling away
from the office, making it much easier to navigate to the
scene of the accident. I just had to roll through a few stop
signs here and there while other cars had pulled to the curb
to let the ambulance by. I wasn't worried—law enforcement
was already occupied.

The accident had happened in a quiet, semi-secluded,
older neighborhood, the body lying a few feet away from
a mailbox, a halo of spilled mail scattered around her head.
A few people stood and watched, just like after the football game, as Chief Henderson knelt next to the body and
Brooks tried to string up some police tape from the mailbox
to a fire hydrant on the opposite side of the street. The wind
kept stealing the plastic yellow tape from him, forcing him
to start over.

I drove up as close as I could, pulled over, and got out,
mindful to bring my notebook and pencil with me. I speed-
walked toward the body, my hand itching to pick up my
phone and tell Daisy, only to fall away when I remembered
our last conversation. I wasn't sure if she was still in this
with me, or not.

It wasn't until I saw the coils of red hair that it dawned on me who I was looking at.

Brooks saw me coming and abandoned the crime scene tape. The wind caught it and blew it into a tree, rolling out a tether, but Brooks didn't notice. He was too busy rushing to meet me on the sidewalk.

"Evangeline?" I asked.

"You shouldn't be here," Brooks said.

"So it is Evangeline?" My heart sank. I didn't know much about Evangeline, but I knew she at least had one son. Did she have a husband? Any more children? I tried not to think about the horrible phone calls that were going to be received today. I stared at her hair, which was really all I could see from my vantage point. "But who would have a grudge against her?"

Brooks glanced over his shoulder at the chief, worry rolling off of him. "We don't know."

I sucked in a breath, only just now realizing what this meant for their case. "You don't know because you thought Evangeline was Coach Farley's killer. Your lead suspect is lying in the middle of the street right now."

"Um, yeah, so there's been a development in our case."

"I should say so. She didn't run over herself. Is she dead?"

He shushed me. "No, she's not dead." I felt a sense of relief. He added, "And you really should go before he hears you."

"No, Brooks," I said, trying to get a better look at Evangeline. Two paramedics had brought a back board and stretcher to her. They were hurrying, but not panicking. I prayed that this meant she would be okay. "I'm the press. This is exactly where I should be."

"He won't want you here."

I gritted my teeth, my hands clamping tighter and more indignantly around my pencil. "Then that makes it even more important that I am here." There was no way I would allow the chief sweep this one under the rug. Evangeline deserved better. The last thing I wanted was her mother to see her name in the paper for being dead.

I could see in Brooks' face that he agreed with me... and that he didn't want to. I felt bad about putting him in such an uncomfortable position. But then I remembered that it wasn't me who was putting him in that position. It was Chief Henderson, and if Brooks didn't like it, maybe he shouldn't have left KCPD.

He gave in. "Just...fine, stay...but, for your own good, don't bring up Paulie. Not now. I'll see if I can get him to set up an interview with you so you can show us what you've got. It's going to be tough for him to accept, though. It's his son."

The grip around my pencil loosened. "You don't have to worry. I don't think it was Paulie anymore," I said.

"What?"

"I talked to Agnes Tellerman and she said it was definitely not a Jeep that hit Farley."

Relief washed over his face. "That's great news."

"Or it's horrible news, because if it wasn't my top suspect and it wasn't your top suspect, and it wasn't Wickham or Kermit, who was it?"

He seemed to consider this for a long time, then shrugged. "Back to square one, I guess."

I sighed. "Can you at least point me to a witness?"

He shook his head. "There weren't any."

"What? It's the middle of the day. How is that even possible?"

"Look around." He gestured toward the trees and tall

hedges around the houses. "Nobody sees anything around here. And apparently, nobody heard anything either. It wasn't until that guy over there came out to go to work that he saw her and called it in. No idea how long she's been there. But I don't think very long. The mail usually gets here after noon, they said."

My mind swirled, trying to absorb everything he was saying. Back in Chicago, if someone ran you down in the middle of the day, there'd be so many witnesses coming forward, the police would be turning people away.

"What happened?" I asked as I waded through the crowd, hoping someone had seen something and just hadn't told the police yet. "Anyone see what happened?"

"I heard a car screech and didn't think anything of it," an older lady said, her hair wrapped up in curlers. "I'm deaf in one ear, you know, so I'm not sure which direction it even came from."

Seemed everyone had a similar story. *I was in the shower. I had on my headphones. I was talking to my mother. I was watching TV.*

Truly, nobody saw anything. Or they did, and they weren't talking. But, given the worried looks on their faces, I doubted that.

Slowly, I made my way to the front of the crowd. The paramedics had loaded her up and taken off, sirens sounding.

I watched as they wheeled her away, and the chief silently inventoried the space where she'd been. With the grim centerpiece gone, the neighbors all began to drift away. But not me. I was interested in what Chief Henderson found on the scene. This time, I wasn't going to walk away until he did. I wasn't going to miss a single thing if I could help it.

He sifted through the mail, then dropped it into a bag. Picked up a cracked cell phone and bagged it, too.

"Was she talking on the phone when she got hit?" I called.

The chief glanced at me, then did a double take, his face clouding over with insta-rage.

"Brooks!"

Brooks looked like he wanted to saunter away with the residents. "Sir?"

The chief pointed at me with the bag of phone. "I told you to keep her away."

Brooks's focus ping-ponged between us, then he straightened up, cleared his throat, and stood tall, separating us. "Sir, she's the press. She's here because it's the scene of an accident."

"Attempted murder," I said.

"She also knew the accident victim."

"Victim of an attempted murder," I said.

"And she..." I could see him measuring his words, could imagine him weighing whether or not he was about to step on toes that would make his life miserable all over again. His jaw tightened as he made the decision. "She has the right to be wherever she wants to be. It's a free country. Chief."

The chief chewed his bottom lip, taking in everything Brooks said with a look of growing disgust. "She has a right, does she?"

"Yes, sir," Brooks said, steely, resolute. Handsome.

Chief Henderson stepped around the crime scene and came toward me, angrily gesturing with the plastic bags that he had—one in each hand. "Well, you may have a right to be here. But you don't have a right to get involved in my investigation. And you don't have the right to make public accusations against my son."

"I didn't." It came out a whisper. I would be lying if I said I wasn't just a little bit afraid of Chief Henderson. And I felt awful. Even though I knew that my intentions were right, I could see how the things I'd said could feel to a father who just wanted to protect his son. "I never pointed any fingers.."

"Everyone is listening. They know exactly who you're not talking about."

Wait, what? Really? Everyone? Why didn't that feel like a victory? "I'm sorry," I said, suddenly wishing that nobody had been listening.

He waved a bag toward me again. "You can stay here, but if you step one toe over that line right there, I will arrest you." We all looked to the police tape, which was still unsecured and waving in the wind. "Brooks, fix that," he snapped, and went back to work.

I watched silently as he continued to bag things. An earring. A single house slipper. The wind blew and a balled up piece of paper tumbled away from the scene and butted against the toe of my shoe. I looked at it and then at the chief, who didn't seem to notice. Had it been on the scene, or had it simply been blowing around, the same way the coach had coincidentally dropped on a hair net with long, red hair in it.

Slowly, carefully, I stepped on the paper. Then dropped my pencil, then bent to retrieve it. In the same motion, I picked up the paper and slipped it into my pocket.

The chief, finished and pleased with his work, went back to his car, got in, and sat there writing into a pad of his own.

"Is that it?" I asked.

Brooks looked up. He'd been trying to wind the tape back onto the spool, but it was just a wad of unruly plastic. "Looks like it," he said. "Anything interesting?"

I thought about the paper in my pocket. I wanted to share it with him. After all, he had just gone to bat for me against the chief, which was surely going to blow back on him in a bad way. And he had done it for me, which told me he either really liked me or really believed I had a right to investigate the case. Maybe he even believed I could solve it. Either way, he believed in me. But it wasn't him I didn't trust; it was the chief. That chief was undoubtedly doubly motivated to get rid of me now, and I didn't want Brooks getting caught in the middle any more than he already had. "Nope. Plain, old crime scene, I'm afraid."

He shuffled a few steps sideways so we could hear each other better. "Between you and me, he doesn't have a clue who's behind this now. Do you?"

I shook my head. "Not anymore. Any chance this was coincidence?"

He shrugged one shoulder while he re-wound a section of tape that he'd just finished winding only for it to get caught in the wind again. "Awfully big coincidence, don't you think?"

"You think someone was just trying to shut her up?"

He lowered the tape and stared at the spot where Evangeline had just been lying. "If so, it may have worked."

The Hibiscus was known for a lot of things, and one of them was their hot chocolate, which was thick and chocolaty and piping hot and dolloped with a huge mound of homemade marshmallow cream. Cold after leaving Evangeline's street, it was all I could think about.

I shivered my way back into town and stopped in for a cup, noting nervously but gratefully that Daisy's van was parked in the lot. We needed to talk.

She was pulling Brant out of the muffin case when I walked in. "I've told you a thousand times, mister. Stay out of Mommy's muffins." Brant was putting up a pretty good fight, clinging to the edges of the case with both hands and feet. He saw me and smiled and pounded on the glass with the flat of his hand. Daisy grunted and yanked.

"Hollis!" Esther crowed when she saw me come in. Her apron was extra fluffy today, pastel floral with a wide ribbon of lavender lace edging it. It looked home-sewn—the kind of apron that family would keep in kitchen drawers for generations to come.

Daisy's head snapped up, giving Brant just enough time to renew his grip. He burrowed back into the case and grabbed a muffin. Immediately, he crammed it into his mouth. Daisy gave a frustrated groan and went back in after him.

"Sit, sit!" Esther patted the counter at the stool where I usually sat. "You look chilled to the bone. You should be wearing a jacket, young lady. Coffee or hot chocolate?"

"Hot chocolate, extra marshmallow, please." I would worry about the consequences to my waistline later. "Are those pumpkin muffins?"

Daisy turned her attention to me again. "I was burnt out on lemon," she said.

"So is pumpkin going to be the new theme? Because I love a good pumpkin bar with cream cheese icing."

Daisy started to answer, but a muffin sailed through

the air and hit a man in a nearby booth, then landed in his soup. "Hey!" the man said.

"Brant!" Daisy yelled, and went back to her wrestling match.

I still wasn't sure where we stood.

Esther brought me a cup of hot chocolate, then reached around Daisy and snuck out a muffin. She placed a paper doily on a plate, balanced the muffin on top of it, and slid it over to me. "So what's new with the podcast?" she asked, but stepped away from the counter before I could answer. Obviously, Daisy had been filling her in on what was new with the podcast, and Esther, unable to stand the thought of two friends fighting, was trying to bridge the conversation toward working out differences. I was grateful for that.

I took a sip of my hot chocolate. I could feel the warmth slide its way all the way down into my belly. I licked the marshmallow off of my top lip. "Perfect, as usual, Esther." I began the process of pulling the paper off the muffin and splitting it in half so I could smear a pat of butter on it.

"I'm glad you enjoy it, honey. Just wait until you try the muffin. Sublime." She gave a worried twitch toward Daisy, then scurried to the other end of the restaurant.

"You're the one on that show," said a voice behind me.

I turned to three men who were sitting at a nearby table. "I'm sorry?"

One of them stabbed a huge forkful of waffle into his mouth. "That murder girl. You're her."

Well, at least if Daisy left the podcast for good, I had a new name for it: *That Murder Girl.* I sipped my chocolate again and smiled. "Yep, that's me! The *Knock 'Em Dead* podcast. Thanks for listening."

"That whole coach thing," he said, bouncing his knife in

the air. "That's a heck of a story. It's got everybody listening. Everywhere I go, someone's talking about it."

"What coach thing?" one of his friends asked, and the man launched into the story of Coach Farley's death, throwing out Paulie's name, even though I hadn't. I felt sick. Oh, boy. Just because I'd talked about the hit-and-run, people had started suspecting Paulie because they thought he was a troublemaker. And he was—no doubt about it—but troublemaker was a far cry from murderer. It hadn't been my intent to drag his name through the mud, but that didn't mean it hadn't been dragged just the same. I had some damage to undo.

I turned back to the counter and took a nibble of the muffin. My eyes rolled back in my head. No matter what else happened, I could not let Daisy quit the show.

More than that, I couldn't let her quit me.

"You really think that kid did it?" the man asked.

I swiveled again. "No," I said. "I'm sure now that he didn't."

He licked his knife. "So you got a new suspect?"

"I'll record new details tonight," I said. "You should listen. There are some big developments."

His face clouded over. "You're not even gonna give us a hint?"

I shook my head, mostly because I hadn't thought yet what I was going to say. Which reminded me...

I leaned to one side, pulled the crumpled paper from the scene of Evangeline's hit-and-run out of my pocket, and pressed it flat on the counter, smoothing out the edges. It was a receipt. Nothing terribly exciting about it. It was faded, but looked like a pretty standard restaurant receipt. I had a dozen just like it in my purse. All it proved was that Evangeline bought herself some dinner at some point.

Except…

I leaned in further, my heart speeding up in my chest. "Holy…"

Daisy, who had won the muffin case battle and was now holding a very drowsy-looking, crumb-covered Brant on one hip, perked up. "What?"

I studied the receipt again to make sure I was seeing what I thought I was seeing.

"Holy what?" Daisy had gotten closer, and then closer still. Soon she was bent over the receipt, her curiosity winning out over her frustration with me. Out of the corner of my eye, I could see Esther nodding with satisfaction.

"Do you see what I see, Daisy?"

"Mister Wok." She was quiet for a minute and then said, "What am I missing?"

"This," I said, placing my finger near the order. "Look closer."

She squinted. "Sweet and sour chicken—hold the pineapple and green pepper—an egg roll, and a soda to go. So? I mean, their cashew chicken is better than their sweet and sour. The sweet and sour kind of reminds me of chicken nuggets with barbecue sauce. But it's not bad. Better than China Steve."

"And look at this." I stabbed the top of the receipt.

She leaned over farther, then sucked in a breath. "The date."

"And time," I said.

It took her a minute, but then I felt the electricity of alarm surge between us. "It was bought right in the middle of that football game."

"Which means Evangeline didn't buy it," I said. "I was talking to her during the game. This receipt could have belonged to the person who hit her. It could have blown out of the car window or something."

Daisy sucked in another breath. "Someone hit Evangeline Crane?"

"Hit-and-run," I said. "Just like Farley. Only she survived. I got this from the scene."

"Paulie?" she whispered. "But why?"

I shook my head. "Not Paulie. And if the same person who hit Farley hit Evangeline, we know for sure he didn't do that, either." I tapped the date and time again.

"We're back to square one?"

I shook my head again. "Nope. I think I know who it was. How many more lemon recipes have you got?"

She grinned. "So many."

There was an awkward pause between us as we tried to navigate the make-up of our first argument. Would it be this easy? Best friends don't hold grudges, right? "Does this mean you forgive me?"

She shook her head, her smile turning soft. "There's nothing to forgive. We all have to blow off steam from time to time."

"But I shouldn't have blown it at you," I said. "You're my best friend."

She put her hand over mine. "Which is exactly why a little argument could never tear us apart. Besides, we can't break up. We're the voice of this town."

We locked eyes. "This speck," we both said at the same time, and then laughed, which made Brant pop awake. He instantly started stretching for the muffin case again.

"He's stubborn," I said.

"Just like his mama."

"Truth!"

"And, for the record," Daisy said. "I don't care if Parkwood is a speck or a dot or a spot or a blob. It's home."

I liked that. In fact, there was something about a speck that made a home more...homey.

"You know," the man behind me said. This time Daisy and I both turned our attention toward him. "That quarterback wasn't the only one who wanted Farley gone." Everyone at the table except the guy who didn't know the story nodded. "A lot of people hated him."

"That's what I keep hearing," I said.

"He was a cheater," he said.

"I keep hearing that, too."

"He still owes me money from last year's homecoming game."

"He owes you money?" Daisy asked. "Are you saying he bet on the game?"

The guy nodded. "Oh, yeah. Definitely. Goes to places like this when his team's about to play in their town, makes bets with people like us, then cheats to make sure he wins. Comes collecting the next day."

"But when he doesn't win," the guy across from him said, waving around a French fry, "he just disappears."

"Except he's in Parkwood all the time," the third guy at the table said. "I saw him just about every day driving in. Used to go right past my house."

"Now why would he be coming here every day?" the French fry guy said. "And why would he be driving through your neighborhood?"

My questions exactly.

I didn't hear his answer, because it suddenly all clicked into place for me.

I knew who killed Gerald Farley.

And I knew why.

# CHAPTER 23

"I HAVE TO TAKE BRANT HOME," Daisy said, half resisting as I pushed her along. "I don't get what all the hurry is about. I left my favorite delivery basket in there. Hollis. Stop!" Brant stirred, then drunkenly dropped his head back onto her shoulder. "Tell me what is going on."

"It all makes sense now," I said breathlessly.

"Maybe to you."

"Think about it," I said. "The assistant coach said Farley would be moving on soon, right?"

"Right."

"But do you remember what else he said?"

She thought about it. "Um...other than *get out of my office?*"

I nodded, impatient. "Think. What did he say about Farley coming to Parkwood?"

"Okay." She closed her eyes. "Oh, yeah. He said that Farley came here for lunch."

"Not just lunch, though," I said. "Long lunches. He always came alone so Wilma Louise wouldn't get in his way. And he wouldn't let her come to the games here, either."

She nodded, remembering. "Because Paulie Henderson was such a loose cannon. And he never had time for beers with Kermit, even when they won games."

"Exactly. The guys in there said he was in town every day, right?"

A gust of wind kicked up, making Brant stir again, this time with a little whine. She rushed to the van and shut him inside. For the first time in maybe ever, he went into his car seat without a fuss. "Right."

"Did you ever see him around town?"

"Only during games," she said. "I don't get where this is going."

"Where would you expect someone to go for lunch in Parkwood?"

We both turned and stared at the Hibiscus.

"And that guy in there said he saw Farley driving through his neighborhood every day. Which means—"

"He was lunching at someone's house...wait." She gasped. "No."

I nodded excitedly. "Yes. Evangeline said the Farleys don't cook. Like, ever. She seemed to know very specific things about them not cooking. She specifically mentioned Wilma Louise's rickety old crock pot. And she knew that Wilma Louise drove a silver Jaguar."

"You're not saying what I think you're saying."

"Agnes saw a woman with Farley the night of the hit-and-run—a woman who looked like her feet were hurting."

"So? That could have been anyone."

"Evangeline actually complained to me about her feet hurting that very night." I paced, everything fitting so perfectly, I couldn't believe I didn't see it before. "Brooks said their evidence proved Evangeline was on the scene. That's why she was their main suspect. But the woman Agnes saw wasn't in a car. She was arguing with Farley, and then ran off when the hit-and-run happened and was gone before police got there. Why? Why would someone run *away* when they've witnessed a crime like that? Wouldn't they run *to* him to make sure he's okay?"

Daisy shook her head uncertainly. "Because she has a record?"

"Or because she didn't want anyone to know she was there. She was very adamant that I leave this case alone. She seemed so angry at Farley. Brooks had assumed that was leftover from the days of her son being cut from the River Fork team, but maybe it wasn't. And you know what else? When Evangeline showed up at the scene and was talking to me, her hair was down. She'd taken off her hair net, which Chief Henderson found underneath Farley, with red hairs still in it."

"You're not serious."

"I am. And there's more. Oh, my gosh, it's so obvious now. The one and only person who was weirdly interested in details about the case—"

"You," Daisy said.

"Besides me." I waited for her to keep guessing, but had forgotten that I'd been alone when Francine Oglethorpe had all those questions for me. "The banker. And she looked familiar. You know where I've seen her before?"

"Francine?" Daisy looked completely lost. "Oh, I know Francine. She's—" She stopped and clapped a hand over her mouth.

"Yeah. I saw her in a photo on Farley's desk. Three blonde women who looked almost identical."

"Wilma Louise Farley."

"And her two sisters," I said.

"Francine Oglethrope is Coach Farley's sister-in-law. I totally forgot about that." She squinted. "You think she did it? But why?"

"No," I said. "Not her. But why was she so interested in

the case without ever mentioning that he was her family? What else was on the scene of the hit-and-run?"

"The Mercedes hood ornament."

"And…?"

"And…" She thought about it. "A hair net?"

"And…?"

"And a take-out menu!"

"Exactly!" I shouted, clasping her hands in mine. "A take-out menu to Mister Wok's. Where Farley never ate, because he hated Chinese food. But Wilma Louise Farley was a regular there. And when Brooks and I went there for dinner, Mister Wok told us that her regular order was…" I pulled the receipt out of my pocket again and let it dangle in the wind between us.

"Sweet and sour chicken, hold the pineapple and green pepper," we said together.

I saw the light begin to come on in Daisy's expression. "And this receipt was on the ground by Evangeline today," I continued.

"Almost like it blew out of someone's car window or something," she said, reaching out and squeezing my fingers excitedly.

"And here's the other thing. What kind of headlights does a Jaguar have?"

She looked hesitant. "Are they? Yes—yeah, they're circular. A Jaguar has circular headlights."

"But she hasn't been driving it. She's been driving his truck."

"I've literally never seen her drive his truck. It's such a man truck. The license plate even says MANTRK. But, I mean, why would Wilma Louise kill her own husband? And why would she try to kill Evangel—" She gasped again. "No."

I nodded. "Yes. What was the first thing everyone said to describe Farley to us?"

"He was a cheater," Daisy said.

"Maybe they weren't arguing so much as having a lover's spat. Maybe she was angry at him because he wouldn't leave Wilma Louise."

Daisy's eyes were round as saucers. "Are you saying what I think you're saying?"

"Farley was cheating on Wilma Louise with Evangeline, so Wilma Louise ran him over. And then ran Evangeline over. She ran over everybody. Mike was right."

"The husband is always the first to go," we said together.

She flung her arms around me. "Hollis! You solved the case!"

"No," I said. "We're a team. *We* solved it. Now, let's go catch her."

Brooks was sitting in his car just on the other side of my car. As I expected him to be. I had a few minutes to kill while Daisy ran Brant home, so instead of getting into my car, I walked over to his and motioned for him to roll down his window. He did.

"Still babysitting, I see?"

"Be fair, now," he said. "I stuck up for you."

"Yeah, you did," I said. "Thank you for that."

He cupped his ear. "What was that? Did I just hear a thank-you? Say it again. I want to savor it." This time I was sure—he was openly flirting, and I didn't hate it. Okay, I liked it. A lot, actually.

I put my hand on my hip. "Don't press your luck. It was

a rare moment of weakness." I tried to sound tough, but my smile betrayed me.

His mouth dropped open, still turned up mischievously at the corners. "And she admits weakness, too? Someone call the press."

I cocked my head to one side. "Very funny. I suppose I deserved that. I've been pretty hard on you."

He opened his car door, and I stepped back so he could get out. He towered over me; I had to shade my eyes when I looked up. "I didn't take it personally. Truth be told, I like the way you stand up for yourself. And I like the way you go all-in when you've got a lead."

I cleared my throat. "Speaking of leads…"

His eyebrows went up. "I can't wait to hear where this is going."

"It's going to River Fork. I'm pretty sure we cracked your case, Officer."

"Oh, did you, now? Let me guess. It was the captain of the high school chess team. Farley stole his knight."

"Good guess!" I slugged his arm lightly. "But no."

He ducked away from my punch playfully, but then looked at me more closely. "Wait. Are you being serious right now?"

"The news is always serious."

"No, I mean it, Hollis, do you know something? Who is it?"

"That, I'm not going to tell you."

"What? Yes, you are."

"I just want to check out the house, see if our theory has any merit, then we'll talk."

"Talk now. You can't withhold information from a police officer. Especially information about a murder case. It's obstruction of justice."

"Oh, come on, we both know you're going to follow me there anyway. Besides, If I tell you, you'll just tell Chief Henderson, and he'll find a way to keep me out. "

He sighed in frustration. "I'll call him after we get there, how about that?"

"No way. What if I'm wrong? It'll just make him even madder at me. And then he'll have you casing my house twenty-four/seven."

"But what if you're right, Hollis? This could be dangerous. You could be tipping someone off and they'll bolt before I can arrest them."

I pulled my keys out of my purse. "I'm pretty sure about this. It will all make sense when you get there. I promise you that."

Daisy's van pulled in on two wheels, spraying gravel everywhere. She practically jumped out while it was still moving. She'd changed clothes and was now wearing black yoga pants, a black long-sleeved shirt, a black jacket, and a black stocking cap that pushed the spikes of her hair so that they framed her face adorably.

"What are you wearing?" I asked. "And how did you change so fast?"

"Stakeout clothes," she said. "And I'm a mother of four. I get precisely nine minutes a day to myself. I can do just about anything in two minutes or less."

"You look like you're about to rob a bank."

"I bought these pants specifically for this purpose. Well, and because they hide cat hair."

"And to work out in?" I asked.

She snorted a laugh. "Yeah, right, like I ever work out."

"We're going to have to start," I grumbled. "All those sweets are going to the wrong places." Brooks ducked his head, and I was pretty sure I saw him blush.

She clapped her hands twice. "Come on, now, let's go get this woman!"

"Woman?" Brooks said curiously. "But Evangeline—"

"No, not Evangeline," Daisy said, but I clapped my hand over her mouth.

"Brooks is going to follow us there."

She grinned beneath my palm and I let up. "Of course. Don't worry, Brooks, we'll drive slowly so you can keep up."

With that, we both jumped in the car. I had it halfway out of the parking lot before Brooks could even get his door open. We laughed as we wrapped our seatbelts around us while on the move.

"Look out, Wilma Louise, we're coming for you," Daisy cried. "To River Fork!"

# CHAPTER 24

OUR DRIVE WAS A LOT shorter than we anticipated.
We were only two blocks away when we spotted a very
familiar truck. It was parked outside a Dairy Dude walk-up
frozen custard shop, dominating the tiny gravel parking lot.

"Look!" Daisy said, discovering it at just the same
moment that I did. She pointed out the window. "Isn't that
Farley's man truck?"

It was. Enormous, polished to a mirror-like shine,
gleaming tires, NFL stickers on the back window,
MANTRK on the license plate. In the daylight, it was an
even more startling and garish sight than usual. Farley had
been clear in his statement to the world: *I am bigger and
better than you.*

I guess the world had been even clearer in its statement
back to him: *Nope.*

Or at least, his wife had.

Speaking of, Wilma Louise was toddling away from
the window in her high heels, slurping a milkshake while
chatting away happily on her cell phone, her designer bag
dangling from her arm.

"What do we do?" I asked, blowing right past Dairy
Dude in a panic, immediately regretting that decision.
Chicago Hollis would have never driven by. Chicago Hollis

would have been first on the scene. Chicago Hollis would have been greeting police as they arrived, notebook and pencil in hand, questions at the ready, searching out the rookie cop who wasn't skilled yet at keeping things under wraps.

Yes, but Chicago Hollis didn't exist anymore. Parkwood Hollis was still feeling her way. We just did things differently here.

"Go back! Go back!" Daisy shouted, pounding on her window as if that would somehow erase the feet of highway I was putting between us and Wilma Louise.

Parkwood Daisy had things under control for both of us.

I turned into a parking lot, did a quick U-turn, and waited in the driveway for traffic to clear so I could pull back onto the highway. We watched as Wilma Louise opened the truck door and started to climb inside. Even with the little step on the running board, it was too high for her, and she had to lean forward to place her milkshake and purse inside to free up her hands.

"Go, go, go," Daisy chanted, bouncing in her seat. The traffic had cleared and my tires squealed in my startled hurry to get back to Dairy Dude. Wilma Louise glanced our direction, then went back to the arduous process of getting into the truck.

I pulled up alongside her, nearly bumping into a picnic table where two teens were enjoying cones. They both flinched. The girl dropped her cone and the boy started fussing at me. The screen of the cashier window opened and a tattooed and pierced guy—the Dude behind Dairy Dude, I assumed—stuck his head out.

"Hey! That's not a parking spot! Hey!"

Wilma Louise paused to watch the scene unfold. Daisy

and I glanced at each other nervously, then got out at the same time.

I held up one finger at the guy in the window, flung a dollar bill that I'd dug out of my cup holder to the boy at the picnic table, mumbling, "Sorry," and made a beeline toward Wilma Louise. Recognition and panic fell over her like a shadow and she began scrambling double-time to get into the truck, but the narrowness of her pencil skirt was making it impossible to quickly get her foot up that high. I allowed myself one moment of pride that we were recognized.

"That's an awfully big truck you've got there, Wilma Louise," Daisy said. "Mind if we ask you a few questions?" That was my line. I beamed with pride. Who knew—if Daisy could pick up reporter habits, maybe I could pick up baking habits. Not likely, but it was a nice thought.

"I'm busy," Wilma Louise said.

"We'll only take a minute," I said.

"Did you not hear me? You need to move your car!" Dairy Dude hollered.

"This was your husband's truck, correct?" I asked.

"I've got an appointment," Wilma Louise said. She made another attempt to get into the truck, grunting and pulling, but no such luck.

"You know," Daisy said, patting the side of the truck. "If I had a truck this big, I don't know if I'd feel comfortable driving it. Would you, Hollis? It just looks so hard to maneuver."

"I'm talking to you two!" Dairy Dude yelled.

"Definitely not," I said. "Especially if I owned something smaller, like a BMW or Porsche or...oh, I don't know, a Jaguar?"

"Me, too," Daisy said. "I would have such trouble getting into a monster like this one, I'd be much happier running my errands in a little car."

"I'm calling the cops!" Dairy Dude yelled.

By then, Brooks had caught up with us and pulled into the lot on the other side of my car. He looked thoroughly perplexed.

"Ha ha!" Dairy Dude yelled. "Guess they read my mind. You're gonna get a ticket now. Good job, Officer! Doing great work, there!"

Brooks ignored him. "The thing about letting someone follow you is not taking off before he's in the car," he said to me. "What's going on here?"

"Throw the book at her, Officer! Can't have people like her running around Parkwood, just taking spots that aren't meant for parking."

"I mean, what would make you take a truck like this out and about if you had something sleek and small—and much more suited to your wardrobe—at home?" Daisy pointed at Wilma's ensemble. "That skirt and those shoes—wow, where did you get those shoes?—would look great in a Jaguar. Don't you own a Jaguar, Wilma Louise?"

"You guys are in over your heads here," Brooks said. "And you broke about ten traffic laws, by the way."

I turned to him indignantly. "In over my head? I have worked murder cases with much tougher suspects than this one."

Wilma Louise's eyes got big. Dairy Dude's eyes got big. The eyes of the two teens got big. "Murder?" they all said at once.

"I can't talk right now." Wilma Louise was trying doubly hard to get into her truck, but the more panicked she got, the harder it seemed to get for her and she kept plopping back into the parking lot.

"Hey! Why aren't you giving her a ticket?" Dairy Dude yelled. "She's parked illegally!"

"I wonder how many Jaguars there are in River Fork," Daisy said contemplatively. She leaned against the truck as if deep in thought. "Any guesses, Wilma Louise? I mean, since you own a Jaguar and all. Probably not that many. Someone's Jaguar would really stand out in a crowd around here, don't you think?"

"Why are you talking about murder and Jaguars?" Wilma Louise asked. She shook her head. "I've got errands to run, and my milkshake is melting. I don't know anything about murder. And I don't know anything about a Jaguar."

She gave another oomph at getting into the truck. This time she was successful.

"I would like to press charges," Dairy Dude yelled. "Trespassing!"

"Stop yelling!" Brooks and I both hollered at the same time. Dairy Dude's mouth hung open, then he slammed the screen shut and then the window behind it, angrily slapping up a CLOSED sign.

"Hey," the boy said, sadly waving his dollar bill. "I was gonna buy a cone."

"Hollis?" Daisy said.

I turned back to Brooks. "I'm hardly in over my head. My partner and I are solving your case. While you were running around after Evangeline—"

"You were blaming a kid!" He put his hands on his hips.

I matched his hands-on-hips pose. "A kid who publicly threatened to kill Farley! It wasn't that far of a leap."

"Guys?" Daisy said.

"Open up! I want a zebra cone!" the boy said, pounding on the closed window. Dairy Dude shook his head defiantly inside, jabbing his finger at the CLOSED sign.

"At least we knew that our suspect was somehow involved," Brooks said.

"Yeah, she was another victim!" I said. "What kind of victory is that?"

"You guys!" Daisy said, stepping between us, wild-eyed. "She's getting away."

We all turned toward the truck. It roared into life and immediately began backing out of the parking lot.

"No!" I said, scrambling after the truck. "I just want to talk to you!"

But Wilma Louise whipped the truck around to leave the lot.

Brooks had gone back to his car and picked up the radio.

"You distracted me," I said.

"Let's go! Let's go!" Daisy yelled, hopping into the passenger seat of my car. She leaned over and turned the ignition.

"*You* distracted *me*," he said.

"Come on!" Daisy growled from inside the car. "You guys can fight later."

"We weren't figh—okay." I slid in, threw the car into reverse, and went after Wilma Louise.

For such a huge vehicle, that truck could really move. I had my pedal pressed all the way down trying to keep up. Of course, it didn't help that Wilma Louise basically ignored all traffic laws.

Daisy held onto the center console with one hand and gripped the ceiling handle with the other, shouting out directions. "Left! She went left!"

I could see Brooks in my rearview mirror, lights blazing and sirens sounding. To all the world, it looked as if he was trying to pull me over and we were involved in some sort of high-speed chase. I saw people stop and stare as we passed them by, and was overcome with an urge to roll down my window and say, "It's not me! He's not after me!" But a part of me thought maybe he kind of wished he was. After our argument at Dairy Dude, he'd looked like he'd love nothing better than to put me in jail.

However, it was not lost on me that Chief Henderson never joined in the chase. Had Brooks been bluffing when he picked up his radio? Was he letting us solve the case first after all?

Daisy let out a yelp. "Through the square! Oh, sweet muffins, we're going through the square." She rolled down her window and hung the top half of her body out, waving her arms around. "Get out of the way, people! Save yourselves!"

We zipped through the square and past the Hibiscus.

And nearly rammed into Wickham Birkland at Tutor and Oak, missing his fender by mere inches. He instantly got red in the face and stormed out of his car, ranting. I paused and rolled down my window.

"Have you ever thought that maybe it's you?" I asked, then kept going, leaving him looking perplexed at the four-way stop.

Soon we were on the highway, racing toward River Fork. And still no Chief Henderson. I started to feel a curious warmth toward Brooks that was more than just the electricity I'd been feeling. He was a good guy. And he believed in me. He didn't think I was a failure in my career, and he liked the same speck I liked. There was a lot about Brooks Hopkins that was just…right.

Wilma Louise took the first exit into River Fork, jerking hard onto the ramp at the last possible second. I followed her. She rolled through a stop light at the top of the exit, cutting off two oncoming cars. Both honked at her, skidding to a stop. Slowly, slowly, they started up again, backing up traffic in their hesitation and putting at least a dozen cars between us. Shoot. She was going to get away.

"What do you think—pumpkin or apples?" Daisy asked.

"Huh?" I was afraid to take my eyes off the truck, which was getting smaller and smaller in the distance.

"Well, lemon is my favorite, but it's kind of a spring flavor. I was wanting to do something a little more seasonally appropriate. But I can't decide between pumpkin and apples." I flew over a pothole, making her voice break on the word *apples*. She gripped the handle and kept going. "I mean, pumpkin is great. Everybody loves pumpkin. But it's overdone. Although I do have a pumpkin buttercream that is to die for—what?"

I was giving her an incredulous look as I got stopped behind another traffic clog caused by Wilma's erratic driving and confused drivers trying to get out of the way for Brooks, who was still running his lights behind me. I could barely see the truck up ahead now. "This is what you're thinking about right now?"

"What's wrong with that?"

"We're in the middle of chasing down a murder suspect, and your mind is on buttercream."

"I'm a professional," she said. "I have an audience to satisfy."

"Oh, brother."

"What? I stress-bake, okay? And I don't know if you noticed, but this is a highly stressful situation."

The light turned green and I left rubber on the pavement in haste to get to Wilma Louise. We turned, and then turned again. And then we got to a railroad track. The arms had just come down, and we could hear the whistle of the train. "Yes!" I exclaimed, following Wilma Louise toward the tracks. "We're caught up, she's ours n—"

Daisy and I both screamed and covered our eyes as Wilma gunned it and wove through the safety arms only moments before the train sped through.

"Did you see that?" I asked, uncovering only because I hadn't heard a crash.

"Is she dead?" Daisy asked, eyes still covered.

"No," I said. "She got away."

There was a knock on my window, grim-faced Brooks on the other side, reminding me of the first time I met him. I rolled down the window.

"Did you see that? She's crazy. Only a murderer could be that crazy," I said. Not exactly true, but it sounded good. "And now she's gone. And who knows where she went?"

"Eventually she'll go home," Brooks said.

I grinned. " It just so happens we know exactly where that is. Follow me."

# CHAPTER 25

S HE WASN'T THERE, BUT WE didn't expect her to be. We parked our car around the corner to wait. Brooks parked his cruiser behind us.

"You don't happen to have a gyro on you, do you?" I asked.

Daisy looked thoroughly confused. "Huh?"

"Never mind. Stakeout inside joke." So inside, I was the only one who knew it.

"Let's look around," she said.

We got out of our car and I mimed to Brooks that we were going to scope out the house. He mimed back that he didn't fully agree with that decision, but he also looked like he understood now that he couldn't stop me. We canvased the Farleys' yard, peeking into the few windows that didn't have their shades pulled—with me taking the front and east side, and Daisy taking the garage and back. The house looked dusty and unused. Wilma Louise hadn't been home much, apparently. Maybe she'd been living it up since Farley had been run down. Almost like someone who was celebrating.

I sat on the front porch and thought about how jealous it had made me to think about Trace with his bevy of better-than-Hollis women. And that was *after* we'd broken up.

Would I have been driven to kill if we'd still been together and I'd found out he was seeing another woman?

I would like to think not.

But Wilma Louise Farley sure didn't seem the type, either.

Maybe we had the wrong person again. It was possible. She could have been running from us because of all the press surrounding the coach's death. It wouldn't be the first time someone ran from a reporter just to get away from the sensationalism of a story.

Daisy joined me on the porch.

"Do you really think she did it?" I asked.

"Definitely," Daisy said. "Without a doubt."

"How can you know for sure? What if we're just badgering this poor woman over a bunch of circumstantial evidence?"

Daisy started to open her mouth to answer me, but clapped it shut and pointed down the street instead. Farley's enormo-truck was coming, slowly creeping, as if she was watching out for us. Daisy grabbed my arm and pulled me around the side of the house. I waved toward Brooks's car to stay put. I doubted he would, but I wanted to feel for just a second like I had some sort of say.

"I left my notebook and pencil in the car," I whispered.

"So?"

"So I can't take notes."

Daisy blinked at me. "I think you can trust your memory on this one. Come on."

As soon as Wilma Louise opened the driver's side door and toppled out of the truck—chatting on her cell phone once again—we stepped around the corner.

"We have some questions for you," Daisy said in a very TV detective voice.

"Wow," I said. "That's getting better all the time."

"Thanks," Daisy said. "I've been practicing in the bathroom mirror—hey!"

Wilma Louise had taken one look at us, dropped her cell phone, purse, and a shopping bag on the ground and bolted through the yard, leaving the truck door wide open and the person she'd been talking to probably wondering where she'd gone.

"Stop!" I yelled, then ran after her. "We just want to interview you!" Not true, exactly. But close enough. I couldn't arrest anyone—that was for Brooks to do. I just wanted to facilitate her capture so justice could be brought to the city of Parkwood. And to Coach Farley, because cheating is rotten thing to do, but not punishable by death. And to Evangeline, because maybe she loved him, even if loving him was wrong.

I heard soft thumps behind me and saw Brooks running toward us. He wasn't just a good jogger—he was a great runner.

My lungs and legs were already burning. Why had I made so many excuses not to get to the gym? "Wilma... Louise...I just...I won't...uh..." I was for sure slowing down.

But so was Wilma Louise. She'd kicked off her high heels and was trying to navigate her way across a neighbor's gravel driveway barefoot.

"Oof! Ouch! Ow! Ow! Ow! Okay..." she said, gasping for air nearly as much as I was. "Okay...I'll stop..."

Brooks, on the other hand, had not slowed at all. It wasn't me she was stopping for; it was him. But the funny thing was, I was starting to see us as being on the same team.

"I'm innocent," Wilma Louise said as Brooks reached her. "I'm a grieving widow."

"Why'd you run, then?" I asked.

"Because I don't want to be in the newspaper," she said. "I just want my privacy. But I'll talk to you…You're relentless."

"Thank you," I said, and I meant it.

We walked slowly back to her driveway, Wilma Louise and I still trying to catch our breath. I'd pulled out my phone to take notes, even though that was not my routine and I hate hate hated it. Wilma bent to pluck her phone out of the grass. That was when I saw a familiar notebook lying in the grass next to her spilled purse.

"Hey, that's my notebook," I said, picking it up. It was true what they said about criminals revisiting the scene of their crimes. Wilma Louise had visited and had taken a souvenir, apparently. "*You* took it? Why?"

"I wanted to see where you were with the case."

"You could have just asked the police for that," Brooks said.

She rolled her eyes and waved him off. "Pssh. Sure, I could have. But she wasn't going to give up on this case. I also took the notebook to slow her down. If anyone was going to figure out who hit Gerald, it was going to be her. I was worried."

I tried not to gloat. *Don't gloat, Hollis. Gloating is not attractive. Gloating makes you petty and small.*

"Told you," I muttered. Okay, maybe I would gloat a little.

"Why were you worried?" Daisy asked, taking my notebook and flipping through it. "If you aren't guilty. Seriously, Hollis? *There's a new man in town, his name is Frank, and he's delicious?*"

I mean, it didn't sound as bad when it was read aloud like that. "Can we focus, please?"

"Gerald was the love of my life," Wilma said. "Soul mates, really. I wanted to know who killed him." Her chin crumpled and her voice started to wobble. "We had plans, you know, to retire to Florida."

Daisy, who had walked over to the truck, shook her head. "You may want to save—"

"We never had children. We didn't need them. We were so happy, just the two of us."

"You're wasting your br—"

"We were going to go down and pick out a little house this summer."

Daisy sighed, leaned into the truck, and pushed a button. The garage door groaned to life. Wilma Louise froze as the door lifted to slowly reveal a silver Jaguar with a mangled grill and a cracked headlight.

We all just sort of stood there and stared at it, until it dawned on me that Daisy knew the car was there this whole time and didn't say anything.

"You saw it when you looked in the garage window," I said.

She nodded, proud.

"Why didn't you tell me?"

"I started to, but we got interrupted." She shrugged. "Besides, I like big endings."

Brooks turned his back and mumbled into his radio. Soon, we heard a police siren fire up in the distance. He pulled out his handcuffs. "Ma'am, I'm going to need you to put your hands behind your back."

For the briefest second, Wilma Louise looked like she was going to run again. Her eyes went wild and her fists balled.

"He was a cheater!" she finally yelled. "He was a cheater and so was she. What do you care that he's gone? Just let cheating dogs lie." Brooks clicked the handcuffs into place and led her toward his car. "I did everyone a favor," she ranted. "Nobody liked him!"

Which may have been the first true thing she'd said since we met.

# CHAPTER 26

CHIEF HENDERSON TOOK WILMA LOUISE away in his car. But not before yelling at me for a solid two minutes about staying out of police business and obstruction of justice and having a good mind to take me right in with her.

"I'm really sorry I accused Paulie," I said. "Like, really, really sorry."

He launched into a rant about big city media and how it was ruining the country.

"I'll issue a full, public retraction on our next episode," I said. "I promise."

He lectured about rights to privacy and slander laws, and then laid into Brooks for not getting rid of me like he was supposed to.

"I'll bake you your own pumpkin roll," Daisy said, swooping in and linking her arm in the chief's. She whispered, "My signature pumpkin buttercream will change your life."

His yell turned into a grumble and then a mumble and then he let Daisy walk him to his car, talking the whole way about pumpkin muffins and pumpkin cakes, and a special secret recipe pumpkin tiramisu.

"What would I do without her?" I said once they were out of earshot.

"Probably go to jail," Brooks said. "Or at the very least listen to him go on for another half hour or so."

"He's not my biggest fan," I said.

"No," Brooks said. "He's not. I don't think apologizing to Paulie on your podcast is going to help any."

"No, probably not. But I'm still going to do it."

"You should just lay low for a while. Do stories on housewares stores."

"You never needed a toaster, did you?" I asked. He chuckled at his feet. "I didn't think so. And you didn't radio the chief back at the ice cream place, either."

"I radioed him."

"Not the question."

He grinned. "I wanted to give you the chance to see this to the end."

"Thanks," I said. I reached over and pinched his arm lightly. "That was nice of you."

"I keep telling you I'm a nice guy. How did you figure out it was Wilma Louise? We suspected her, but couldn't find anything to back it up."

I shrugged. "A good reporter never reveals her sources. But maybe a good egg drop soup could talk it out of me."

"Deal." The electricity came back and we got silent. It wasn't a terrible feeling, if I wanted to be honest with myself. Finally, Brooks broke the tension. "I know you're bored here."

I looked around. The neighbors had begun to come out and gather round. Someone brought a lawn chair. Someone else brought lemonade. It was a party, and everyone was invited.

"It's not the worst place in the world."

"I like to hear that," he said. "Makes me think you're going to stick around."

Trace popped into my head. He'd found me a job. He'd come all the way down to Parkwood to try to get me back. He'd even brought Tink, and I knew how much Trace hated letting Tink in the car, because the dog hair made his allergies act up, plus *camel hair coats were fur magnets.*

I could go home to Chicago. I could see my mom and Aunt Ruta, let them yell at me that I was letting my hair get split ends and my thighs get too jiggly. Listen to them argue in person. Let them meddle in my life in their adorable old lady way.

I could go back to a big, busy newspaper. Could eat lunch in the company lunch room with Pulitzer winners and their famous friends. I could follow murderers every day, looking for that big scoop, that unique angle that nobody else had. Hot dog rollers could come and go by the thousands and I would never even know about them.

That was what I'd been hoping for. It was what I'd wanted since I arrived in Parkwood. And Trace had offered it to me on a silver platter.

It was my time.

I leaned over and shut Wilma Louise's truck door, then bent to pick up the spilled shopping bag. "I should get back to the office," I said. "Mary Jean will be wondering what happened to me."

# CHAPTER 27

"W HERE HAVE YOU BEEN?" MARY Jean asked as soon as I came in the door. "The biggest story we've seen in a decade and you were out to lunch? I had to send Ernie to the police station to report on the public statement."

I didn't have the heart to tell her Ernie was elbows-deep in giblet gravy over at the Hibiscus.

"I'm sorry, Mary Jean," I said. "I had to...pursue something."

"I certainly hope it was worth it," she said, setting off a huge coughing fit that knocked her back in her chair.

"It was," I said. I could feel Joyce's eyes—and her questions—boring into me. I snaked my hand around to my back and gave her a thumbs up.

"Well," Mary Jean said, recovering, blotting her sweating forehead, "I have a lead for you. The superintendent got new paneling in his office. I need you to cover that."

"Paneling?" I asked, deflated.

*I'm sorry, Mary Jean, I've been offered a job back home in Chicago, and we would never do a story on paneling, because nobody wants to read that. So you'll have to do your own superintendent story. I'm out.*

I wanted to say that.

But I didn't.

Because I knew I wasn't going anywhere. Because as much as I hated to admit it, Mary Jean and her uninspired stories had grown on me without my even knowing it—the same way all of Parkwood had.

"It's quite controversial," she said, then blew her nose.

"Too much taxpayer expense?" I ventured. "Misappropriated funds?" This had potential.

"No, no." She blew again, then tossed the tissue. "Too golden pecan."

"Huh?"

"The superintendent's office has always been mahogany. He's replacing it with golden pecan. His receptionist says she has to wear sunglasses indoors from all the reflection. It's a real hullabaloo over in the district office. People are drawing hard lines in the sand over it."

It wasn't murder. It wasn't even misuse of taxpayer money. It was a *hullabaloo*.

But it still had potential.

"I'm on it, Mary Jean."

I grabbed my notebook and pencil and headed out.

She was going to get the best hullabaloo story she'd ever seen in all her years in the business. I would read it aloud to myself just to be sure.

Trace was waiting on my porch again when I got home.

"You have to stop doing this," I said, dropping my bag on the floor. "One of these days you're going to come away from here with one less kneecap or something."

He laughed. "You know I love it when you act tough. Have you made your decision yet?"

I ignored him. "Listen, Trace. We need to talk."

"There's a one-bedroom for rent in my neighborhood that would be perfect for you," he said. "You might have to get rid of some stuff, of course, but you could just put some of your textbooks up for sale online."

"Sell...my textbooks?"

My journalism textbooks that I'd hung onto to remind me of how hard I'd worked to get where I was. The books that encouraged me to hang on when things got tough and I thought for sure I wasn't going to make it in the bloody world of crime beat journalism. The books that told me there was a reason I was willing to interview mob bosses and drug lords and grieving widows. The books that said, *Hollis, you may be working nothing beats at a nothing paper in the middle of nowhere, but this is only a speedbump on your way to success, because you* will *be a success.* The textbooks that were central to my life in so many ways.

Just...sell them?

"This isn't going to work," I blurted.

"Sure it will," he said. "I'll help you pack. We'll go to Office Max or whatever it is you have here, get some boxes, and work into the night."

"No," I said. "That's not what I mean. This..." I toggled my finger back and forth between us. "Is not going to work."

He sat frozen, trying to take in what I'd just said. I could tell that it did not compute with him. Of course it didn't—it was rejection. And if there was one thing Trace had a hard time comprehending, it was rejection.

"I don't want to pack all night. I have to get up and go to work in the morning. There's a scandal in the superintendent's office and I have to cover it."

"You're going to quit after you turn in the story, though, right?" he said weakly.

"No, I'm not quitting. I don't want to sell my books. And the fact that you don't already know that about me is a huge problem. My things are already home. I'm already home."

"Okay," he said. "Okay. We can take it slower. I get it. You have loose ends to tie up. I'll give you more time. A couple weeks. Or three, if that's what you need. Get rid of stuff your way. Give your two-week notice."

"No, that's not what I mean." I ran my hands over my face and through my hair. "I mean, I'm not going with you."

"Right," he said. "I'll come back for you. I'll probably leave Tink with his au pair, though. Travel messes with his digestive system. He needs his greens for regularity."

I chuckled. Trace, trying to smooth things over, chuckled, too.

"No," I said, exasperated. "I don't want that. And Tink is a dog. He needs a dogsitter who will toss him a Milk Bone every now and then and scratch him behind the ears and take him out to pee on things. That's what dogs need. Not au pairs and greens and regularity."

"Why are you getting so upset about Tink?" he asked. "I thought you loved him."

"It's not about Tink," I exclaimed. "I do love him. I don't want this, Trace. I don't want to leave Parkwood. And...I don't want you. I don't love you."

His mouth hung open, aghast. For once, he was without words. And I found it relieving and also horribly offputting. I felt insta-guilt.

"It's not you," I said. "It's that I've grown to like it here. My life is simpler. My job is simpler. My needs are simpler." King Archie jumped in the living room window and pawed aside the blinds. "The point is...the point is I'm happy. And

I'm sorry. I'm turning you down. Go home. Without me. It's over."

# CHAPTER 28

The Hibiscus was typically packed, even though it was a Tuesday evening. It was dinner time, and I was feeling lighter and freer than I'd felt since moving to Parkwood. There was something about defining your role in a place, and really owning it, that took a serious weight off.

Trace hadn't taken my rebuff well, and I thought I would be sad about that, but...I wasn't. Was I? At least, I didn't think I was sad. Which was interesting, given that I'd been sad and sad and sad about leaving Trace behind for all these months. Actually pining. But it had turned out that it wasn't Trace I was grieving over—not the real Trace, anyway. I'd been pining over an imagined, better Trace. Who was to say it wasn't an entire imagined life?

Somewhere in those months of grieving, I let that life go and built a new one, because I could be certain that this one was real. And, in my opinion, maybe even a better one. At least a livable one.

Daisy was at the Hibiscus, saving me a seat. Her table was a swarm of moving parts—kid arms and legs and torsos and hands and feet. Daisy paused to wave me over and without missing a beat, scooped up Willow and plopped her into her high chair, then shoved a banana in her hand before she could get her indignant screaming fit off the ground.

Mike was sitting across the table, playing—and losing—a game of paper triangle football with Jake. A rogue kick sent the triangle flying into my stomach as I sat down.

"Out of bounds!" Mike crowed, sticking his finger in Jake's face. "Out of bounds! My ball!"

I sat, and Esther, looking particularly fluffy, brought me a glass of sweet tea. "Turkey sandwich tonight, honey? Extra gravy?"

I wasn't sure if my gut could take another round of those giblets, but I couldn't resist them. And from the semi-miserable faces around the restaurant, I guessed I wasn't the only one. "Sure," I said. "Why not?"

Esther scurried off, and Daisy leaned in. "She's working on a new recipe. Shepherd's pie. The secret is buffalo meat, but don't tell her I told you that, or she'll reveal the secret to my pumpkin tiramisu."

"Definitely going with pumpkin, then, huh?"

She shrugged, pushed her bangs out of her eyes, and flung Brant back into a chair, where he was immediately hit in the temple by the triangle football. He started to wail, but Daisy never even stuttered. Just pushed a cup filled with chocolate milk his way. He instantly stopped crying. This woman was a master.

"It's popular," she said. "It's delicious and I have a bunch of recipes. Tons, really. But I was thinking of going with something a little broader."

"Like…dessert?"

"Too broad. Like pie. Everyone loves pie, and my granny's pie crust will knock out a full grown man, I can tell you that much. I'm starting with pumpkin tiramisu pie. A blend of a blend of a blend. It's what they call fusion these days, I guess. You keeping with the poisoning theme?"

"Nope, it's time to move on," I said. "I'm toying with jealous rage."

"You mean like Wilma Louise Farley?"

"Something like that."

"Evangeline's awake, by the way. Lucas, I saw that. Michael, do something about him."

"She is?"

She nodded. The paper triangle hit her on the side of the head, but she didn't seem to notice. "I ran into her sister at Vacuumulate. She's a little worse for wear, but she's gonna make it.—Jealous rage, huh?" she pondered, picking a cherry out of someone's Shirley Temple and eating it. "Wives on the edge." She flicked her eyes toward Mike. "I like it."

"Whatever. You wouldn't touch a hair on that man's head."

She sighed. "You're right. He's a big child, but he's mine." She grinned wickedly and tilted her head toward the door pointedly. "Well, look who's here."

I turned and looked where she'd been not-at-all-subtly indicating and saw Brooks walk in. He was wearing plain clothes—jeans and a button-down shirt, open to reveal a college T-shirt beneath.

"You should go get him," Daisy whispered.

"What? No."

"I'll hold down the fort here," she said. "I'll make sure none of these crazies takes your food."

"It's not about that," I whispered. "I don't know if I'm ready for—" I felt a hand on my shoulder. I was not at all surprised to find that it was the warm hand of Brooks Hopkins.

"Hey, Daisy," he said. "You still making those cherry chocolate chunk muffins?"

"Of course," she said. "Plus a lot of lemon poppyseed. I mean, a lot. Two for the price of one today. Blue line special."

He chuckled. "Actually, I'm not here to eat." He touched my shoulder again. "I came to see Hollis."

I felt my cheeks burn in a not-entirely-bad sort of way. "Me?"

"Outside?" he asked, and I thought I detected some underlying shyness there.

"Okay," I said. "Sure." But I wasn't feeling okay and sure at all. I was feeling nervous and tingly and really, really unsure.

I followed him outside. He led me to a bench next to the front door and we sat.

"I just wanted to thank you," he said.

"Thank me? For what? I was nothing but a pain for you guys."

"Not true." He laughed. "Okay, a little true. But you also made me think outside the box. Look at other suspects. You have great skills. You know that, right?"

"Actually," I said, "I kind of do know that. But it's still good to hear it. And a lot of the skills were Daisy's. She's a natural."

"For the record, I thought it was Paulie, too. The whole time."

"You did?"

He nodded. "It made sense."

I grinned. "It did, didn't it?"

"Wilma Louise officially confessed. Gave the whole statement. I've gotta admit, I feel a little sorry for her."

"Me, too," I said. "Imagine being so wrapped up in a guy like Farley?"

"A lot of restaurants are going to miss her business," he said. "I know Mister Wok will. She was his most dedicated customer."

"Maybe we can sneak her in an egg roll every now and then," I said.

He chuckled. "Nope, they would never allow it. You could get a lot of contraband inside an egg roll."

"Hmm, you're right." I kicked a rock and watched it skitter underneath the car in front of us. "Like an Uzi. People are sneaking those in through Chinese appetizers all the time. I did a story on it."

He started to argue, but then caught the look on my face and cracked up, and there were those two little dimples again. I melted, and I didn't even try to stop it from happening. "You've got an interesting sense of humor, Hollis Bisbee."

"I'll take that as a compliment."

"You should."

We sat there for a few more minutes, watching cars pull in and out, including a severely frowning Wickham Birkland, whose car was sporting a brand new dent in the front fender.

I pointed at it as Wickham walked past. "Corner of Tutor and Oak?"

Brooks sighed. "Yep."

We chuckled, then fell silent again. It was one of those uncomfortable, expectant silences, but neither of us seemed to want to—or be able to—break it.

"I should probably get back in there," I said when it got to be too intense. "I've got a celebration to be the center of."

"Yeah, yeah, of course," he said.

I stood, then he stood, and we both just kind of hovered awkwardly. He looked like he wanted to say something, and I was pretty sure I knew what that something was. Dang, his eyes were so blue.

We both started talking at the same time, and then laughed breathlessly.

"Congratulations on your arrest, Officer Hopkins," I said.

"Same to you, Miss Bisbee," he said, and I edged away, still hoping he would come out with it.

He never did.

When I gave one last look before going inside, he was sitting again, his head in his hands, as if he was deep in thought.

I kind of liked it that way.

# CHAPTER 29

"WELCOME TO THE *KNOCK 'EM Dead* podcast!"
"Where murder and muffins meet!"
"I'm Hollis."
"And I'm up to my eyeballs in pie!"

I had given up on trying to make Daisy conform to a script. In fact, I'd given up on making Daisy do a lot of things. I figured it was her podcast, too, and people liked her exactly as she was. In fact, most people in Parkwood still believed this was a cooking podcast and I was interrupting her with my murder stories.

Hey, success was success, and I would be a fool to fight it.

"That's Daisy, for all you pie-lovers out there."

She held up a gorgeous dessert toward the microphone as if the audience could see it. She knew they couldn't, but still did it out of habit. Or superstition. I wasn't sure which. "Huckleberry," she said. "Now, I know that's a summer pie. But I don't see any reason why we can't have summer in our podcast nook—"

"Corner."

"And, don't worry. Next week I'll dish up something special for your Thanksgiving Day menu planning. I think everyone's going to be feeling a little energized after their turkey dinner with the recipe I have in store. But first, huckleberry. I have a story about huckleberry pie—"

"So listen, Daisy, before we get into any stories or to-day's secret ingredient or our new theme, I need to do something."

She looked panicked. Last time I'd hijacked the podcast with something serious to say, we'd ended up angry at one another.

"I have a retraction I need to issue. I didn't say any names in my last podcast about the Coach Farley murder, but some people were pretty convinced that a certain person ran down Coach Farley. But police have cleared him—in fact, he was never an official suspect—and Coach Farley's own wife, Wilma Louise, has plead guilty to one count of attempted assault with a deadly weapon and one count of voluntary manslaughter. My apologies to everyone for pre-maturely reporting."

"Hollis, that was really nice," Daisy said.

"It's the right thing to do," I said.

My phone rang. It was the *Chronicle Weekly.*

"Hollis?" Joyce's voice came out tinny and urgent. "Mary Jean wants you to come in asap. There's some break-ing news coming in over the scanner, and she wants you to be our lead reporter to follow it."

"Wait, what? What kind of news? Lead reporter? Me? Not Ernie? Are you sure? Did she really say that?"

"Are you going to ask questions all day or are you going to come?"

"I'll be there in ten minutes."

I whipped off my headphones and dropped them on the table, then turned off the recording equipment.

"What's going on?" Daisy asked, taking hers off, too.

"Breaking story, I don't know what. Gotta go." I grabbed

my bag, double checked for my notebook and pencil, and then stopped at the front door. "Is Mike home?"

Daisy grinned. "You bet he is."

"Let's go."

I opened the front door just in time to see Brooks pull up in front of my house. He was back in uniform. He got out, stood by his car, folded his arms, and shook his head.

"We're going to have to shake my babysitter," I said with a sigh. Though I couldn't help smiling just a little when I said it. I would have been disappointed if he hadn't shown up.

"Not a problem." She fired off a quick text to Mike, then joined me at the front door. "Look at us—editing our podcast, making pies, solving crimes, shaking the fuzz. Girl, we are legit!"

We high-fived.

That was all I wanted from the very beginning, really.

## THE END

# CHERRY CHOCOLATE CHUNK MUFFINS

*A Hallmark Original Recipe*

Hollis and her best friend Daisy have a new podcast called *Knock 'Em Dead*—"Where murder and muffins meet." They talk about cold cases, and Daisy throws in some baking tips for good measure. Murder comes right to their small town when a local high school football coach is killed in a hit-and-run. But it's no mystery why Daisy's Cherry Chocolate Chunk Muffins are a favorite in Parkwood: this recipe is to die for.

**Yield:** 12 muffins (12 servings)
**Prep Time:** 25 minutes
**Cook Time:** 20 minutes
**Total Time:** 45 minutes

# INGREDIENTS

Cherry Chocolate Chunk Muffins:
- 2 cups all-purpose flour
- 2 teaspoons baking powder
- ½ cup unsalted butter, softened
- 1 ¼ cups granulated sugar
- 2 teaspoons vanilla extract
- 2 large eggs
- ½ cup whole milk (or buttermilk)
- 1 cup semi-sweet dark chocolate chunks
- 1 (one-pound package) frozen tart red cherries, thawed, drained (reserve juice)
- Dark Chocolate Ganache:
- ½ cup semi-sweet dark chocolate chunks
- ¼ cup heavy whipping cream

Tart Cherry Glaze:
- 1 cup reserved tart red cherry juice
- 5 tablespoons granulated sugar
- 2 tablespoons cornstarch

# DIRECTIONS

1. Preheat oven to 425 degrees F. Spray muffin pan with non-stick cooking spray and line with paper liners.

2. To prepare muffins: whisk together flour and baking powder. Set aside.

3. Cream butter, sugar and vanilla in mixing bowl until light and fluffy. Add eggs, one at a time, and mix until blended.

4. Alternately, add flour mixture and milk to mixing bowl; mix on low speed just until blended. Fold in chocolate chunks and drained cherries.

5. Using an ice cream scoop, portion batter evenly into muffin cups.

6. Bake at 425 degrees F. (without opening oven door) or 6 to 9 minutes or until muffins rise ¼ to ½ inch above the paper; reduce heat to 350 degrees F. and bake an additional 6 to 10 minutes or until a toothpick inserted in center comes out clean. Cool on wire rack for 5 minutes, remove muffins from pan. Makes 12 muffins.

7. To prepare chocolate ganache: measure chocolate chunks in microwave-safe container and heat in 20 second increments until melted (about 45 to 60 seconds). Add heavy cream and stir until smooth. Microwave 15 seconds and stir to blend. Drizzle over muffins.

8. To prepare cherry glaze: combine cherry juice, sugar and cornstarch in small saucepan. Whisk until smooth. Stir over low heat until mixture thickens to a glaze-like consistency. Drizzle over muffins.

Thanks so much for reading *The Game Changer*. We hope you enjoyed it!

You might like these other books from Hallmark Publishing:

*The Secret Ingredient*
*Love On Location*
*Beach Wedding Weekend*
*Love at the Shore*
*A Country Wedding*
*Sunrise Cabin*

For information about our new releases and exclusive offers, sign up for our free newsletter at hallmarkchannel.com/hallmark-publishing-newsletter

You can also connect with us here:

Facebook.com/HallmarkPublishing

Twitter.com/HallmarkPublish

# ABOUT THE AUTHOR

Jennifer Brown is the award-winning author of young adult novels *Bitter End*, *Perfect Escape*, *Thousand Words*, *Torn Away*, and the *Shade Me* series. Her acclaimed debut young adult novel, *Hate List*, was chosen as an ALA Best Book for Young Adults, a VOYA Perfect Ten, and a School Library Journal Best Book of the Year. Jennifer is also the national bestselling author of several women's fiction novels, including *The Sister Season* and *The Accidental Book Club*, under the pseudonym Jennifer Scott. She lives in the Kansas City, Missouri, area with her husband and children.

Turn the page for a sneak peek of

# Out of the Picture

## A Shepherd Sisters Mystery

# TRACY GARDNER

# CHAPTER ONE

S AVANNA SHEPHERD BREATHED DEEPLY, CLOSING her eyes for a moment to savor the crisp fall air that was somehow sweeter on this side of Lake Michigan. Those vast blue waves with beautiful whitecaps made it seem more like an ocean; she'd never tire of it. It was good to be home.

Savanna let the small poodles lead her down the sandy sidewalk. They knew the way by heart. Even though she'd grown up here, Savanna was still acclimating to her little beach town after spending over a decade in Chicago. At the age of thirty, it was strange to think about her old life, due west across the lake. Her twelfth-floor apartment, her job as art authenticator for a prestigious gallery, and her fiancé Rob had been replaced with a small pink room at her sister's house in Carson, an art teacher job at an elementary school, and her Boston terrier Fonzie as her most constant companion.

It wasn't that Savanna missed her old life. It was more about the whiplash feeling from so many changes in such a short time. She knew she was lucky to fall into the teaching position just as the schoolyear was starting. And wow, had she ever missed her sisters.

The three girls had been inseparable growing up. As the middle sister, with Skylar two years older and Sydney two years younger, Savanna had fully embraced returning to her family. It was kind of a bonus that Syd was totally fine with giving her a place to stay while she figured things out. The time she'd spent lately hanging out with her sisters made Savanna acutely aware of all she'd missed over the last several years.

As they approached Caroline Carson's house, Duke pranced in circles around Princess. Savanna bent to untangle the leashes. The poodles were primped and fluffed and smelled like a flower shop, courtesy of Sydney's grooming salon, Fancy Tails and Treats. Along with the poodles, Savanna was delivering a little paper sack of gourmet dog biscuits Sydney had made herself. After Savanna's very first day at Carson Elementary School, she'd stopped by the salon to bring her sister a coffee and had ended up volunteering to return the poodles to Caroline.

The Shepherd sisters had grown up thinking Caroline was their grandmother. Even after they were old enough to understand that the families were just close friends, Savanna remembered spending Sunday afternoons and long summer days on Caroline's wraparound porch. Spotting the pillars of the wide front entrance, Savanna could almost smell the lemonade and sunscreen from her youth. The Carson mansion was gorgeous and stately, the rear of the house overlooking the lake and its rolling dunes.

Princess and Duke were having trouble containing their exuberance as Savanna tried to sidestep them on the wide stairway to the porch. She hadn't seen Caroline in almost five years. She'd wanted to come home for the funeral when Mr. Carson had passed last year, but she hadn't been able to get away from work. She was equally excited and nervous to see Caroline again, and she also couldn't wait to see what had changed in the Carson art collection.

The beautiful pieces on the walls of this house had inspired Savanna to go into art authentication. She'd always enjoyed doodling and painting, but she'd learned about the Masters program while she was an undergraduate in college, minoring in early education but majoring in studio art to earn her BFA.

The poodles scrambled wildly onto the porch, pulling Savanna smack into a tree. Well, not a tree, but a tall stranger who'd just stepped out the front door. Savanna looked up to find herself staring into the bluest eyes she'd ever seen. She watched them crinkle at the corners, making her suddenly aware she was standing there, gawking, mute. He had a shock of unruly black hair, cut close but longer on top, and a few faint freckles across his cheeks.

"Hello." His voice was deep and quiet. He placed one large hand lightly on her upper arm, steadying her as she stepped back.

After tripping over a leash, Savanna regained her balance. She looked down and found the poodles had taken the opportunity to weave themselves in and around both hers and the stranger's ankles.

She laughed, trying to extricate herself. "Here." She finally scooped up Duke. "Would you mind?" She handed the poodle to the man and he took it, smiling at her and making her more flustered. What was she doing? How did she know this man would just hold a random dog? Too late now, she thought, unclipping Duke's leash and unwrapping it from their legs while Princess sprung into the air, pawing at Duke.

"Oh, gosh," Savanna murmured, capturing a squirming Princess and glancing up at the man again. "I'm so sorry!"

"Don't be." He laughed. "I love these two."

She frowned at him without meaning to. She thought she knew everyone in town; who was this man claiming to know Caroline's poodles? And why was his smile making her all warm and stupid inside?

"I'm Aidan. And you are …not Sydney."

Savanna shook her head, disconcerted. How did he know Sydney? "I'm not. I'm Savanna. Shepherd."

Understanding dawned on him. "Aha! A third Shepherd sister!"

"Yes. How do you know my sisters?"

"We take our dog to Fancy Tails. And I've crossed paths with your sister picking up Caroline's poodles before. And your other sister Skylar is my attorney. Not that I need a lawyer," he interrupted himself. "Just, y'know, for things that come up. Nothing bad. Financial stuff. She's great. They're both great," he finished awkwardly.

Savanna heard one thing in Aidan's explanation, and it had nothing to do with him needing Skylar's services—*we*. As in, "We" take our dog to Fancy Tails.

This ridiculously cute man was taken. Of course. How could he not be?

He said, "Your sisters must be happy to have you back."

"I'm thrilled to be home. I haven't seen Caroline yet, so I offered to deliver these two." She gestured at the little dogs, now back on their leashes.

He nodded, stepping aside and holding the door open for her. "It was nice meeting you." The deep timbre of his voice sent a pleasant little zing through her.

Aidan who? But Savanna's mother had raised her with good manners. There was no polite way she could ask him to define who he was to Caroline. "Nice meeting you too,

Aidan." She took his offered hand, surprised at how warm his was. She let go, noting that he held on just a beat longer.

"Maybe I'll see you around." He turned and headed down the front steps.

Savanna stood in the doorway and watched his retreat. Okay, she'd have to sneak details out of Caroline. She was pretty sure he was married, but now she mentally kicked herself for not noticing if he wore a ring. And, on the heels of that, she kicked herself again for even wondering. After everything Rob had put her through, she'd sworn she was done with men—for a good while, anyway.

Savanna reached outside and rang the doorbell before closing the door and unclipping the poodles. She didn't want to just walk in and startle an old woman. "Hello? Caroline?"

"Hello, dear. In here," the familiar voice called.

Savanna peeked into each room as she made her way to the back of the enormous house, knowing she'd find Caroline in the parlor. The best room in the mansion, it spanned the entire west wing and had more windows than Sydney's whole house. Sunset on Lake Michigan was breathtaking, just as Savanna remembered it. She stood for a moment in the doorway, basking in the orange and pink light spilling over Caroline's wingback chair. If she lived here, she'd never want to leave this room.

Caroline rose, reaching for her cane as she spoke. "Now, Sydney, you must take this. You do such good work on my babies." She turned toward Savanna with cash in hand, and then her face lit up.

"Not Sydney," Savanna said for the second time today, smiling and wrapping Caroline in a warm hug.

"Oh, my! I'd heard whispers... I'm so glad to see you, Savanna!"

Caroline carried her age well. She had to have been ninety. She was still tall, though not quite as tall as she'd been when Savanna was a child. There was a regal air about her, in her mannerisms, her gait, the way she spoke. Savanna spied *The New York Times* on the table beside Caroline's chair; she was obviously as sharp as ever.

"I've missed you so much!" Savanna said, giving her one extra little squeeze before letting go. "You look exactly the same. How can that be?"

The older woman chuckled. "You always were a good fibber." She held Savanna at arm's length and looked her up and down. "Lovely, my dear. You look wonderful. It seems leaving the city and that idiot man has been just what you needed."

Savanna's eyebrows went up in surprise. "Sydney told you?"

"Skylar told me. She'd like to find him and give him a piece of her mind, you know."

Savanna laughed. "Oh, no." She shook her head. Rob wouldn't know what hit him. "Yeah, my sisters weren't too happy when he broke off the engagement. Well, that's not true. I think they actually are happy it's over. They never liked him. They weren't great at hiding it. But I'm okay." She gave Caroline's arm a little pat. "I promise."

"Of course you are. I think"—she leaned in, curling one arm through the crook of Savanna's elbow—"he did you a favor. You belong here, with your sisters. I'm glad you're home. Now, how about a refresher? We've acquired some exquisite work since I last saw you. Let me show you, and you can tell me what you know from your fine art degree. And I want to hear all about Chicago."

Caroline kept her arm linked through Savanna's and they began in the library, Princess and Duke following closely. Dark cherry wood was everywhere Savanna looked, and stacks of books reached far over her head. An imperial staircase led up both sides of the room to a catwalk stretching across it. The whole presentation was breathtaking, even to Savanna, who'd grown up devouring the Nancy Drew and Hardy Boys collections on these shelves. The railing along the catwalk above gleamed, and just below it, Savanna was stunned to see an actual Minkov hung on the wall. She gasped.

Caroline followed her gaze up to the painting.

"Is that a Sergei Minkov?" Savanna already knew the answer, but she had to ask. She'd only ever seen his work in books.

"It is. Everett fell in love instantly, the same as you. He had to have it." She chuckled and lowered her voice in a poor imitation of her late husband. "'I don't care what it costs, Caroline. That piece belongs in our library.'"

"Wow," Savanna breathed. "I've never actually seen one in person. May I take a closer look?"

"Of course."

Savanna left Caroline to rest a moment at a reading table, a few books scattered across the top. She moved as close as she could to the painting, an imposing size even in the huge library. It was exquisite. Most Minkovs were valued in the hundreds of thousands or higher, and that wasn't taking into consideration the year, the period, the size, or the individual piece. Even for collectors such as Everett and Caroline, even in a town known for its long history of an esteemed art community, this was an incredible acquisition. She doubted if any of her peers in Chicago had ever seen a real Minkov in person.

"There's another, in the dining room," Caroline said. "Come, I'll show you."

Savanna was seriously impressed. Another? She listened as they passed through the living room and Caroline pointed out two paintings Savanna recognized, one a Monet and the other by an early nineteenth-century artist, Francois Laurant. The Minkov in the dining room was smaller than the painting in the library, but no less amazing.

"I hope these are insured, Caroline," Savanna murmured. "I'm not sure you realize what you have here."

Caroline gave Savanna's arm a little squeeze. "Absolutely, don't worry. Your sister handles all of that for me—insurance, copies of paperwork, everything. Everett was always so smart about finances and legal things, and Skylar has been a big help in recent years."

They circled around back toward the parlor, passing the grand staircase, and Savanna noticed three faded rectangular outlines, bare spots, on the wall on the way up the stairs. "What was there?"

"Ah! That was a…Matisse, I believe, and a Rothman, and an early Laurant, I think—a painting of the Roman canals. I have trouble keeping them all straight. There are too many." She glanced at Savanna. "I've begun some cleaning since losing Everett. We found a new home for the Rothman that was there and moved the other two for now while the stairway gets redone. My neighbor Maggie has her husband helping with construction." She gestured in the direction of the house next door.

Back in the parlor, Savanna shook her head. "You're busier now than when I left ten years ago." She smiled at Caroline. "Why are you renovating? Your house is gorgeous."

Caroline clapped her hands suddenly, excited. "Oh my, I just realized. You don't even know, do you? You have to come. We're planning a grand party here for my ninetieth birthday next month!"

Savanna's face lit up. "Really? I came home just in time then, didn't I?"

Caroline leaned forward in her chair. "Savanna. I wonder if you might consider doing me a favor? At least think about it."

"Anything."

"A mural. Can I commission you to paint me a mural? That wall." She nodded toward the north end of the room. "Everett and I always felt it should have a seascape. After all the years here, it almost seems I can see it. It would complement our view." She glanced out at Lake Michigan. "And you had the talent—I remember your artwork. Would you do it?"

Savanna was taken aback. She hadn't painted—not seriously—in years. She'd messed around a little, but Rob had made her feel as if it were a waste of time, and she'd stopped making the time to do it. She'd dabbled a little since coming back to Carson, but...the idea of a mural was both exciting and daunting. "Caroline, I'm flattered. But you haven't seen my work in ten years. I'm not sure I can meet your expectations. Why not just hire it out?"

"Because I want you to do it."

———

Get the book! *Out of the Picture* is available now.